# THICKER THAN WATER

# THICKER THAN WATER

## A Leo Waterman Mystery

# G.M. FORD

THOMAS & MERCER

Text copyright ©2012 by G.M. Ford
All rights reserved.

Printed in the United States of America.

Published by Thomas & Mercer
P.O. Box 400818
Las Vegas, NV 89140

ISBN-13: 9781612183787
ISBN-10: 1612183786

*For Arnie*

# Chapter 1

My old man was right. From the very beginning, he understood that leaving a pile of money to a guy like me just wasn't a good idea. It didn't take a genius to see I wasn't the sort who'd stash the cash and then trot off to work the following morning. That part was easy. I'd been a slacker since birth. As far as I was concerned, Manual Labor was a former governor of California.

What took insight on his part was realizing that I also wasn't the type to fritter away ninety percent of it on whiskey and women and then waste the rest. To his credit, he recognized that I was moored somewhere between lazy and crazy and thus my draconian trust fund had sprung to life.

I think it was the paper route that sealed the deal. I was fourteen when I signed up to deliver the *Seattle Post-Intelligencer*. My first job other than mowing lawns. He tried to talk me out of it. Took me into his office, a dark sanctum from which I was otherwise forbidden, and put on his most ominous Big Bill Waterman scowl. Said it was a hell of a responsibility...neither rain nor sleet nor dead of night, and all of that...but I was too stoked to listen to reason and eventually badgered him into signing the parental paperwork.

I lasted a week and a half. A particularly bad spate of weather combined with a persistent head cold quickly doused my ardor. He ended up having his driver/bodyguard deliver the papers until they could get somebody else to take over the route. Early on, he told his cronies, it had cost him three grand. By the time of his death, that accursed paper route had supposedly cost him a house on the Amalfi coast.

So he doled out the ill-gotten bundle with the stipulation that I didn't see the first installment until I reached the ripe old age of forty-five. Wasn't like he had a wealth of options. I was, after all, his only child. The sole issue, as it were. What else was he going to do? Leave the pile to the cat? Despite his well-founded misgivings regarding my work ethic, in the end, blood turned out to be thicker than Little Friskies.

At that point, I'd been attending the University of Washington for the better part of seven years and was inching triumphantly toward full junior status. He must have figured the only way to avoid perpetual tuition and a life-time roommate was to find me something useful to do. As I spent a great deal of my free time reading detective novels, he just naturally figured that's what I'd like to do with my life, which probably explains why the he pulled a thousand strings and finagled me a King County Private Investigator's license.

As a private eye, I had my moments. I plied the trade for the better part of twenty years, made a decent living, got myself in the papers on a number of occasions, made the front page once or twice, and, I'd like to think anyway, managed to help quite a few people in their times of need.

Being a PI is a touchy business. People hire private investigators only out of desperation. When all else has failed, when the cops have moved on to something more current, when your friends are sick of hearing you bellyache about it, only then do people go out looking for a gumshoe. Most of the time they're not even clear what it is they want. Somewhere in their hearts they know there's virtually nothing a PI can do that can't be better accomplished by a modern police department. It's just common sense, but that's not the point. The point is that if they're ever going to be able to look at themselves in the mirror again or ever get a good night's sleep, then they're going to have to be able to tell themselves that they've done absolutely everything they possibly could. That's where private dicks come into it. We're kinda the last bent straw in the milkshake of their lives.

My forty-fifth birthday rolled around about six months back and the timing couldn't have been better. The advent of no-fault divorce combined with the digital revolution had reduced my calling to little more than data input. As skiptracing and bail recovery held little appeal, I found myself at a middle-aged crossroads. Had it not been for my old man's long-ago insight, I'd probably be working in a Burger King by now.

Instead, I was stretched out on a chaise lounge in the backyard of the family manse, a cold one hard by my elbow, kicking back, enjoying the intermittent sunshine, watching the remnants of my father's political machine stumble and cavort around a pile of fresh topsoil like decadent earth trolls.

Big Bill Waterman's political empire hadn't survived his passing. Before he was cold in the ground, several of his closest confidants were indicted and later convicted on a laundry list of charges ranging from fraudulent appropriation of public funds to immigration-law violations. City and state government spent a decade and over three million dollars trying to wrest his considerable estate back into the public pocket—and out of mine—but failed miserably. Even in death, he was slicker than they were.

The local press had a field day with it. For the better part of a month after his death, his face adorned section A of both papers, as the newshounds sought to sell papers and grease the slow-turning wheels of justice. All of which made it kind of hard for me to mourn my father's passing. The guy in the paper—the one they accused of all those improprieties—that big, scowling visage bore scant resemblance to the man I'd always called Dad. To me, my dad was just my dad. All the hoopla made it so I wasn't quite sure which one of them was real and which one wasn't, which of them deserved my sadness and which deserved his fate...or either... or neither...or both.

There weren't many of his old cronies left anymore. Most of them had passed away. All that remained were a couple of minor functionaries who'd managed to avoid the dragnet, the last of the crew of drunks and reprobates for whom I still felt a certain sense of personal responsibility. No telling what course their lives might have taken had they not become entwined with my old man and his backroom dealings.

Back when I was a full-time PI, I used to invent work for them. By that time, they'd succumbed to serious substance abuse and perennial homelessness and needed all the help they could get. Besides, if you could keep them conscious, they made excellent surveillance operatives. In urban society, the homeless and destitute have become virtually invisible. We treat them like some kind of nasty apparition and subconsciously train ourselves to look the other way. They could loiter outside a building for days without anyone taking the slightest notice.

These days I find them odd jobs whenever I can. Today it was gardening, replacing a couple of ancient rhododendrons that had perished over the winter. Coupla days back I'd stopped by the Eastlake Zoo, told Manny, the daytime bartender, that I was looking for a little landscaping help on Saturday. Free beer and a shovel. A little pocket money on the way home. Tell the boys if they happened to stop by. Manny picked his teeth with a matchbook and said he'd pass it on.

Five of them showed up. Late, drunk, and in shambles, but that was to be expected. George Paris was one of the originals. Somewhere around seventy now, he had a face like a satchel and a body to match. George used to be a prominent local banker. One of the cadre of financial specialists who hatched the serpentine scheme to launder my old man's money. Just far enough down the authority ladder to avoid criminal prosecution, he'd been summarily cast adrift by the bank, divorced by a well-to-do wife, and jettisoned into the streets like a discarded gum wrapper. For the past twenty years, he'd bounced from gutter to gutter. Blown by the wind, fueled by an ocean of cheap booze and bitter memories, he'd managed to maintain both his keen intelligence and his acidic sense of humor.

Ralph Batista wasn't so lucky. Bleary-eyed and thin as a wire, he'd been a midlevel official for the Port of Seattle when my old man died and the excrement met the proverbial cooling device. Served short time in the county lockup on a plethora of charges relating to the smuggling of human cargo through the port and then was likewise cast upon the streets. The years hadn't been as kind to Ralph as they'd been to George. Decades of self-abuse had cut his functional IQ in half. Ralph wandered through the world, looking for his next drink in a constant state of wonder and semi-confusion. If it weren't for George looking out for him, he'd undoubtedly have been dead by now.

The other three I'd picked up along the way. Billy Bob Fung had a thick Tennessee drawl and skittered through his days in a state of mild amusement, nodding and smiling at everything that went on around him. If you'd put a gun to his head, cocked it, and told him you were about to blow his brains out, he'd have grinned that gap-toothed grin of his and said, "Yeah, man. Yeah. Go for it."

Large Marge and Red Lopez were regulars at the Eastlake Zoo and two of the more sentient examples of an otherwise insensate crowd. The kind of people who reminded you that it took only a couple of bad decisions to start your life circling the bowl. That the line between the middle class and out on your ass was thinner than a piece of Denny's bacon.

Marge was, as advertised, large. Almost as tall as I was. A former working girl, she'd been reduced to penury by a series of bad relationships and a serious heroin jones. You wanted to end up with your front teeth in your shirt pocket, you just put your hand on Marge somewhere she didn't want a hand put. Apparently Marge would be rendering no further services.

Red was an Inuit from somewhere up in the Northwest Territories and a sad example of the genetic intolerance to alcohol so common among his people. Four drinks and he was either on all fours barking at the ants or out stone-cold, drooling among the peanut shells. With Red, you didn't have to wonder what his problem was. It was his penchant for exposing himself in public places that most seriously curtailed his career opportunities and so vexed the local authorities. His habit of whipping it out and asking "Ain't it a beauty?" proved to be a social faux pas too serious to surmount, earning him repeated stretches behind bars and a level-one sex-offender designation. He and I had reached an accord. I wouldn't show him mine, if he wouldn't show me his. So far, so good.

They had an interesting approach to landscaping work. First they drank all the beer. Forty-eight of them. Quick as you could say, "Ticonderoga," they were up to their ankles in empties and the cooler was bare. Suitably fueled, they bent to the pick-and-shovel work, digging up the dead rhody and casting it aside. By the time they finished the exhumation, Billy Bob Fung was on his lips, facedown in the loam, snoring softly. The other four dragged him out of the way as they bantered and bickered their way through the planting of the first new bush.

That's when things took a sudden sloppy turn. Probably my fault. I should have seen it coming. Lots of people in this world you wouldn't want to have a gun. Some you wouldn't want driving cars. Still others you wouldn't want making the final decision on anything at all, no matter how minor. These guys...these guys you wouldn't even give a garden hose. Not with water anyway. I don't know what the hell I was thinking.

By the time I pulled my mind from the many faces of my old man and my eyes from the slate-gray clouds moving in from the West, all three of them were breaded like veal cutlets. Head to toe. Covered with mud. Soaking wet. Brown M&M's with eyes.

Ralph slapped his muddy hands together and reckoned how he'd just step inside the house and clean himself up a mite.

I came out of the lawn chair like a Scud missile. "Nobody's going inside the house," I announced.

The cleaning service had made its weekly appearance yesterday and I had no intention of letting these maniacs trash the joint. Bad enough that I felt guilty about not doing my own housework. If I had to have it done twice in the same week I may have been forced to take holy orders, pledge myself to poverty, and that kind of stuff.

I pointed at the other rhododendron. "Plant that damn thing," I said. "I'll go inside and get you all some clean clothes."

"We're getting a little parched too," George grumbled to my back as I headed for the house.

"Plant it," I growled over my shoulder.

I was gone for the better part of ten minutes. All the way up to the attic, where I'd come across the old trunk several weeks back. I couldn't keep a smile from creasing my lips as I hoisted the steamer up onto my shoulder and tiptoed down the narrow stairs, through the kitchen and out the back door. Sigmund Freud would have had a field day with me.

They'd managed to muscle the bush into the ground. The poor thing looked like it had survived a hurricane. The beleaguered shrub leaned east at about a thirty-degree angle. Leaves littered the ground around the base. I made a mental note to straighten it out after they left. Wouldn't want to hurt their feelings. They were hosing each other off as I came out the door.

I set the trunk on the back steps, flipped the brass fasteners, and lifted the lid. A pair of worn leather straps prevented the lid from flopping all the way open. Inside were my father's clothes. I guessed that his sisters must have packed them up after his funeral, expecting that I'd donate them to charity or something, but somehow I missed the memo and wasn't aware of their existence until I stumbled upon them while poking around the attic one rainy February afternoon.

The sight of his tweed overcoat, rough to the hand and big enough for a four-man tent, nearly took my breath away. I stepped aside and gestured at the trunk. "Have at it," I said.

Ralph was too far gone to recognize his own mother. Billy Bob was down for the count. Red and Marge had never met my father, so none of them had a clue.

George, on the other hand, knew immediately. His red-rimmed eyes ran over my face like an ant colony. "These are...," he began.

"Yeah," I said. "They are."

He sat on the step next to the trunk and stared off into space.

Marge, Red, and Ralph rummaged through the mound of clothes like mad moles.

For the sake of modesty, I encouraged Marge to use the back porch as a changing room. Red and Ralph shed their sodden rags right there in the backyard. After appropriating most of a tuxedo, Marge disappeared up the stairs.

Ralph Batista naked was more than I could bear. I turned away and went back to studying the rapidly approaching weather. The spaces between the steel-gray clouds were disappearing. The wind had begun to freshen in the trees. That's when I heard the magic words. "Ain't it a beauty?" Red Lopez inquired.

I cringed and studied the sky harder.

"Leo," George said.

I kept my face averted. "Is he dressed yet?" I asked.

"Leo," George repeated.

When I met his watery gaze, he threw his bloodshot eyes toward the corner of the house.

She was standing on the flagstone walkway, her purse clutched in front of her with both hands, the little going-to-church hat resting atop her head like a thorny crown. All things considered, she was doing a pretty good job of pretending there weren't two naked winos standing there on the lawn, one of them wanting to know what she thought of his prominently proffered package.

Normally I would have been greatly amused by her discomfort. Problem was, the sight of Iris Duval meant that somewhere in the universe pigs had officially taken wing. The mountain had come to Mohammed, and nothing but disaster could possibly have impelled Iris Duval to come looking for me.

■　■　■

Iris Duval had a disapproving mouth. The more she disapproved of something the thinner her lips got. The sight of my face had always puckered her up tight enough to stamp license plates, and today was no exception. She never said a word and never took her eyes off my face as the crew got dressed and lurched their way around toward the front of the house.

I took her inside and invited her to sit on the sofa, asked if I could get her anything, but she just glared me off, so I left her standing in the middle of my front parlor looking out through the open door while I stuffed the crew into a cab and sent them on their way, fifty bucks apiece burning a hole in their pockets, an extra twenty to the cabbie for putting up with the singing.

A light rain had begun to fall, darkening the pavement, hissing softly onto the magnolia leaves as I stood in the driveway and watched the cab roll out through the gate. I didn't want to go back inside the house. Didn't want to hear whatever it was that Iris had come thirty miles to tell me. Avoidance was a specialty of mine. You name it, I could pretend it didn't exist. I liked to tell myself it was better than taking Prozac.

Don't get me wrong. I'm not claiming eternal sunshine or anything like that. I'm only human. Like most folks my age, I've got a long list of regrets. Things I wish had turned out differently. Things I'd like do-overs on. That's the way life is, trial and error.

If there was any aspect of my past that haunted me on a daily basis, however, it was Rebecca Duval, Iris's daughter. In a couple of weeks it would be three years since we'd parted ways, and I still wasn't "over it." Truth be told, I didn't want to be "over it." The sense of longing I felt whenever I thought of her connected us in a way I didn't understand but wasn't prepared to abandon. Pain was something and something was better than nothing.

In a perfect world, I could have blamed her for walking out on me. Called her a faithless ho and drunk myself to sleep at night. But what can I say? She wanted somebody with the same hopes and dreams as her own, not some over-grown kid who played at being a private cop and whose only real ambition was to live to be forty-five. Who could blame her? I could miss her, but I couldn't blame her.

We started back in the fifth grade. For reasons I'll never understand the powers-that-be were determined we learn to dance. The well-rounded young person or some such tripe. So Thursdays after lunch, they'd bus Seattle Preppies like me over to Holy Names Academy to trip the light fandango with the Catholic girls. Talk about awkward. The airborne hormones were thicker than string cheese. Exhibiting great social sensitivity and *savoir faire*, they matched us up accord-ing to height. As Rebecca and I were both a head and a half taller than anyone else in the room, we were a natural fit. She found my clumsy attempts at dancing hilarious, and there was absolutely nothing about her that didn't amuse or excite me, so we just kept dancing, year after year, until she walked off the floor and took the music with her.

I took a shallow breath and started for my front door. Iris hadn't moved. She stood on the carpet, rigid as a fence-post, her mouth thin enough to pass for a scar.

I took my time. Moving slowly, thoroughly wiping my feet before closing the door. I swallowed a sigh, turned, and ambled her way.

She just couldn't resist. "Nice crowd there," she commented.

I'd long ago decided that life was too short to trade one-liners with Iris. We'd already said what we had to say to one another, on several occasions at great length and at top volume. No point in going over that same old pile of beans again. A tedious moment passed. The silence was deafening.

I finally broke the spell. "What can I do for you, Iris?"

Funny I should ask.

"I haven't heard from Rebecca in over a week," she said.

My body began to vibrate. Felt like I'd dropped a quarter into one of those old-time Magic Fingers motel beds, and was lying there waiting for my fillings to shake loose.

I did what people do in moments like that. I tried to come up with a scenario that would explain the unexplainable. Maybe she did this. Maybe she did that. Perhaps this, perhaps that. I led a rather rich fantasy life, but nothing whatsoever came to mind.

A day seldom passed when Rebecca didn't speak with her mother. Usually more than once. A week was impossible. The family mythos depended upon it. The promises of deferred gratification demanded it. As the saga went, Iris had sacrificed everything for her daughter. Held down three jobs. Scrimped and saved, and then scrimped and saved some more. The undisputed queen of the single mom-dom, trudging onward and upward after the death of her shiftless, alcoholic husband. Putting her daughter through the University of Washington, through med school, through a pathology residency. All of it, and I mean all of it, a tribute to grit and steely feminist determination.

"What's Brett got to say?" I asked.

Brett Ward. The guy Rebecca married a couple of years back. A seriously handsome rake of a guy who drove a Porsche and sold yachts for a living. Snappy dresser. Fast talker.

Iris's glare went halogen. "He says they had a fight. Says she walked out on him. Just packed a suitcase and left. Said she needed to get away and think. Brett says he doesn't know where she is." She started to add something but stopped herself.

"You believe him?"

"No."

"What else?" I prodded.

"He came to my house looking for her. Drunk." She made it plain that she was holding something back. I went along for the ride.

"And?"

"He had a gun."

"Really?"

"I saw it in the waistband of his pants."

"What else?"

She met my gaze. "He said he thought she'd probably come running back to you. Said he was going to come over here and find her. Drag her back home."

"Haven't seen him," I said with a glum shrug.

"Of course you haven't," she scoffed. "You whipped him like a dog. He wouldn't dare come over here and bother you."

I winced. Knocking Brett Ward stiff wasn't something I was proud of. First off, it was too easy. He was drunk; I wasn't. I was big; he wasn't. Secondly, it was childish on both our parts. He made it a point to invite me to his bachelor party, just so he could tell his friends he had. "Hell, Bob, I even invited the big idiot." He'd already won the girl, but just had to rub it in. Wanted to show his buddies how thoroughly he'd defeated his rival.

Oh, I admit it. I should never have taken him up on it. I was being just as childish as he was. Worse yet, I saw trouble coming, right from the start. I could have nipped it in the bud and stopped him while he was working up the nerve. I could have walked right out of the Waterfront Restaurant and taken a cab home. But I didn't. I let him paddle all the way up Stupid Creek. Let him get his blood in a boil to the point where he felt confident enough to take a poke at me and then walk off. I coldcocked him right in front of his friends and family. Party's over. Thanks for coming, folks.

Not one of my finer moments.

I asked Iris the obvious question. "What about the people at work? Vaughn...Sandy..." Rebecca was the chief forensic pathologist for King County and, although nobody was truly indispensable, she came pretty close. As far as Rebecca was concerned, the only excuse for not showing up at work was death in the family...your own. Another integral part of the Iris-as-hard-working-heroine myth. That was subplot 3-B, about how Iris instilled proper values in the girl.

"She took an indefinite leave of absence," Iris said.

My mouth hung open. "When?"

"Two weeks this Thursday."

"Did you know she was going to do that? Was she planning something?"

"Never said a word to me."

A strange situation was getting stranger by the moment. The idea that Rebecca Duval hadn't bothered to discuss something like an indefinite leave of absence with her mother was absurd. Another quarter dropped into the Magic Fingers slot. The vibrating escalated to jackhammer proportions.

"You been to the cops?" I asked.

"They checked with the people at the medical examiner's office. Said she arranged her own leave of absence." She anticipated my next question. "Listed 'personal' as the reason." She tore a hand away from the purse and waved it. "Even interviewed and hired a temporary replacement for herself. Other than that, the cops said she was an adult and entitled to go wherever she wanted to go. Said they didn't have time to be out looking for people who left of their own volition."

"They've got a point," I admitted.

"Do I have to explain this to you?" She didn't wait for me to answer. "Do I?" she shrieked. She sensed she was getting a mite shrill and pulled herself together.

"Could she be pregnant or something?" I asked.

"I'd have known," Iris said, without hesitation.

And she would have. And we both knew it.

Once again I rooted around for an explanation and came up empty.

"The relationship…," I began. "I mean, before the night they had the fight and she walked out on him…I mean… how was it going? Were they…"

"Like all relationships," she hedged.

"How's that, Iris?" I wasn't about to let her euphemize the question out of existence.

I understood that this was hard for Iris. She'd given Brett Ward her personal seal of approval. To admit that everything had gone less than swimmingly would be tantamount to admitting she'd been wrong...and we certainly couldn't have that, now could we?

To my astonishment, she came right out with it. "Rocky," she said. "They'd been having some trouble lately."

"Trouble about what?"

"What do couples argue about?" she shot back.

"You tell me."

Her neck got stiffer. Her lips all but disappeared. "She wouldn't tell me. She just said they were working it out together."

"Working it out how?"

She swallowed hard. "I think they were seeing someone."

"Therapy?"

"I think so."

"You know who?"

"Whom," she corrected.

"A name," I growled.

She shook her head and looked away. "No idea," she said.

"I'll make a couple of calls," I said.

"Find her," she demanded. "Get out there and find her."

"I don't do that kind of work anymore," I said.

"You don't do any kind of work anymore?" she snapped.

I refused to allow myself to be drawn into her spurious web of contention. "There's nothing one man can do that the SPD can't do fifty times better."

"Unlike you, Leo, the police have other things to do."

"Yeah," was all I could think to say. "They do."

■  ■  ■

"Same damn thing we told the mother," Marty Gilbert said.

After all these years, Marty was still skinny. He'd been a beanpole in high school and taken quite a bit of good-natured ribbing about it, but his thin genes were paying compound interest in middle age. While the rest of us fought love handles, Marty had put on maybe five pounds in twenty-five-plus years.

As we spoke, he was seven months from early retirement and holding down the second shift watch commander's desk at the East Precinct. Marty was no fool. No sense risking your ass on the street when you're staring your twenty-five in the eye. He was gonna desk-duty his way out the door and right into that condo he and Peg had bought down in San Diego, so they could get out of the rain and be near the grandkids.

"Rebecca made plans to leave. She left. Other than that it's none of our business." He allowed his hands to fall to his sides and made a resigned face. "And after meeting the mother..." Marty gave discretion its due and let the rest of it hang.

I resisted the urge to chime in on the subject of Iris Duval.

"I'm worried," I said instead.

"People go through changes, Leo. You, of all people, ought to know...there's no telling what goes on behind closed doors."

I turned my face aside, hoping he wouldn't sense my grudging agreement.

"What did Brett Ward tell you guys?"

"Same thing he told the mother. They got into it. She packed up and left. He hasn't seen her since. What did he tell you?" Marty asked.

"He's not answering his phone and his mailbox is full." I cut the air with an angry hand. "I ran by their place on the way over here. Neither car is in the garage."

"Last time I checked, that wasn't illegal either," Marty noted.

I walked over to his desk, peeled a piece of paper off his note pad, and scribbled a single short line. *Recent credit card activity and phone logs? Her car?*

Marty glanced down, casually picked it up, and fed it into the shredder beneath his desk. He clapped me on the arm. "Wish I could do more to help you, buddy," he said. "I'll keep my ear to the ground. I hear anything, I'll give you a jingle."

We shook hands for the sake of surveillance cameras. I thanked him for giving me some of his time and headed for the door.

A relentless rain had nearly cleared Twelfth Avenue East. Everybody who had a place to go had up and gone. Those without shelter were hunkered down in doorways and under trees. I pulled my coat over my head and sloshed across the street.

As my old friend Joe Ruggio liked to say, "Living in Seattle is like being married to a beautiful woman who's sick all the time." But what the hell, if the weather were better, half of Orange County would have moved up here by now. As it was, the city was nearly impossible to get around. A couple of million more people and we'd have L.A. gridlock redux, so I counted us lucky and noted for the umpteenth time that life is mostly a series of highly dubious trade-offs.

I rolled away from the curb, made a quick right, and headed down Pine Street. My tires hissed and splashed through the rapidly gathering rainwater as I passed the ball field, bumped over Broadway, and started down Olive. Toward downtown. Toward South Lake Union, Millennium Yacht Sales, and Brett Ward.

South Lake Union was, as the wags liked to say, "an area in transition." What had, for most of the city's history, been an enclave of mom-and-pop businesses was now in the process of being gentrified out of existence by Paul Allen and his minions at Vulcan. Money talks, and he had more of it than anybody except his old Microsoft partner, Bill Gates, so he got to turn the neighborhood into just another collection of condos, IT companies, and supposedly upscale office buildings that looked more like old-school Soviet bloc architecture than anything you'd want to immortalize on a brochure.

Like I said, money talks.

I rounded the corner on Fairview and cast myself headlong into what was known locally as "the Mercer mess," the extreme south shore of Lake Union, where a dozen seemingly random lanes of traffic from all over the city converged, bumping and grinding around the south end of the lake in a horn-honking frenzy reminiscent of rush hour in Beirut. I forced my way into the right lane and bumped over the curb into a nearly empty restaurant parking lot.

Two minutes and eight bucks later I was hustling across the puddled pavement. A blue and white sign on the side of Daniel's Broiler read, "Millennium Yacht Sales." The red arrow pointed down the wide concrete stairs. I loped down the stairs, two at a time.

Millennium had occupied that spot for as long as I could recall. Even as the street level business had morphed from one thing to another over the years, from commercial boatyard to its present incarnation as an upscale steak joint, the yacht dealer had always been sitting just below, collecting the rent, bobbing along at water level, looking out over the marina.

A brass bell tinkled several times as I pulled open the door and stepped inside. The room was empty and quiet, but otherwise looked like a yacht dealership should, all brassy and woody and nautical. Ocean Alexander posters. An entire wall of boat photos. On the wall directly in front of me, the sales staff each had a framed picture with a little brass plaque enumerating both their names and years of service to the company. Five men, two women. Third from the left, Brett Ward grinned out at the room.

According to most folks, Brett Ward had charisma, that special something that lights up a room and draws every eye his way. Personally, I'd never seen it. It needs to be said that my views on the subject of Brett Ward should certainly be taken with a substantial grain of Freudian salt, as I was the loser in our little love triangle and as such must be considered to be, at best, unreliable, but even with that proviso, I'd never seen what it was that so attracted people to him. To me, he was just full of crap. A good-looking, elbow-fondling, affable sort who remembered everybody's name and erogenous zones and just kept running his lips until he'd steered you wherever he wanted you to go. How anybody could take the guy seriously had always baffled me.

But they did, a fact that had forced me to the conclusion that being full of crap was perhaps a far more important part of life in the modern world than I had ever given it credit for being. As Facebook and Twitter and their ilk allowed us a far wider circle of friends, the depth of those friendships got more and more shallow, until eventually you were a petri dish in the ocean of life.

My ruminations were interrupted by the squeak of a door and the sounds of muffled footsteps. The guy who walked into the room looked like he'd just left the helm after an exhaustive ocean crossing. White hair and matching mustache, the Monopoly man on the bounding main. Crisp Ralph Lauren polo complete with ascot hiding his sagging neck. Pressed slacks. Topsider boat shoes, no socks. All he was missing was the little captain's hat with the gold braid. Avast, matey.

Took him all of three seconds to make me for a noncustomer. No proffered hand, no welcoming smile. He stopped coming my way and stood his ground.

"Help you?" he asked.

"I'm looking for Brett Ward."

"Brett's not with us anymore," he said.

I threw a glance at Brett's picture on the wall. Commodore Commodious here was up there too. Far left. Bigger plaque than the others: Harvey Jorgensen, Founder-Owner.

He read my mind. "Just haven't gotten around to taking his picture down," he said with an air of nonchalance.

"You know how I can get a hold of him?"

"I believe I have his number."

"He's not answering his phone."

He found a pained expression. "Then your guess is as good as mine."

I looked around the room again. "Pretty quiet," I commented.

"Lunchtime," he said.

"Guy worked for you for a long time," I said.

"Salesmen...they come, they go."

"Ten to twelve years, wasn't it?"

He didn't answer.

I wanted to see how he'd react. "The downturn in the economy must be tough on the yacht business," I ventured.

"For some people," he said imperiously, the implication being that the kind of people who bought yachts from dealerships of *his* magnitude...those people hardly noticed fluctuations in the tawdry, street-level economy.

"What did you say your name was?" he asked.

"I didn't."

"That's right," he agreed. "You didn't."

"Leo Waterman."

"Aaaaah," he said as if confirming some previous notion.

"Any idea what Brett's doing these days?"

"Big Bill's boy?" he asked.

"Yes indeed."

"I knew your father."

"Everybody knew my father."

His eyes narrowed. He took a step forward. "As I recall, you had a physical altercation of some sort with Brett."

"A momentary misunderstanding," I assured him.

"Aaaah," he said again. "If the look of him was any indication, Brett got considerably the worst of that little failure to communicate."

"Luck of the Irish."

He frowned. "Is Waterman Irish?"

"No," I said. "It's not."

Like so many before him, he didn't find me amusing. He rubbed his palms together in a gesture of finality. "Soooo... unless I can interest you in a yacht..."

"Not today," I said.

"Wish I could have been more help," he said.

"Thanks," I lied.

He padded back down the hallway, turned left into his office, and closed the door.

Something about the silence unsettled me. I was overcome with an eerie feeling, a sense of displacement, as if the world had somehow shifted five inches to the left while I wasn't paying attention. The discomfort nearly made me stupid. I was in a fog. I started to wander back out into the rain, caught myself, and instead walked over to the wall of employee photos and took out my notebook.

. . .

Instead of turning right and heading back up to my car, I stepped out the door and walked down three stairs. The late afternoon rain had grown more insistent and the wind had decided to stop fooling around and blow full time, a steady fifteen or twenty knots, I guessed. Over on the public section of the dock, the metal forest of sailboats rocked back and forth as the rush of air slapped halyards against masts, rapping and pinging like a symphony of tone-deaf tinkers.

From where I stood, not a single empty slip was visible. Looked like Jorgensen had fifty or so boats for sale. Even with my limited arithmetic, this was a big inventory. Lotta money tied up during a very slow economy. I hunched down into my jacket and strolled out onto the dock.

The oversized motor cruisers bobbed nervously in the roiling water, squeaking and groaning their discomfort. Each boat was festooned with several of Millennium's trademark blue and white signs. The tide was all the way in. Lines and fenders fought to keep the shiny playthings from ripping themselves to pieces on the concrete dock. Somewhere out in front of me a mashed fender screamed its displeasure.

They kept the big brutes out at the far end of the dock where they had more room. According to the sign, a one-hundred-and-five-foot Nordlund was a real steal at $3.99 million. The ninety-two-foot McQueen from the mid-1980s was marked down to seven hundred thousand bucks and had, if the sign were to be believed, a highly motivated seller. I was betting that "highly motivated" didn't begin to cover it.

I spied a pair of feet sticking straight up in the air, moving rhythmically as if pedaling a bicycle. Above the growl of the wind, I heard a curse and then the guttural grunt of physical exertion. Once, twice, and then three times. Another curse blew off to the south like airborne litter. Curious, I jammed my hands into my pockets and wandered in that direction.

The boat was a late 1960s Tollycraft, maybe forty-eight feet. I sidled over to the stern and peered down onto the deck. The engine compartment was propped open. Assorted wrenches were strewn here and there on the deck. Individual pieces of what appeared to be a water pump lay scattered among the tools.

The feet belonged to a guy in a pair of filthy pinstriped coveralls. He'd crawled headfirst as far down into the bulkhead as he'd been able. I watched as he tried to lever himself back above decks and once again failed. More colorful cursing ensued. He'd gone so far down into the bilges that getting himself back on deck was no longer a straight line and required something of a contortionist.

"Need a hand?" I inquired.

"No…no…I'm…uh…I'm okay…"

"Okay," I said without moving.

This was hard for him. I could tell. Manly maritime types don't like being rescued. Bad for the testicularity. It was, however, getting late in the day. Night was fast upon us, and the prospect of spending the evening wedged in the bilges of a fifty-year-old motor cruiser held limited appeal, even to the saltiest of souls.

Didn't take long for sanity to rear its head.

"Hey!" he hollered.

"Still here," I said.

"Yeah…maybe I could use…you know…"

Took us three or four minutes to wiggle him all the way out. Tore a jagged hole in the shoulder of his coveralls in the process, but at least he was right side up.

He was pushing fifty, with a weathered, windblown face, and a body lean and lithe for a guy his age. He ran a greasy hand through his hair and introduced himself as Neil Robbins.

"'Preciate the help," he said disgustedly. "Had to practically dismantle the exhaust system just to change the damn water pump," he complained. "By the time I got it outta there wasn't nothing left to lever myself out with."

He began to pick up his tools. I stood on the rolling dock and watched as he worked at making the Tolly ship-shape. I looked around the marina. Still not an empty slip in sight. "Looks like there's no shortage of work to be had," I commented.

"The work's easy," he growled. "It's gettin' paid that's the trick."

"Tough times," I said.

"Used to be, three of us couldn't keep up with the work. Now..." He threw a greasy hand in the air. "These days I gotta work on whatever I can."

"Nobody pays his boat mechanic first."

"Or second or third..." He found a hose and washed off the deck. "These days we get 'em back way more often than we ship 'em out."

I gestured with my head. "Millennium looks like its hanging in there."

He shook his head. "They're circling the bowl," he said. "Wasn't that he owned the building, he'd be out on his ass like the resta them. That's the only damn thing keeping him afloat, 'cause he sure as hell ain't moving any boats."

"How long you been busting knuckles around here?"

"Nine years."

"You know any of the salesmen?"

"Sales associates," he corrected with a malicious grin.

I laughed.

"They're all gone. All off selling refrigerators or something."

"You know Brett Ward?"

"At least he could actually drive a boat," the guy said as he gathered the water pump parts and stowed them in the lazarette. "Some of these yahoos..." He rolled his eyes.

We both knew exactly what he was talking about. While society at least goes through the motions of making sure someone knows the rules of the road and is prepared to operate a motor vehicle in traffic, no such precautions are deemed necessary when it comes to boats. Anybody with gas money and a watery wish is permitted to operate a boat, which, of course, produces predictable results, particularly among the big boat set.

For reasons best left to psychoanalysis, there seemed to be a feeling among the well-to-do that the skills necessary to operate the vessel were transferred along with the title. After all, these were people who'd attained a certain level of success and thus had displayed a certain level of competence. They were good at things. Why shouldn't they be good at operating a yacht?

Usually they had to lose an anchor or crash into the fuel docks or run over half-a-dozen bow lines and foul the prop before they figured out that boats don't just turn left when you want them to, that little things like the wind and the tide and the forces of motion and inertia affect boats in ways theretofore unimagined. At that point they either get somebody to show them how to properly slide a vessel of that size around and then practice their little hearts out, or they read the handwriting on the wall and hire a professional to do it for them. Still others just kept bumbling around. The SPD water cops and the Coast Guard were busy all year long.

He threw his tool bag over his shoulder and held out a hand. I yarded him up onto the dock in a single smooth motion. Wasn't till he was standing beside me that he realized how big I was. He looked up and grinned. "It was you stuck in there, we'dda had to gut her to the waterline to get your big ass out."

I held up a testifying hand. "Not me in there," I swore. "Nobody in the history of mechanics has ever been less adept with a wrench than I am. I can turn a thirty-dollar job into a nine-hundred-dollar job in about as much time as it takes to sneeze."

We started down the dock side by side.

"Ward...he was the first one outta here," the guy said. "Then the big blonde honey from the desk." He waved his free hand in the air as if to shoo the breeze. "After that, they all just melted off into Neverland, one by one."

"Any idea what Ward's doing now?"

He stopped walking and looked up at me. "What you wanting him for?"

"It's kind of personal," I said.

"You ain't the cops."

I shook my head. "No."

"Bill collector?"

Another shake.

"Process server?"

"Like I said, it's personal."

That was good enough for him. As far as this guy was concerned some things were best left unsaid.

"By then Jorgensen was mostly usin' him as a repo man anyway. The dealership had all these units up in B.C. that was way behind in their payments. Most of 'em not even fighting it. Wanted to give the damn boats back." His expression said, "You know how people are when money gets tight." He started walking again. "Mr. Ward...he'd fly on up there, get all the Canadian paperwork straight and then run 'em back down here."

I made a show of looking around again. "Doesn't look like Jorgensen needs any more inventory," I commented.

"Shit no," he agreed. He waved his calloused hand again. "Ward had some other deal goin' on. Musta worked out something directly with Northwest Maritime." He shot a glance up at the office. "That's the lender Jorgensen uses for Canada. Ward musta made some kind of deal with them. He was cleaning 'em up someplace up on Northlake and wholesaling them off somewheres, gettin' whatever he could for the bank."

He looked up for the briefest of moments and smiled. Above us in the front window of Millennium Yacht Sales, Jorgensen stood with his arms folded tight across his chest, gazing down on us like the lord of the manor.

"Taking a slice for himself and avoiding the middle-man." He smiled and flicked another glance at Jorgensen. "Bound to be better than *not* sellin' yachts for a living."

"Were there hard feelings about his leaving?" I asked.

He shook his head. "Not as far as I could tell," he said. "I got the impression Harvey was glad Brett found something else. The handwriting was on the wall by that time. The economy was full scale in the shitter. Wasn't nobody buying boats. They were all standing around the office pickin' each other's ass."

I followed him up a set of metal stairs onto the side deck of Daniel's Broiler. The deck was desolate and deserted. Inside the window, half-a-dozen early diners chewed con-tentedly on fifty-dollar steaks and gazed out on to the tur-bulent waters.

"He have any particular friends on the crew?"

He thought about it. "Used to go to lunch sometimes over at Hooters with that Ricky guy."

"Ricky?"

"Ricky, Richie…Something like that." He cut quotation marks in the air with his greasy fingers. "One of the sales associates. He's sellin' shoes up at the Northgate mall. I seen 'em when I went up there with my sister the other day." He grinned. "He pretended not to recognize me."

I trailed him up the remainder of the stairs, up along the back wall of the kitchen where the smell of seared meat coming from the massive exhaust fans was strong enough to paralyze vegans, and then up and out into the parking lot, where I thanked him for his help. He said it was no big deal, resettled the tool bag on his shoulder, and strode off.

I stood in the rain and watched him disappear into the gathering darkness, then ducked my head into the wind, and began jogging toward my car.

■  ■  ■

When you poke your nose into other people's business for a living, it's best to operate from the assumption that somewhere out there somebody's still holding a grudge. Lots of people in this world just aren't able to take responsibility for their actions, so they decide that the only reasonable thing to do is to shoot the messenger. That's how private investigators end up with their skulls cracked and their noses broken, or worse yet, gunned down by some out-of-his-mind, about-to-lose-everything husband or wife.

Since I stopped working, I'd gotten out of the habit of looking over my shoulder. I told myself that was because I was in the best physical shape of my life and therefore ready for anything, even if I wasn't paying attention. Truth was, I went to the gym every day in order to fill time rather than to exercise any sense of professional responsibility. No doubt about it, I'd lost whatever edge I'd once possessed, presuming, of course, I'd ever had one to lose.

I wanted to make it all the way downtown to the King County Coroner's Office before everybody went home for the day. Going through the middle of the city at that time was out of the question, so I planned to get myself up onto Capital Hill, just far enough from the I-5 to avoid the commuters, and then make my way south through the neighborhoods.

If I'd taken any other route I'd never have noticed them. My mind was in outer space. I was bellyache-worried and not paying the slightest attention to the world around me as I turned right off Fairview and started up Eastlake.

The derelict smokestacks of the old Seattle City Light steam plant seemed to be giving me the finger as I rolled up the grade, past ZymoGenetics and the back of the Fred Hutchinson Cancer Research Center, up to the top of the hill, where a forest of concrete pillars suddenly sprouted on my left and the roar of the freeway began to seep into the car's interior.

As I crested the grade, I checked the surrounding area. Three blocks down, along the front of REI, a knot of traffic shimmered in the rain. Brake lights threw jagged shafts of red on the asphalt. I slowed to a crawl. A moment later the light changed and suddenly the street was empty. I fed the car a little gas.

I checked the rearview mirror. Back at the bottom of Eastlake Avenue, a white Cadillac Escalade with British Columbia plates was moving uphill inside a self-generated cloud of mist, its otherworldly white halogen headlights bouncing this way and that as it navigated the minefield of potholes.

I crested the hill and veered hard into the right-hand lane, getting as far from the concrete divider as possible, before swinging back to the left, gritting my teeth hard as I swung across three lanes, barely avoiding the concrete traffic island designed to prevent precisely this grossly unlawful maneuver.

I made it with an inch to spare and was halfway up the ramp, driving over the freeway, congratulating myself, checking the mirrors for cops, when I saw that the Cadillac had not only performed the same illegal maneuver but had also closed the distance between us by half.

I had a "hmmmm" moment. The first time I'd seen them, they had their lights on, and now the driver had turned them off. And it wasn't like visibility had improved either. Quite the contrary. It was getting darker and drearier by the second. A steel ball bearing rolled down my spine. Why no lights?

I could understand how my scofflaw maneuver might have nurtured the worst instincts in my fellow citizens and I sorely regretted being such a poor role model, but the lights? The lights made no sense at all unless somebody was trying a little too hard to not be noticed. The *Twilight Zone* theme began to toot in my head.

A dry laugh escaped my throat as I eased up to the stop sign. "A bit paranoid or what?" my inner voice asked. Hell, on my worst day it took me several hours to piss somebody off enough to be following me over hill and dale. I'd been looking for Rebecca for only an hour. So...unless I was about to set new annoyability records...

Just as sanity was about to prevail, I checked the mirror again. The Escalade was standing still, wipers swishing back and forth, big silver raindrops plopping all around, the driver refusing to get closer to me. That's when my other voice piped in.

"Only one way to find out," it said.

Almost without willing it so, my foot jammed the gas pedal all the way to the floor, sending the car roaring up Belmont, the tires whirring for traction on the steep hill, the scream of the engine drowning out the rising weather.

A hundred yards up the hill I swung a hard right onto Bellevue. As the car fishtailed once and then righted itself, I mashed the brake pedal to the floor, threw the transmission into reverse, intending to jam the car into a narrow alley between apartment buildings. Or at least, that was the idea.

I used to drive a Fiat, a little POS whose only virtue was that it didn't take up a lot of space and was relatively easy to push by hand. My recently acquired Chevy Tahoe, however, while far more commodious for a man of my dimensions, regrettably was also considerably less accommodating.

The scream of warping metal and the tinkle of broken glass made it apparent that both my depth perception and my driving skills had suffered the same ignoble fate as my wariness. The passenger side of my car was no more than an inch from the Sir Galahad Apartments. I checked the rearview mirror. It was gone.

Worse yet, the driver's side was no more than a foot from the north wall of Bellevue Court. No way I could open the door. I stewed for a few seconds, resigned myself to the ignominy of it all, and lowered the rear window. Nothing like crawling around the inside of an automobile to give a man a little humility. Accompanied by a symphony of grunts and groans, I extruded myself over and around two sets of seats, and finally crawled out the back window feetfirst, where I stood precariously on the plastic bumper, hanging onto the ski rack for all I was worth, looking out over the length of the Tahoe toward the rain-slick street.

Worst of all, my little maneuver had failed to fool my pursuers. Just about the time I had steadied myself on the bumper and looked back over the length of the car, they stepped into the mouth of the alley. Two of the strangest-looking dudes I'd ever laid eyes on. The little guy was under five feet tall. Big round glasses half the size of his head. Looked like Peter Lorre as Mr. Moto.

His partner was downright reptilian. Leather-scary. More zippers than a set of slipcovers. Big, square noggin sporting a platinum blond flattop hairdo. With lightning bolts cut into both sides of his head, he looked like something straight out of a comic book. Captain Carnal maybe. Definitely not something you'd bring home to mother. Or bring home, period.

Zipper-head curled a disdainful Elvis lip. "Tight fit," he said.

"They're not making alleys like they used to."

He nodded at the broken mirror. "Looks bad," he said.

"Speaking of bad looks," I said, "you need to do something about yours, man. This leather zipper-head thing you've got going on here..."

The corners of his eyes narrowed. "Smart guy, huh?"

"Also, whoever writes your dialogue definitely needs to be replaced. That old film noir shit..."

Apparently I touched a nerve. The Elvis lip straightened itself. "You sayin' I'm stupid?" he demanded.

"Perish the thought," I deadpanned.

"You're sayin' I'm stupid." Not a question this time. Apparently he'd had some previous experience along this conversational tack.

He took a step back and surveyed the scene. That's when I realized that the other guy was nowhere in sight, but I didn't have time to ponder. Zipper-head was looking for some way to get back to where I stood, without coming over the top of the car.

Mr. Moto popped back into view. They exchanged a glance.

"You best mind your own business and butt out," Zipper-head said. "You been puttin' your face where it don't belong."

"You followed me all over the city just to tell me that?"

"I see you again, I'm gonna fuck you up."

"Providing you remember."

He was going to go into it again. The stupid thing. I could tell.

Mr. Moto toddled around the back of the Escalade and pulled himself into the driver's seat.

"He got blocks on the pedals?" I asked Zipper-head affably.

"Next time I'll let you ask him yourself," he promised.

I smiled. "I'll leave myself a note on my BlackBerry."

Without another word, he launched a karate side-kick at the front of my car. If he was trying to impress me, it worked. The whole car rocked from the force of the blow. I heard the headlight shatter and fall to the ground. He stepped to the left and duplicated the maneuver on the other headlight, with much the same result.

"Next time it'll be your lights I put out," he promised.

Before I could come up with another snappy rejoinder, he turned and ambled back toward the Escalade, slithering with a loose-hipped lizard swing as he crossed the street and climbed into the car.

I stood where I was until the Cadillac hissed out of sight.

*     *     *

By the time I got my car towed to the Chevy dealership and signed my life away for a rental car, it was quarter to nine. Took me another half hour to get over to the mall at Northgate and canvass the shoe emporiums, so, by the time I'd finished my first pass of the stores, they were less than a half hour from closing.

He must have been on a break or hanging out in the back room the first time I strolled by. Second time I walked past the All-Star Sports store, he was standing at the cash register chatting with a customer.

Richard Waters, aka Ricky, was a good-looking young fella. Smooth, even features and good hair. Bright red polo shirt with an embroidered logo on the chest. He'd put on a few pounds since his Millennium photo, but it was him all right. Probably eating more starches and less steak than when he was in the yacht business, I figured.

He handed a purple plastic bag to the customer and waved him on his way. Soon as the customer turned his back, the boyish smile disappeared and then, a coupla seconds later, so did Ricky.

I waited for one of the other clerks to ring up a customer, and then, with the counter area finally deserted, slid through the opening, past the "Employees Only" sign and into the dusty back room.

Floor-to-ceiling unpainted metal racks awash in shoe boxes. Dirty bathroom on the left, battered metal desk on the right. Nobody'd swept the floor in a month.

He had the back door propped open with a storage bin and was standing outside power-smoking a cigarette. His eye caught my movement.

"Hey, hey," he said. "Didn't you read the damn sign? You can't be back here."

I ignored his admonition and kept coming. When he flicked the butt behind himself and slid the storage bin aside, I bellied him back through the doorway and out into the service road that ran behind the mall.

A quarter mile of green dumpsters, cardboard balers, and loading docks. He tried to swim his way around me but I straight-armed him backward. While he fought to regain his balance, the door slammed shut on its own.

Half-a-dozen brightly painted garbage trucks were lined up along the back of the mall. The roar of diesels mixed with the whine of hydraulics to form a wavering wall of sound, punctuated now and then by the rap of metal on metal as the trucks banged the last flattened remnants from the big green trash containers.

"You crazy?" he yelled above the din. "I'm gonna have to walk all the way around the fucking building to get back to the store."

"You don't answer my questions you're not going to be able to walk around the building," I promised with a smile.

He took a step backward. His boyish face clouded. "You kiddin'?" he asked.

"If I was kidding, I'd be wearing a balloon hat and no pants."

Somewhere in his head a lightbulb went on. "You're the guy."

"What guy?"

"The guy from the bachelor party. You're the one who…"

"Yeah," I said. "I am."

The admission had the desired effect. He showed me a pair of cautioning palms. "Hey, I don't want any trouble here," he assured me.

Guys like Ricky never do; that's how they keep those boyish good looks. But something in his expression caught my eye. Something furtive and pained.

"I'm trying to find Brett Ward," I said amiably. "He doesn't answer his phone and his mailbox is full."

"How would I know where he is, man?" he whined. "I haven't even talked to the guy in a couple of months. We worked at the same place. Went out to lunch once in a while. Went to a Huskies game together one time." He threw his palms at the ceiling and shook his head. "That's it, man."

The adamant denial struck a discordant note. He was trying way too hard to convince me that he didn't know anything. "If you needed to find him, what would you do?" I pressed.

"Call his old lady, I guess," he answered quickly.

"She's missing too."

"Then how in hell am I supposed to…"

I straight-armed him again. He staggered back two steps.

"I'm not feeling very patient," I told him.

Ricky checked over his shoulder, thinking about making a run for it.

"I'm a lot quicker than I look," I warned him.

He took me at my word. "Come on, man. I've got a wife, a kid, and another on the way. I need to make a living here. I can't take any more of…"

"Any more of what?"

He pressed his lips together and looked away.

A lightbulb went on in my head. "I'm not the first person to come asking about Brett Ward, am I?" I tried.

He set his jaw and looked away. "I can't, man," he said finally. When he turned his gaze my way, his eyes were on the verge of welling over. Obviously, something had happened. Something that could make a grown man cry.

"What happened?"

He turned his face away again.

The scream of hydraulics filled the air, making it impossible to talk.

"They said they'd come back," he said when things quieted down.

I put a reassuring hand on his shoulder. An ongoing shiver ran through his body like an electric current. He flinched and hunched his shoulders.

"'They' who?" I pressed.

He shook his head and hunched harder.

I took a shot. "Blond flattop hairdo? Lightning bolts cut into the sides?"

Had he been able to tie his shoulders in a knot around his neck, I believe he would have. "That Koontz guy...," he began.

I couldn't believe it. "You know that guy?" I asked.

"He's famous, man," Ricky whined. "Jordan Koontz. He's that Canadian mixed martial arts fighter who killed the guy in the ring up in Vancouver. Remember? The one who attacked the referee when he tried to stop the fight. Busted the ref's neck. Banned from MMA for life. Ended up going to prison for a while."

As a matter of fact, I did vaguely remember. Five or six years back, it had been all over the news. As I recalled, the referee suffered some degree of permanent paralysis. The Canadian bluenoses had gone wild. The incident had nearly led to the banning of mixed martial arts in Canada.

"And the other one," he snuffled. "Little Asian guy with big round glasses, he just held the gun on me. Koontz, he made me…" He wanted to blurt it out, but couldn't bring himself to do it. I watched in silence as he backed up and tried again. "He took his hand and…" He shook his head in resignation. Not only was he unable to spit it out, but by now I was pretty sure I didn't want to hear it. Whatever he had to say would surely drag me to a place I didn't care to visit.

I took a step back and waited while he pulled himself together. He looked out over the line of trash receptacles and composed himself. Minutes passed. When he turned back my way he'd dried his eyes and had the look of a guy who wanted some payback. "There was one weird thing with Brett," he said. "Something I didn't tell those guys."

"What's that?"

"Brett's wife sent a stripper to the office for his birthday." He held his cupped hands in front of his chest in the international sign for "tits out to here." "He'd been gone for months and months by that time. It was weird that she didn't know."

"And I suppose the rest of you sent the girl on her way with a nice tip in her pocket."

He grinned sheepishly and shrugged. "You know, man. She was there, you know, ready to do her thing, all paid for and all. Seemed like we might as well, you know…"

I helped him out. "You let her do her thing. So she wouldn't feel bad."

"Yeah."

I watched as something crossed his mind.

I poked him in the chest with a stiff finger. "What?"

"I gave Brett a jingle. You know, a one-guy-to-another kind of thing. Told him about the stripper showing up at the office. Just in case it came up, you know, in conversation or something like that."

"You remember the girl's name?"

He thought about it. "Sherry, Cherry, something like that." He held up a finger as if to ask for a moment, dug into his back pocket, and came out with his wallet. He was one of those guys who makes a point of collecting business cards from everyone he meets. A salesman's habit. You never know, you know.

Took him a minute of sorting through a fistful of cards but eventually he came up with a gold business card. Embossed belly dancer. Merry Storm. Exotic Dances for All Occasions. Seattle phone number at the bottom right.

"Thanks," I said, pocketing the card.

"Hey look," he said. "I got to go. We're closing up. I got to be there."

"Go ahead," I said.

I stood on the asphalt, amid the roar and rumble of the garbage trucks, and watched as Ricky limped down the road like he was coming home from a colonoscopy. Forty yards down, he stopped and turned back my way. He yelled above the din.

"That blond one...he's one a sick bastard. You better..."

"I'll be careful," I said.

Halfway down the mall, Ricky found another store's back door open and ducked inside.

# Chapter 2

Ah, the heady aroma of the morgue in the morning. The bouquet opens with a piquant whisper of formaldehyde, and then as the palate slips into play, segues smoothly into earthy undertones, prior to a surprising finish that clings to the roof the mouth with the zeal of a Catholic communion wafer.

When I was younger, I had a much stronger stomach. I used to go downstairs, stand behind the thick glass windows, and watch as Rebecca and her colleagues performed their grisly duties. That's where I learned that autopsy strategies were as individual as the people doing the saw work.

Rebecca treated the dead with great reverence. Her table was always neat and clean and the bodies were draped this way and that so as to keep prying eyes like mine from seeing anything they didn't have to. She always said that people deserved the same dignity in death that they deserved in life.

Vaughn Tisdale, on the other hand, was all blood, guts, and veins in the teeth. He treated the dismemberment of a corpse as if he were parting out a 1967 Chevy. Red to his armpits. Body parts scattered hither and yon. Great gobs of goo everywhere. The fact that Rebecca thought very highly of his work made it plain that pathology allowed for different strokes for different folks. Metaphorically speaking, of course.

These days I stayed upstairs in the office area. That's where I found Vaughn Tisdale. Vaughn was a big, fleshy guy with a bale of curly red hair clinging stubbornly to the back of his head. He was sitting at his desk, staring at a silver toaster, waiting for a pair of Pop Tarts to make an appearance. As usual he was wearing a three-dimensionally soiled smock and an even more execrable pair of latex gloves.

He looked up from the toaster. "Hey, big fella," he said. "Long time no see."

"The girl out front said Sandy was out of town."

"Conference of some sort. Iowa or someplace, as I recall."

Which was a pity, because Sandy McGinty managed the business end of the county morgue operation like a pit bull manages a kitty cat. Sandy was known as a micromanager of subatomic proportions and would surely have known whatever there was to know, whether the knowers knew it or not. If that makes any sense.

"Iris Duval came to my house yesterday afternoon."

"Lucky you," Tisdale joked.

"Iris tells me she hasn't heard from Rebecca in over a week."

Vaughn rocked forward in his chair. The Pop Tarts popped. He ignored them. "How can that be?" he asked.

"I was hoping you could enlighten me."

"I just know what everybody else knows." He snagged the nearest tart and, irrespective of how hot it must have been, swallowed half of it. "You know how Rebecca is, Leo. She's pretty damn self-contained." He took another bite and the tart was gone. "Not one of those people who put their personal business in the street, if you know what I mean, and I know you do."

"So nobody down here knows anything about the specifics. Anything about what was going on that required a leave from her job."

He accessed the second tart. "The rumor mill says she's having problems with the hubby." In two quick bites the pastry disappeared. "I can tell you this; she was taking long lunches on Mondays and Fridays. If you ask me, they were getting some professional help for whatever problems they were having."

"Why do you say that?"

"She alluded to it once." He wiped his mouth with his sleeve. "She was sitting on the wall outside reading over some folded-up paperwork. I asked her, you know just conversationally, how things were going. She said she had some homework to do before today's session."

"Session, huh?"

"That's what she said."

"You're right. Sounds like marriage counseling."

Vaughn nodded. "And those people are always giving the happy couple these vitriolic little assignments to complete between sessions. You know..." He raised his voice an octave and a half to Julia Child's pitch: "'I want both of you to write down the five things you most detest about one another. We'll share the next time we see each other.'" He ended with one of the waxiest grins I'd ever seen.

I laughed aloud, despite my mood and the cold, empty feeling in the pit of my stomach. "You sound like you've had some experience in these matters of the heart."

He made a disgusted face. "I've been married five times, Leo. My head's been shrunk more times than a virgin wool sweater."

"But you've got no idea who they were seeing."

"Nope," he said. "I can tell you one thing, though. Coupla weeks after she started taking long lunches, I asked her if maybe she couldn't bring me back a sandwich or something. She showed up with this great big belly-bomb of a sandwich."

"Yeah?"

"I know where the sandwich came from."

"Where?"

"You know, that place with 'Corned Beef' painted in red on the side of the building. Up there close to the freeway."

"Mike's Market."

He nodded. "And there's absolutely no place to park in that frigging neighborhood. Anyplace you could legally put the car would cost you more than the damn sandwich."

"Rebecca's a very frugal girl," I said. "That wouldn't work for her."

"So you have to figure she was already parked when she went for the grub."

"You're thinking those big office towers across the street."

"That's what I'm betting," he said as he dusted crumbs from his gloves and pushed himself to his feet. "Nice talking at you, Leo," he said. "But I've got some more bowel sections waiting for me downstairs."

I didn't offer to shake hands.

．　．　．

The Metropolitan Park Towers sat at awkward angles to one another on opposite sides of Minor Avenue, as if a skyhook had dropped them in place and wherever they landed was where they stayed. A quick perusal of one building's directory made it apparent that if Rebecca had been seeing someone in these the buildings, I was going to need a lot more information. If I was doing the math correctly, between the two buildings there were somewhere in the vicinity of four hundred tenants, many with remarkably uninformative company names like Internal Solutions Corporation, which as far as I was concerned could have involved anything from integrated business software to gastrointestinal distress.

The rain had momentarily relented, so I bought myself a latte and a cheese Danish from the Starbucks on the ground floor and repaired to the outdoor plaza to contemplate my next move. I used the brown Starbucks paper napkin to dry the bench and then sat there under steel wool skies asking myself how I could get a line on Rebecca's marriage guru.

When a long-term relationship breaks down, people often feel the need to take a side and, while Rebecca and I still had a few mutual friends, most of the people we used to spend time with had chosen one camp or the other. Add that to the fact that couples tend to hang out with other couples and it was safe to say that the diameter of my social circle was considerably smaller than it had been a few years back.

By the time the Danish disappeared and the dregs of the coffee were cold, I had a pretty good idea what I was going to do. I hated the idea to the very depths of my childish soul, but I was going to do it anyway.

If anyone other than her shrink knew what was going on in Rebecca's life, it would be Monica Muller. They'd been friends and confidants since grammar school. It had always been my understanding that they shared whatever girlie secrets girlies shared with other girlies.

First problem was that Monica and I had never been terribly fond of one another. Nothing personal really, just something about being rivals for Rebecca's time and attention. Second was the fact that Monica had gotten remarried since I'd last been in contact with her, and I had no idea what her new last name was.

I did, however, have a pretty good idea of how I might find out, so I got on the horn and starting making calls to the other side of the great social divide. Took me nearly an hour and half and a dozen calls to people who were no longer speaking to me before I worked my way to Judy Lombardi.

Judy refused to give me Monica's number but said she'd leave her a message saying that I'd been trying to get in touch. I gave her my contact information and told her to say that Iris hadn't heard from Rebecca for over a week and had asked me to look for her. She said she would. I told her it was an emergency.

I was on the phone trying to come up with a number for Fran and Larry Fitzgerald when call waiting began to vibrate. Number blocked. I thumbed the button.

"Leo Waterman," I said.

"Judy said you called." Her tone held all the warmth of a walk-in freezer.

In a perverse way, it was nice not to feel compelled to go through all the long-time-no-see bullshit that precedes getting around to what it was you really called about, so I dispensed with the niceties and got right to it. I told her about Iris Duval coming to my house. About Rebecca's leave of absence. About being unable to contact Brett Ward. I was prepared to keep talking until she either came around or hung up on me, but that was all it took.

"I haven't been able to reach her either," Monica said. "I've been worried."

"Do you know what's going on?" I asked.

"Just that they were having some sort of trouble in their relationship."

"But you don't know what?"

"She wouldn't say."

A fact that was troublesome in its own right. If Rebecca wasn't telling Monica, she wasn't telling anyone, which I suppose explained why she'd felt the need to hire somebody to listen to her. The hole in my stomach got deeper and colder.

"I don't have to tell you how out of character this is for her."

Long pause. "No, you don't," she said finally.

"Everybody seems to think that she and Brett are seeing somebody about it."

"They are," she said without hesitation.

"You know who they're seeing?" I asked.

"She," Monica corrected. "He only went twice."

"Do you have a name?"

Longer pause as she tried to decide whether or not to tell me.

"Rachel Thoms," she said finally. "She's in one of those office buildings..."

"Right by the interstate," I finished for her.

"If you already knew, Leo, why call me?" she asked disgustedly, and hung up.

●　■　●

East Tower, seventeenth floor, suite 1751. Rachel Thoms, MSW, ACSW, LICSW, Relationship Analysis. I eased the door open and took a seat in the waiting room. I could hear the dull mumble of voices in an adjoining room but made it a point not to listen.

The room was carefully designed to promote peace of mind. All muted browns and yellows. Fresh fall floral display on the central coffee table. Three small still lifes and a big painting of a suspension bridge arching into a distant, fog-shrouded shore. Either a transformation metaphor or an invitation to jump. I wasn't sure which.

Thirty-five minutes later, the door on the opposite side of the room opened and an anorexic young woman in her midtwenties stepped into the room. She was strangling a hankie and dabbing at her bloodshot eyes. One look at me and she bolted across the room like an Olympic speed walker, snuffling a garbled curse in my direction as she streaked out into the hallway and slammed the door.

The next woman through the door was most everything the first one wasn't and then some. She wasn't skinny and she wasn't crying. Like the first woman, however, she also wasn't in the least pleased by my presence.

She was a handsome woman. Five-ten without the shoes. Big boned and big featured, with a thick head of chestnut hair pulled to the back of her head and pinned up. The kind of woman who looked you dead in the eye and challenged you to bring it on. The kind of woman you'd like to climb up on the furniture and then dive into. I restrained myself but couldn't help but notice that, despite that cold steel feeling in my gut, my blood had begun to redistribute in a rather unwelcome manner.

"You violated that woman's privacy," she said.

"I'm sorry. That certainly wasn't my intention."

"Didn't the girl at the desk tell you to wait downstairs?"

"I skipped the desk and came straight up here." I anticipated her next question. "I was afraid you wouldn't see me."

She blinked once and picked at her tweed skirt. "And why would I refuse to see you?" she asked.

"I'm looking for Rebecca Duval," I said.

I watched as the veins and tendons in her neck tightened. She cocked her head like the RCA dog and took a moment to look me over.

"You'd be Leo Waterman," she said.

"Yes, I would."

She folded her arms over her luxurious chest. "As you must know, Mr. Waterman, I can't discuss my patients. Just admitting that she *was* a patient..." She let the self-admonition peter out.

"She's missing," I said.

She did that cocking of her head thing again, making me wonder whether the gesture might be shrink body language that showed the patient you were listening.

"Missing in what sense?" she wanted to know.

I gave her the *Reader's Digest* version of the story. Not surprisingly, she was a good listener.

"That's very worrisome," she said when I finished.

"I'm scared to death," I admitted.

"Perhaps you should contact the police."

"Been there, done that," I said, and then told her what Marty Gilbert had told me.

She checked her watch. "I've another patient in five minutes," she said. "You're going to have to go."

"Anything you could do that might help me find her..."

She waved me off, walked across the room, and opened the door to the hallway. The sound she made when moving would have been illegal in seven southern states.

"The relationship between a patient and her therapist is a sacred trust," she said as he pulled the door all the way open.

I took the hint and stepped out into the hall. "This is an emergency. If you could just...," I began.

"Do you have a business card?" she interrupted.

I fished around in my wallet and came out with an old, tattered private eye card with somebody else's number written in red pen on the back.

She slid a pair of red half-glasses onto the end of her nose. I watched her eyes slide over the surface. She gave me a curt nod, stepped back, and closed the door.

■ ■ ■

Five hundred seventy-seven dollars and twelve cents. That's what it cost to replace the Tahoe's headlights. Throw in another two hundred or so for the mirror, yet another forty-seven for the rental car and insurance and I was out eight hundred bucks or so, five hundred of which was coming out of my pocket. Not to mention I had to listen to a lecture from the guy in the body shop about how the space-age polymers in the headlights were warranted to withstand everything short of small arms fire without cracking or breaking, and that however I managed to smash them without demolishing the front of the car should probably be avoided in the future. I gritted my teeth and assured him I'd be more careful.

So it's no surprise that my mood was about as sunny as the weather as I headed back toward downtown in a cold drizzle. A full day's work had yielded nothing other than the fact that I wasn't the only one looking for Brett Ward, which made the situation all the more troubling. Worse yet, whatever was going on involved those two hired freaks in the Cadillac. Freaks who had managed to instill an absolutely primal fear in Ricky Waters. Guys who'd hurt him in ways he didn't want to talk about. No doubt about it. I didn't like it one bit.

My phone began to tinkle in my pocket. Normally, I don't answer the phone while I'm driving. First of all, it's illegal to have a phone in your hand while driving in the state of Washington. Absolutely everybody still does it, but technically it's illegal. Second, and more to the point, I don't flatter myself to imagine that my doings are of sufficient import as to require immediate attention. Ninety-nine percent of the time whoever is on the phone can wait till I get to where I'm going. The other one percent are wrong numbers.

Today, however, feeling hollow and somber, I immediately began to pat myself down looking for the phone. Must have looked like I was on fire, slapping this pocket and that, trying to locate my personal device. All I managed to do was to weave from lane to lane like I'd had a stroke. An irate chorus of horns snapped my attention forward just in time to avoid rear-ending the FedEx truck in front of me.

I gulped air and got the hell off the road before I hurt somebody, pulling into a strip mall parking lot and jamming the car into Park in front of a *pho* parlor, before resuming my search for my phone, which had by that time ceased tinkling.

Took me the better part of three minutes to figure out it was an e-mail message and then retrieve it. No subject. Sent from a Hotmail account. Marty Gilbert, I figured, trying to help me out but taking no chances with his pension.

No message, but attached was a spreadsheet packed with tiny numbers. Screens and screens and screens of them. I zoomed in, turned the device sideways, and worked my way across the top line like a stadium reader board. Rebecca Ann Duval. MasterCard number such and such. Transactions. Date. Location. My eyes clicked back to the date like a slot machine settling on the cherries. The card had been used yesterday. I scrolled back to the left and started down the list of transaction dates. Her MasterCard had been used multiple times every day for the past two weeks or so.

My emotions bounced around like a ping-pong ball. One part of me wanted to be joyous. To exalt. Another part warned me not to get ahead of myself. All it meant was that somebody had used the card. That's all it meant. I kept telling myself that.

．  ．  ．

I stopped at the house for long enough to pack an overnight bag and use the computer to read the rest of the information Marty had sent me. It was all there in black and white. For the past week, Rebecca had been charging food, drink, and sundries at the Alderbrook Resort and Spa. Same thing with the phone. All of her phone calls had originated from that same out-in-the-middle-of-nowhere area code. Most of them to a Seattle number I didn't recognize.

An hour after I'd arrived back at the family manse, I was on the road again, heading downtown toward the Pier 56 Ferry Terminal where I could catch a ride over to Bremerton from whence I could drive to the bottom of the Hood Canal, which really wasn't a canal at all, at least not in the man-made sense, but rather was a long, thin fjord within a fjord whose sole claim to fame was that it separated the Kitsap Peninsula from the Olympic Peninsula and thus required a bridge.

Forty minutes on the ferry followed by an hour and a half's driving would get me down to Union, where the Alderbrook Resort squatted by the dark shores of Puget Sound. The place had been there forever, since 1913 or something. Started out as one of those resorts where, as was the fashion of the day, outdoorsy city people in bowler hats and high button shoes abandoned their privileged lives in favor of sleeping in tents, and otherwise communing with nature. Same people you saw in the old photographs, climbing Mount Rainier dressed for a garden party. Hardy souls those.

I googled the Alderbrook website while waiting for the ferry. Nearly a hundred years and half as many owners later, the Alderbrook had moved upscale with Irish linens, four-star restaurant, world-class spa, eighteen-hole golf course, and all. Your year-round getaway destination. I took the virtual tour and then booked myself a room.

By the time I rolled through Belfair, it was mostly dark and I had a plan pretty much worked out. I opted for discretion. I needed to satisfy myself that Rebecca was okay without invading her privacy or looking like a complete fool if maybe she and Brett were reconciling and making wild whoopee in the woods.

If I started showing photos around the lobby and asking questions, I was bound to attract whatever passed for security, at which point all hope of anonymity would be out the window, so I'd decided to fly under the radar, which, my brain noted, wasn't going to be easy if the place was deserted. In the past hour I'd passed maybe a dozen cars, the majority of which were headed in the other direction.

I needn't have worried. The parking lot was jam-packed with luxury vehicles. The rich rumble of laughter and voices spilled from the front of the main building as I gave the kid my bag and started up the wide front stairs. In between the two sets of double doors, a reader board welcomed the twenty-third annual Pacific Northwest Cosmetic Dentistry Association to its annual get-together. SmileFest, I guessed.

Place looked like some Hollywood set designer's conception of a wilderness experience. The Pasadena Ponderosa. Giant fireplace crackling at the far end of the room, urban art on rustic walls, lots of thick, rich-looking furniture arranged this way and that, at least a dozen separate seating areas where guests could commune in bucolic luxury.

I registered as Tom Van Dyne, one of several borrowed identities I'd used back when I'd worked as a PI. The real Tom Van Dyne was serving life without the possibility of parole down in Pelican Bay, so I didn't figure he'd mind me co-opting his identity. He might be doing forever for offing and then partially consuming both his wife and his mother, but thanks to me he had a perfect driving record and his credit was top notch. The way I saw it, the guy ought to be grateful.

The gorgeous East Indian girl at the desk volunteered that SmileFest was drawing to a close. Only the awards dinner remained and they were staging that little gala next door in the Vancouver Room as we spoke.

I let the kid carry my bag all the way to my room. His name was William and he was taking a couple of semesters off from Central Washington University to raise funds for grad school. I slipped him a five on the way out. I'm all for education.

The room was as advertised, sumptuous and nobly appointed. As was my habit, I hung my things in the closet, and then unpacked. Something in me feels more settled and at peace if I take my things out of the bag and stow them in the dresser drawers. Don't ask me why.

After delivering my shaving kit to the bathroom, I sat down on the edge of the bed and looked around. The digital clock read 6:02. I stretched and yawned. I lay back, half on, half off the bed, and closed my eyes. Just gonna rest for a second.

• • •

Sometime during the two hours I was out cold, I'd sleepwalked most of the rest of me up on the bed, where I awoke to find myself lying crossways with my lower legs hanging over the edge of the mattress. Wasn't until I sat up that I realized everything from my knees down was fast asleep. I sat on the bed, stomped my feet several times, and began massaging life back into my lower legs.

I don't generally remember my dreams, but as I sat there trying to knead some feeling into my calves, I recalled where I'd been for the past couple of hours. I'd been involved in a frantic pursuit, trapped inside a rotting Victorian mansion, where one shabby room led to another and another, to deadfalls and trap doors and secret staircases, where toothless, wild-haired maniacs barred my way at every turn. I saw it all in a single somber second. I saw a terrified Rebecca, stretching, reaching for me but always just beyond my grasp. I cried out to her and then the movie faded to black.

By nine thirty, I'd showered, shaved, and stuffed myself into a suitable pair of trousers and a Tommy Bahama shirt. I'm not much of a dress-up guy. I'm pretty sure my tenuous relationship with fashion dates to my childhood. For reasons I've never fully understood, my parents had a nearly uncontrollable urge to dress me like a miniature FBI agent. Birthdays, Easter, Christmas, you name the occasion and there I was in some old photo, squinting into the sun, wearing a Mike Hammer porkpie hat and a John Cameron Swayze trench coat with enough epaulets to tie down a load of lumber.

The Overlook Bar lived up to its billing. It overlooked the dining room, which in turn overlooked the dark waters of Puget Sound, thus allowing me to scan the dinner crowd without actually being among them. It was a big room in the shape of a fan. From above, it looked like a galaxy of flickering candles with waiters flitting from flame to flame. Beneath it all, the clink of flatware and the dull undertones of conversation rose from the room like a long, low musical note. I ran my eyes over the tables one by one, taking my time, making sure. No Rebecca.

I must have unconsciously sighed or something, because the bartender who'd been kept busy by a succession of waiters fetching drinks for their tables, suddenly looked up from the cash register and ambled in my direction. Mr. Nondescript in a black shirt and matching trousers. Maybe fifty or so. Fit and trim for a guy his age. Good teeth shining in the semidarkness. The gold name tag read "Bruce."

"How ya doin'?" he asked.

I assured him I was peachy and ordered a Heineken.

He swept his eyes over the dining room below. "Looking for someone?"

"Old girlfriend," I said.

"Sometimes it's best to just let 'em go," he offered with a knowing smile.

"Can't live with 'em, can't live with 'em," I joked.

Before we could continue our manly repartee, a piano began to tinkle the opening bars of "Body and Soul." On my way in, I'd somehow failed to notice the grand piano squatting in the front corner of the room, an eight-hundred-pound oversight that suggested I might be a bit more overwrought than I was willing to admit.

The lady at the piano had a delicate touch and a nice sense of timing. She slid into the chord changes much the way I imagined she'd slid into her blue cocktail dress.

Bruce poured my beer and set it on a cardboard coaster. "What makes you think your friend's way out here?" he wanted to know. "This is seriously off-season for this place. Soon as the tooth and wallet specialists hit the road, this place is gonna be deader than heaven on a Saturday night."

"I ran into her mother the other day," I said. "She thought Rebecca said she was coming out here to get away from it all."

"'Away from it all' we got plenty of," he conceded.

Seemed like Bruce wanted to talk, so I decided to take a chance and push a little harder. "I figured, you know, what the hell, I had some business out in Port Angeles, figured I'd stop by." I shrugged helplessly. "You never know," I said.

"Yeah," he offered. "I know how it is."

"Figured she wasn't going to be hard to find. There's not that many six-foot-two inch women traipsing around the Pacific Northwest."

My description straightened his spine and flexed the muscles along the side of his jaw. He noticed that I noticed and slid himself to the far end of the bar with a bit more nonchalance than the moment called for. I watched as he busied himself with a stack of receipts, then poured a club soda over ice and delivered it to the lady playing the piano. He leaned in close and whispered in her ear. She said something. He shook his head and then whispered some more. As he walked away, she pulled her eyes from the keyboard for long enough to flick an inquisitive glance in my direction.

Once back behind the bar, Bruce experienced an overwhelming need to straighten and dust his liquor inventory. He found a white metal stool, climbed up onto the middle step, and dusted the shelves, top to bottom, one at a time. I listened to the piano and sipped at my beer as he worked his way in my direction.

When the passage of time and empty state of my beer glass made it impossible for him to ignore me any longer, he inquired, "Another?"

"Was it something I said?"

He stepped over to the register, pulled a stack of credit card receipts from beneath the cash drawer, and shuffled his way toward the bottom of the pile. He separated one from its brethren, returned the rest, and slid the drawer shut.

"This your friend?" he asked.

I took the receipt from his hand. Chase MasterCard. Rebecca Ann Duval.

"That's her," I said.

The pianist segued into a stately version of "Take the 'A' Train."

"Maybe it's best," Bruce said resignedly.

"Maybe what's best?"

"That you stopped by," he said. "Sometimes these things just work out." He waved a knowing hand. "You know—cosmically."

"Ah," I said, as though I knew what in hell he was talking about.

A waiter arrived with a drink order. Bruce ambled down to the far end of the bar and got busy mixing up a couple of mojitos.

By the time the waiter had disappeared with the drinks, the song had moved to Cyndi Lauper's "Time after Time," and Bruce was leaning on the bar in front of me.

"Way I hear it...," he began. "They had to send security out to her cabin this morning."

I tried to remain calm. "Really," I said. "How come?"

"To get her out of there."

"She wouldn't leave?"

"Not from what I hear."

"Why did they want her to leave?"

"All of a sudden her credit was no good."

"Any idea why?"

"I hear the bank turned her card off."

Of course they did. The minute Marty Gilbert requested Rebecca's credit card history, Chase security had automatically been notified. Police inquiries make banks nervous and banks take very few chances with their own money. Your money, they'd bet on a Tijuana cockroach race. Their money is a whole different story. The frequency of use, combined with the unusual geographical location of the charges and a police inquiry, had set the bank's algorithms to dancing the tarantella. Bingo. Stop payment.

"So what happened?"

The telling made him nervous. He double-checked the surrounding area. "Hey...," he wheedled. "...you know I'm just the messenger here. I probably shouldn't even be..."

I reached over and put a hand on his shoulder. "No trouble from this end," I assured him. "Just tell me what happened."

He wiped the corners of his mouth with his thumb and forefinger. "Last week or so she was here..." He paused again. "One of the locals...a real jerk..." He stopped talking, trying to choose his words carefully. "His name's Teddy. Teddy Healy. Teddy's a first-class pain. Comes down here, puts the moves on every female under sixty. Gets in fights with patrons." He waved an angry hand. "Teddy's just a pain."

"What's Teddy got to do with this?" I pressed.

"He was all over her," Bruce said. "Buying her drinks. Buying her dinner. Trying to work his way...you know..."

"Into her pants," I finished for him.

"Yeah," he said.

"Was she going for it?"

"Not at first."

"But he wore her down."

His turn to shrug. "Looked that way to me."

A trio of waiters arrived with drink orders. Bruce straightened up.

"Why do you say that?" I pressed.

"She...you know, after they threw her out of the cabin..."

"Yeah."

"She left with Teddy." He looked over his shoulder at the impatient trio of waiters. "You want to know about Teddy, ask Patty." He nodded at the piano lady. "She can tell you a lot more about Teddy Healy than I can."

.  .  .

Patty's age was hard to tell. She could have been a hard-driven thirty-eight with a lot of city miles on her, or a well-preserved fifty-five that had been garaged and only driven on Sundays. Either of which worked for me.

I remembered my reaction to Rachel Thoms earlier in the day and wondered why, all of a sudden, I found myself physically attracted to women. I hadn't thought about women in years. At least not in that way. I'd been way too busy feeling sorry for myself to be concerned with such tawdry urges and now, all of a sudden, at the least appropriate moment imaginable, I was like a slumbering bear, suddenly out of hibernation and lumbering around the neighborhood looking for a meal.

I sipped at my beer and wondered, for the umpteenth time, about the walking contradiction that was Leo

Waterman. I spent an uncomfortable twenty minutes wandering through the ins and outs of my tortured psyche before I finally came to my senses. Too much introspection always made my head hurt, so I simply leaned back against the bar and listened to the music.

She played another couple of numbers and finally ended with a flourish that said tonight's musical interlude was over. As the last strains of a tune I didn't recognize floated through the air, I slid from my stool, and walked toward the piano at the far end of the room.

She saw me coming, retrieved a sequined clutch purse from inside the piano bench, and staged a hurried exit. Like I told Ricky Waters, I was faster than I looked. I made up the distance in half-a-dozen strides and stepped around her.

"Might I have a word?" I asked in my most courtly manner.

Apparently, chivalry wasn't my strong suit. She turned her shoulders, slid past me, and started down the stairs at a dainty lope.

I trailed along in her wake. Past the phones and the elevators, past the dazed-looking concierge sitting at his desk, and out into the lobby, where she finally tired of me filling up her rearview mirror and stopped walking. She turned to face me.

"You don't seem to be getting the message," she said.

"The bartender said…"

She went shopping for angry but came back from the store with scared. "Bruce is an idiot. He needs to learn to mind his own business."

She caught me reading her anxiety and started walking again, faster now, heels clicking on the polished wooden floor, veering left toward the Dutch door to the left of the reception desk. Checked luggage and coatroom.

Not wishing to loom, I stayed at a nonthreatening distance as she retrieved a long, black wool coat and shouldered her way into it.

Newly armored, she exchanged a few words with whoever handed her the coat, and then walked over and stood as close to me as personal space considerations would allow. "Do I have to call security?" she asked in a low voice.

Up close and personal, she was about my age. Middle to late forties somewhere. She'd had work done. Good work. Expensive work. You had to look closely around the corners of the eyes and the backs of her ears to see the spiderweb traces. Fifteen more years, four excellent plastic surgeons, and she'd begin to have that startled "what the hell just happened?" look they get when modern medical technology has gone one step too far in its quest to stave off the ravages of time. But for now, the illusion was alive, well, and working just fine.

Not only that, but she'd meant what she said about calling security. I could feel it. This was the only chance I was going to get so I went straight to it.

"I'm really worried about a friend of mine," I said.

Apparently she didn't share my anxiety. She turned and walked away.

As for me, I stayed right where I was. Further pursuit would almost certainly result in answering pointed questions from square-headed people, so I just stayed put. Either the magic of human decency was going to work, or it wasn't.

She straight-armed one of the massive front doors and disappeared from view.

I waited.

A minute passed.

And then two.

Before the door swung open and Patty walked back inside with a look on her face that said her worst fears were confirmed. I was still standing there. Right where she left me. Not doing a thing that would give her an excuse to call security. She swallowed a curse and ambled in my direction, taking her time, making me wait.

"What are you, the jilted lover?" she asked.

"Not the way you mean it," I said.

"What way's that?"

"The way where I just can't seem to get on with my life. Where I'm following her around, making an ass of myself. Stuff like that." I shook my head and looked her in the eye. "Nothing like that."

"No?"

"I skulked off into the bushes like a gentleman."

Her eyes crinkled at the corners. "Maybe you didn't love her so much after all."

"Maybe I respected her choice," I said evenly.

We had a short staring contest. "Big, tall gal?" she asked.

"Yep."

"Blonde?"

"More like brown."

She shrugged. "You know women and their hair."

I said I did.

"What's your story?"

I gave her the condensed version. No names, places, or dates.

"Why would the mother come to you?"

"I used to be a private investigator."

"What do you do now?"

"As little as possible."

"Which explains her choice of partners, I guess."

"More or less," I admitted.

She walked away from me again. Out into the center of the lobby, to a pair of cowhide club chairs. Yee ha. She removed her coat and sat down on one of the former Guernseys. I wandered over and occupied the udder.

"Your friend's got trouble," she said as I settled in.

"This Teddy character?"

"Yeah. Teddy Healy."

"Rebecca can take care of herself," I said.

Her eyes clouded. "Not with Teddy, she can't."

"Why's that?"

She thought about it for a second. "He's got a real nose for weakness. One minute talking to a woman, and he knows what she does and doesn't like about herself. It's uncanny. He's like a lion looking at a herd of zebras and immediately being able to pick out the slow and the weak."

"Rebecca's neither of those."

"Neither was I," she said.

I believed her but didn't want to say so. My silence seemed to make her uncomfortable, so she began to talk. Seemed Patty Franklin was from L.A. Learned to play piano from her grandma. Worked the L.A. club circuit. Wasn't getting rich but playing jazz beat the hell out of bag lunches in a cubicle. She'd been here in the tulles for about three months, tending to an estranged father who was dying of colon cancer. Back then, his doctor claimed he had a month to live, but the old man seemed hell-bent on defying the odds. No telling how long he was going to be with us. She hated the Alderbrook, the state of Washington, the weather, and every other damn thing around here and was going to be back in SoCal about five seconds after her old man cashed his chips. Whenever in hell that turned out to be.

Pops had a sister who came over most nights and helped out, so Patty took the gig at the hotel just to keep her chops honed and her spirits uplifted. An old friend of hers had once said that the most miserable creatures on earth were people who got stuck caring for other people. At the time, she'd thought he was just being mean-spirited. Lately, though, she'd changed her mind.

Teddy Healy was nothing like her type. Not even close. She didn't do rural. Back in L.A., she'd have sent him on his way without a second look. But she was bored and horny and miserable about being stuck out in the woods so she let him buy her drinks. Listened to his pathetic redneck chatter for a month or so before…before she had a few too many one night and found herself at his place.

She caught herself running off at the mouth and looked away from me. I could feel the ambivalence churning inside her. Part of her wanted to cough it up like a fish bone. To finally tell somebody what had happened between them, and how she'd been forever damaged by the experience. Another part of her was so consumed by shame and self-loathing that the very idea of anyone else knowing the details was more than she could bear.

"All the more reason I need to find Rebecca," I said, hoping we could keep this thing on track.

The rush of feet and the sound of voices pulled my attention over toward the desk, where the last toothy knot of dentists was checking out. A parade of bellboys and car jockeys was carting their baggage out through the big front doors. They toodle-ooed the hired help and followed their belongings into the great outdoors.

"He's got a place on Prescott Creek."

"You think that's where they went?"

"I know that's where they went. That's what he does. He gets you out there where nobody's going to interrupt his..." She censored herself. "By now he's got her so coked up she'll..."

"How do I get there?" I interrupted.

"You'd never find it. It's a driveway off a dirt road. Way the hell out there."

"Show me."

"Pfffft," she scoffed. "Like I'm gonna get involved with that."

"Maybe it's time Teddy got what was coming to him," I suggested.

I watched as the idea took a bite out of her. As I'd hoped, the prospect of retribution held a certain primal appeal. Human beings are like that. You do them wrong enough and they start making up little seek-and-destroy Clint Eastwood movies in their heads. Ninety-nine percent of the time, nothing happens because, first of all, the opportunity never presents itself, and secondly, because they don't really have the balls to do anything about it, even if it did. Tonight, however, Patty Franklin found herself traipsing among the other one percent. Here she was, face-to-face with the possibility that her revenge novella could, quite possibly, come true, a prospect that excited her in a way and to a degree with which she wasn't particularly comfortable.

"You don't know what Teddy's like," she hedged.

"What's he like?"

"He likes to humiliate people."

"He's not going to humiliate me," I said.

"He's got this little…" She searched for a noun but came up empty. "This piece of lead, I guess. It's wrapped in leather. It's got this loop that goes around his wrist." She made a striking motion with her left hand.

"A sap?" I tried.

"Yeah. Yeah. That's it. A sap. He always has it in his pocket."

"I'll keep that in mind," I promised.

"He's quick with it."

"You've seen him use it?"

She hesitated a beat. "Out in the parking lot one night… some drunk followed me out of the bar, started hitting on me." She rolled her eyes. "Poor guy was stone cold before he ever knew what hit him."

"I'll keep that in mind too."

"Know what Teddy did?"

"What did he do?"

"He pissed on the guy, and then left him laying there in the parking lot." She showed her palms to the ceiling, as if to ask the universe, "What's with that?"

"Show me how to get to Teddy's place," I said again.

This time she thought about it. She threw a glance over at the checked baggage window. I watched as she ran her revenge movie again.

"I'll change my clothes," she said.

．　．　．

"Leave the keys," Patty said as I jammed the Tahoe into Park.

She insisted I park out in the road. Made me turn the car around so it was facing back the way we'd come. Not taking any chances, this girl.

I popped the car door and stepped out onto the shoulder. Faded signs on either side of the driveway said it all. Posted. No Trespassing. No Soliciting.

The house was forty yards away at the top of a little rise. Big decaying two-story from the late fifties, with a ramshackle, brokeback roof that had needed replacing a decade ago, and a pair of dormers looking out over the yard like raised eyebrows. Down below, a wide front porch ran the length of the house. Here and there a post or two was missing from the railing. Half-a-dozen hanging baskets, complete with dead plants, decorated the underside of the porch roof.

I looked over at my car.

Patty had crawled over into the driver's seat. She rolled down the window. "You even look like you're going to lose and I'm out of here," she said. "I'll call 911 as soon as I'm back in cell phone range, but I've spent all the time with Teddy Healy I'm gonna."

We'd run out of cell phone bars three or four miles back, just as we turned off the last of the paved roads. She'd been right. I'd never have found the place on my own. She put the window up, adjusted the seat, and started the car. The doors locked by themselves.

I walked up the incline toward the house. The sound of my crunching feet played counterpoint to the gurgling sounds of the surrounding forest. It had rained earlier in the day and the woods were alive with the sound of water dripping and sinking and otherwise moving downhill.

Overhead, the ancient Douglas firs creaked and groaned as the intermittent wind swirled their heavy branches.

I was within twenty yards of the porch when the light to the left of the door blinked on, and there he was. Bare-chested, fastening the last couple of buttons on a pair of 501 jeans, he strutted onto the porch in his bare feet.

The laird of the manor threw an angry hand my way. "Didn't you see the sign, asshole? No trespassing. Get the fuck outta here 'fore I hurt your sorry ass."

He'd once been buff, but time and excess had taken their toll. The last bulky remnants of years in the weight room had migrated south. The upper portion of what had once been a broad muscular chest was morphing into a passable pair of breasts, while the bottom half of his torso had begun a permanent pilgrimage toward his waist.

"You best walk your big ass back to the car," he said with a malignant grin.

I kept moving his way. His face and torso were covered with a light sheen of sweat; the roots of his curly black hair sparkled in the dim light.

"I'll need to have a few words with the lady," I said.

He smirked at me. "Who the fuck are you? Comin' out here tellin' me what you need. Don't nobody give a rat's ass what you need, asshole."

"I need to speak with the lady."

He slipped his right hand into his pants pocket.

Behind him, the drapes covering the big bay window quivered. I watched as a woman's silhouette peeked out between the curtains. Teddy caught the shift in my focus and looked back over his shoulder. The head immediately disappeared.

He gave me a big smile. "Oh, you neeeed to," he sneered and stepped off the flagstone walkway. "Well, why in hell didn't you just say so, pilgrim? If I'd known you neeeeded to...well, hell." He bowed at the waist like a cavalier and swept a hand elegantly across his body, gallantly inviting me to pass.

I took him up on it, but not like he'd planned. I stepped even farther onto the lawn and passed him on the opposite side, too close to his right side for him to be pulling anything out of his pocket. His shithouse grin got bigger and bigger right up to the point where I gave him enough space.

Patty was right. Teddy boy was real quick with the skull-buster. I was looking for it, but it damn near didn't save my bacon. The business end of the cudgel whistled so close to my face I could feel the breeze in my nostrils as it went zipping by.

I pushed his upper arm hard, using his own momentum to send him staggering several steps before he was able regain his balance.

Teddy looked surprised. I was guessing he hadn't missed in a while. He was so accustomed to his victims immediately going down in a drooling heap that he had to take a moment to regroup before attempting anything more strenuous.

That's when his bloodshot, baby blues got mean. I looked into those eyes and saw the nasty little bug-squashing, fire-starting, pet-torturing kid he used to be. A chill went coursing down my spine.

He sensed my discomfort and dispensed with the grin. No fooling around anymore. He crouched and began to shuffle my way, left foot forward, twirling the sap in a tight circle as he sidestepped in my direction.

"You pretty quick for a big boy," he said.

I kept my distance, mirroring his movements, moving to my right into the middle of the overgrown lawn. As far as I was concerned, the more space the better. I had to be careful. Anything that sap hit was immediately going to cease functioning, so the sooner this tussle was over the better it was going to bode for me.

He feinted with the sap—once, twice—and then tried to kick the legs out from under me. I jumped backward, avoiding the sweeping leg, but turned an ankle on something lying hidden in the grass and went to one knee.

That's all the advantage Teddy was looking for. Had me right where he wanted me. He raised the leather-covered lead above his head, took three quick steps and gave it his all, trying to cave in the top of my skull with a single downward stroke.

Instead of trying to skip out of range, which was what he was expecting, I stepped closer. Nose-to-nose. Up close and personal. On the way in, I raised my right shoe and brought it down hard on his bare foot.

The sap nearly amputated my left ear in the nanosecond before it plowed into the top of my shoulder. The whole left side of my body went numb. I stifled a groan, reached up with my right hand and grabbed the wet hair at the back of his neck. He raised the sap again, looking for the killing stroke. Launching myself forward and up, I head-butted him full in the face, with everything I had behind it.

I heard the cellophane crackle of his nose breaking and then his anguished cry of pain. Before he could recover, I pulled him even closer, holding him in a bear hug as I pistoned my knee into his groin several times.

The air left his lungs in a single locomotive whoosh. His face was painted with gut-ache and disbelief. He stared at me, as if looking for an explanation.

I dug my right foot into the ground and put my shoulder behind a straight right. Drove it smack into his already broken and bloodied nose. He yowled like a dog, staggered backward, and plopped down in the sitting position on the wet grass.

I know what they say about not kicking a guy when he's down, but I wasn't taking any chances with this jerk. I reared back and gave it everything I had. Teddy's teeth snapped together with a sickening crack; his eyes rolled out of sight. He went over backward with his legs still pinned under him and his arms spread wide like he was making snow angels. I stood over him, breathing heavy, fists balled and ready, but Teddy Healy was in the arms of Morpheus.

I walked over, pulled the leather thong up over his hand, and pocketed the sap. His breathing was wheezy and wet. I turned toward the house. The simple motion nearly tore off the top of my head. I tried to roll my shoulders but nearly fainted from the pain.

Mercifully, I didn't have to kick in the door. The front parlor was awash in overstuffed furniture and overflowing ashtrays. A moth-eaten deer head stared down into the room, looking as if he didn't think much of the place either. A big set of keys and red leather purse sat on the battered and burned coffee table.

I heard someone moving around in the next room. The sound of a squeaking bed. Up squeak, down squeak. I grabbed the keys and bellied my way through the doorway.

She was standing on the bed hopping up and down trying to get into a pair of jeans. Apparently she'd been unable to locate her underpants and, due to the extreme circumstances, was now preparing to venture forth *au naturel*. I moved my gaze up to her tearstained face.

She had a serious mouse under one eye and a full-scale shiner brewing in the other. Finally, she pulled the jeans over her hips and zipped up.

I underhanded her the key ring. She trapped it against her chest and gawked at me like I was a man from Mars.

"If I were you," I said, "I'd take his truck and get yourself out of here while you've still got the chance."

I didn't have to say it twice. Without another word, she bounced down off the bed and made for the door, tucking her shirt in as she hurried over the littered floor, slowing only long enough to find her jacket and snatch her purse from the table.

I followed her outside. I was walking at an angle now, one shoulder lower than the other. I felt like I was limping on both legs. I could feel blood dripping down my collar and made the mistake of reaching up and touching my ear. My hand came away wet. A low groan escaped from my chest.

Out on the lawn, Teddy Healy was crawling toward the house on his hands and knees. I sighed and headed his way. Teddy was just the type to be a gun nut. Since I didn't want to have to worry about getting shot in the back of the head on my way out of here, I walked over, drew my foot back, and gave him another shot to his face. He rolled over on his back and spit blood on his bare chest.

I quickened my pace as much as it would quicken. A sudden gust of wind waved the ancient trees like ghostly dancers. All around me bits of airborne debris swirled in the angry night air, like I was being blended into a giant forest milkshake.

The gray Dodge Ram came out of the garage like a bottle rocket, engine roaring, tires spewing gravel into the air, as she fed the pickup way too much gas for the conditions. I managed one brief peek at her face as she came by and was left with the image of her teeth, locked in a skull-like grimace as she white-knuckled the steering wheel with both hands.

I held my breath as she roared down the hill out of control, toward Patty and the Tahoe. She crimped the wheel hard left and locked up the brakes. I tried to wave at Patty, to warn her, but moving my shoulder nearly made me pass out.

The Tahoe began to slide, its tires chattering sideways over the ruts. I saw Patty cringe in the driver's seat and waited for the sound of the impact, but, somewhere in the middle of the slide, defying all laws of physics, the big Dodge found purchase and yanked hard left as if it was on trolley tracks, missing Patty and the Tahoe by inches, then fishtailing twice before righting itself and screaming off into the darkness.

I stood and listened until the sound of the engine melted into the wind. When I pulled my eyes back to the Tahoe, the driver's door was hanging open and Patty was standing on the road, her eyes the size of saucers, pressing one hand on her chest, as if to keep her heart from escaping. As I walked her way, her face told me everything I needed to know about how I looked.

"You drive," I said as I limped around the front of the car and, with great difficulty, pulled myself into the passenger seat.

She reached over and helped me fasten the seat belt. "Jesus," she huffed. "You ought to see your ear."

Out in the middle of the lawn, Teddy Healy had struggled to his feet. The thick blood basting his chest shone pure black in the moonlight.

"Let's go," I said.

Didn't have to tell her twice either.

■  ■  ■

I remember the early parts of what was to follow. How I went loose in the passenger seat and allowed the safety restraints to keep me in place as Patty steered us back to civilization. I remember Patty driving around to the back of the hotel and taking me in through the kitchen, and up the service elevator to my room.

Next thing I recall, she was helping me sit up in bed, trying to get my shirt off, before finally giving up because I was being no help. I remembered taking some pills of some kind. Somehow or other she got me into the bathroom, although I don't remember a damn thing about the trip.

The twenty minutes it took to clean up my ear will forever be etched in my memory, however. Filed under P for pain. I must have passed out at some point because the next thing I knew she'd somehow commandeered a professionally equipped emergency medical kit and was in the process of putting my ear back together.

"You're gonna need to have somebody look at this," she kept saying.

Nothing made sense. I felt like I'd walked in on the last five minutes of a foreign film and just couldn't for the life of me make heads or tails of it, so I closed my eyes and dreamed.

When I opened them again, it was dark in the room. The digital clock read 3:09 and my left ear felt as if it was about to burst into flame. Patty was asleep on the other bed. She'd pulled half of the bedcover over herself and looked like a great big taco. I blamed the drugs for making me silly and went back to sleep.

       ■   ■   ■

The door to my room banged against the wall with a sound-barrier boom. Reflexively, I jolted straight up in bed, and then immediately wished I hadn't. I groaned in pain and hugged myself. I felt like the Tin Man after a rainstorm.

Seven forty-one in little red numbers. No Patty.

"Washington State Patrol," a rough voice shouted.

They came through the door in single file, screaming over and over for me to keep my hands in sight, crouching behind ballistic shields and moving fast. They had me hand-cuffed and facedown on the floor before I'd fully come to my senses.

"Somebody want to tell me what's going on here?" I asked as they jerked me to my feet. I asked again and was met by the same stony silence. Apparently, telling me why I was being cuffed and stuffed wasn't part of their job description.

As also might be expected, the tactical squad proved remarkably unsympathetic regarding the condition of my ear and pain in my upper extremities as they marched me downstairs to a small conference room in which a single folding table and six chairs had been set up immediately to the left of the door.

A plastic pitcher of ice water and the obligatory six glasses sat on a red plastic tray in the center of the table. Somebody'd drawn the Kool-Aid face in the condensation on the outside of the pitcher. Very festive indeed.

One of the black-visored storm troopers stayed behind to make sure I didn't go dashing off into the sunrise. He stood directly behind me, cracking his knuckles on the MAC-10 hanging from a lanyard around his neck. They left me to cool my heels for the better part of half an hour before the door opened and three men came strolling into the conference room. Two square-headed Washington State Patrol troopers and a guy in civilian clothes.

Cop Handbook 101: Crowd the suspect, get inside his personal bubble where other people generally don't tread. The uniformed cops pulled chairs close enough to study the contents of my ear canals. One of them dropped a brown file folder on the table, while the other produced a handheld voice recorder.

The civilian took his time carrying a metal folding chair from the opposite side of the table and setting it down in front of me. Our knees touched once he finally got around to sitting down. I didn't much like playing kneesies with this guy, but bitching about it didn't seem like it was going to get me anywhere I wanted to go, so I resolved to keep my mouth shut and get through this as quickly as possible.

He was a lean fifty-something with those narrow little cop eyes that look like they've spent a lifetime scanning the horizon. He introduced himself as Detective Sergeant Bradley. By the time he'd removed his hat, hung his coat on the back of the chair, and folded his scarf into eight precise little squares, my resolve to shut up was all but gone.

"You want to give me a hint here?" I asked.

He gave me the smarmy half smile you generally reserve for hearing bad news about somebody you don't like, and leaned in even closer.

"Looks like you had a tough night," he commented as he reached behind himself and wiggled his hand into one of his jacket pockets. I watched as he eased something out. A second later, Teddy's skull-buster bounced once on the table and then came to rest.

The cop was looking at me like it was Christmas morning and I was that shiny, red fire truck he'd been asking for. "You ever seen this before?" he asked.

"Yep," I said. "I took it off a guy named Teddy Healy last night."

His horizon eyes flickered. I'd put myself at Teddy's house, right where he wanted me.

"Took it off him?"

"We had a tussle."

The uniformed cops chuckled in two-part harmony.

"A tussle?"

"Is there an echo in here?" I asked.

The uniformed cop on my left smacked me in the back of the head and slid a photograph on the table in front of me.

Teddy Healy, lying on his back in the grass. Pretty much like I'd seen him last night, squashed nosed and bloody-faced, except in this photo, Teddy was sort of a teal color and had a neat little bullet hole decorating the right side of his forehead.

"He was standing up when I left him," I said.

He smiled that smarmy smile again. That was the second time I'd put myself at the crime scene. As far as he was concerned, things were going swimmingly.

Normally, I would have played with this guy for a while, but this morning I was in way too much pain to avail myself of the pleasure. "I wasn't alone," I said.

"Excuse me?"

"Somebody was with me."

"And who might that be?" he inquired evenly.

I told him.

He sat back in the chair and frowned. "The piano player?"

"That's her," I said.

The cop on my left got to his feet and marched out of the room.

Detective Sergeant Bradley kept hammering at me for another twenty minutes. How come I'd registered under an alias? Was I aware of the fact that the real Tom Van Dyne was not only a serial murderer, but also a cannibal? Did I know that identity theft was a felony, punishable by a fine of this much and jail term of such and such? Was I aware that my private investigator's license had lapsed and was no longer valid and so on and so forth, it went on and on like a bad dream. We both knew he was just wasting time, waiting to hear whether my alibi checked out, so I humored him and coughed up a judiciously edited version of what I was doing there and why.

About the time I was running out of evasions and half-truths, the other state trooper came bopping back into the room. He bent at the waist and whispered at length into the detective's ear. Bradley whispered back and the trooper nodded.

I watched the uniform reach into his pants pocket and pass Bradley something under the table. The detective peered down into his own hand for several moments. His lips nearly disappeared as he turned whatever it was around in his fingers, checking it out from all angles. He and the trooper exchanged emphatic whispers again.

Bradley heaved a sigh. When he finally met my gaze, his disappointment was palpable. Cops like things simple. You know, Mom catches Pop flying United with the next-door neighbor and blows both of them into the middle of next week. That sort of thing. Mysteries hold little or no appeal for cops, especially in these economically troubled times, when duty rosters are short and overtime unthinkable. He made a locking-the-door motion with his free hand. The trooper to my right got to his feet, pushed me forward in the chair, and removed the handcuffs.

Bradley waited until I'd rubbed some life back into my wrists and tried unsuccessfully to untie the knot that was my shoulders before he threw what looked like a stainless steel washer up onto the table, where it wobbled to a stop next to the sap.

"Ever seen that before?" he asked.

I poured myself a glass of ice water and drank it. "What is it?" I asked when I was finished.

"GPS tracking device."

"Nope," I said.

"We found it attached to your car," he said. "Up under the bumper, on the air conditioning compressor."

I remembered Mr. Moto disappearing from view while my car was stuck in that damn Capitol Hill alley. Hadda be him, I figured. When I didn't say anything, Bradley got to his feet, gathered up his outerwear, and ambled for the door. He leaned his back against it, allowing the troopers to precede him into the corridor.

Heartsick that he wasn't going to be able to send me to the penitentiary for the rest of my life, he settled for having the last word. He broke out his wolf grin and said, "So I guess your friend wasn't looking to be rescued."

I matched him tooth for tooth. "Turned out she wasn't my friend," I said.

# Chapter 3

I'd like to tell you how I used my vast array of private eye skills to ferret her from hiding, how I tapped shady contacts, called in overdue markers, and annexed secret databases known only to illuminati such as myself. It would make a great story, but unfortunately, it wouldn't be true.

Truth was, all I had to do was to pull out my notebook, open to the page where I wrote down all the Millennium Yacht Sales employees' names and go online to White-Pages.com. There she was in black and white. Rosemary De Carlo, 2573 Harrison Avenue East, #309, Seattle, 98102. Badda bing.

Last night in Teddy's boudoir, I'd recognized her the second I'd managed to focus on her face. How had that boat mechanic Neil referred to her? "The big blonde honey from the desk," if memory served. The one who left the dealership right after Brett Ward went off to repo boats for a living. Turned out that Neil was right on both counts. She was at least six feet tall in her stockinged feet and, while she certainly wasn't Rebecca Duval, I could personally attest to the fact that she was a real blonde.

Suffice to say that my exit from the Alderbrook Resort and Spa ranked highly on the Martha Stewart social stigmata scale. Apparently, my early morning tryst with law enforcement, combined with a leaking ear bandage the size of a baseball mitt, had considerably lowered my GDI (Guest Desirability Index). I checked out amid a sea of averted eyes and shielded whispers, all of which I belligerently chose to ignore.

My ear throbbed like a boil as I drove the sixty miles to the ferry and caught a ride back to the mainland. I stayed in my car and held a one-man brood-fest for the forty-minute passage. If I was worried before, now I was terrified. I couldn't imagine a scenario where Rebecca willingly gave up her identification and credit cards. Worse yet, the only reason I could think of as to why somebody would want the world to believe Rebecca Duval was alive and well was that she wasn't.

Soon as the ferry workers dropped the safety chain, I bounced the Tahoe off the boat and began to drive like a maniac, weaving in and out of traffic, taking crazy chances just to gain a car length or two, none of which did any good of course, as I-5 South through Northgate was a traffic knot twenty-four hours a day, but at least I felt like I was doing something.

Twenty-five seventy-three Harrison was just what I expected. Capitol Hill personified. One of those brick, mid-sized—somewhere between twenty and thirty units—apartment buildings this part of Seattle was absolutely lousy with.

For the first time all day, I got lucky. Small lucky, but lucky nonetheless. As I was walking up the front walk, a thirty-something woman and a four- or five-year-old girl came out the front door holding hands. The woman held the door for me. The little girl threw her head all the way back and looked up at me, all sticky-mouthed and stupid.

"He's biiig, Mommy," she slurped.

The woman smiled a weak apology and towed the kid toward the street.

I stepped into the foyer. Four-story walk-up. Old-fashioned brass mailboxes on the left. A gateleg table where the mail carrier probably left packages. Other than that, everything was carpet. A bold floral print of such power and complexity you could have slaughtered livestock on it and, once the fluids dried, nobody would have noticed.

Three-oh-nine was the back right corner apartment. I stood directly in front of the peephole and knocked hard. Nothing happened for a moment and then I heard the sound of her feet trying to be quiet. The peephole darkened.

"Remember me?" I asked.

Nothing.

"I'm not going anywhere," I said. "Open the door. We need to talk."

Again nothing, so I knocked harder and longer this time.

"Go away or I'm calling the cops," she whispered through the door.

I raised my voice several decibels. "Good," I said. "You do that. We can all have a nice little chat about identity theft. About obtaining goods and services under false pretenses." I rambled on, doing my best Perry Mason impression, making it up as I went along.

Still nothing, so I got louder. "Not to mention the fact that Teddy Healy took a bullet in the head sometime last night..." I paused for effect. "...which, I imagine, the local cops would very much like to have a few words with you about," I finished.

I heard the dull thump of feet on the stairs. A pair of lank-haired skater types in oversized sweatshirts and skinny jeans gave me the hairy eyeball as they carried their skateboards into an apartment down the hall, checking back over their shoulders every few steps like they were the building centurions or something.

I waited. Inside the apartment, chains began to rattle. She peeked out. The mouse under her eye looked a little better than it had the last time I'd seen it. The shiner, however, was in full bloom. Puffed up like an egg, several shades of purple and green, the eye was very nearly closed. The slit that was still visible was bright red.

"Shhh," she hissed.

"We need to talk," I said.

"How'd you find me?" she demanded.

"Great cunning and dare."

"What?"

I was past the snappy rejoinder stage, so I put a big smile on my face and pushed my way into the apartment as gently as possible, moving around her as much as I was able, brushing her aside when I had no other choice. Quite frankly, the girl looked like she'd had about all the abuse she could stand. I almost felt bad about bracing her for information. Well, maybe not bad, but it did occur to me.

The place was shabbier than it was chic. Too many knick-knacks, doodads, and votive candles for my liking. Looked like she had passable taste but a serious shortage of folding money. On the far wall, the metal mount for a flat screen TV hung empty and forlorn, like some kind of post-recessional wall art denoting the end of civilization as we knew it.

"Here's what you're going to do for me," I said.

Her lumped-up face filled with "oh God, not again" concern.

"Not like that," I assured her. "What you're going to do is tell me everything you know about how and why you found yourself at the Alderbrook Resort registered under the name Rebecca Duval. You're going to tell me where you got her ID and everything you know that might help me find Brett Ward." She started to speak but I stopped her with a cautioning finger. "You do that and I'll forget about you. You screw around with me and I'll put you together with cops."

I made the Boy Scout's honor sign.

She took me at my word. "That son of a bitch," she said.

"I take it we're talking about Brett Ward."

She nodded. "Called me about a week ago. He knew things were tough for me. Knew I was having trouble making the rent since my unemployment ran out. Said he needed me to go out to this place in the woods and pretend to be his wife. She's some kinda doctor or something. Said it had something to do with insurance. Said I could eat, drink, and be merry on her dime. No problem. Just stay in character. Call him if I need anything. He'd slip me a few bucks when it was over."

"And you went for it."

"I've been eating a lot of Top Ramen lately," she said defensively. "A week in a spa on somebody else's dime was just too damn good to turn down."

I could see her point but didn't say so. "You sleeping with him?" I asked.

"Not lately," she groused. "Lately Bretsey's got..." She made quotation marks in the air with her fingers. "Bretsey's got 'erection issues' all of a sudden."

"How lately?

"Last couple of weeks."

"So?"

"So he picks me up here, gives me her ID and credit card, and then drives me way the hell out into God's country to the Alderbrook, and leaves me there. Says he's gonna be back to get me in a week or so, have fun, and then he drives off."

"And all of a sudden the credit card wasn't good anymore."

"I tried to call him." She shook her fist in anger. "Son a bitch deserts me out in the middle of nowhere. Won't answer his goddamned phone. No money, no nothing!"

I watched in silence as she started to lose control of herself. Tears rolled down her bruised cheeks. "And then that Teddy pig…he…what he did…" She looked at me with that horrible red eye, as if she needed something from me, understanding or forgiveness perhaps, it was hard to tell.

Whatever it was made me uncomfortable, so I changed the subject. "How long had you and Brett been sleeping together?"

"Coupla three months," she sniffled.

"Where?" I asked.

"Where what?"

"Where did you guys hook up?" I looked around the room. "Here?"

She shook her head and said, "At his place."

"His condo?"

"No, no. Never there. He's got this office out by the Ballard Locks."

I pressed her for details, but all she knew was how to drive there and get laid. Somewhere between the Ballard Locks and Shilshole Bay was the best she could do. On the ship canal side. Big old boathouse. Used to be painted green but most of the paint had long since peeled off. Seemed Brett kept a little love nest behind the boatyard office. Classy guy, that Brett.

I kept at her until she ran dry. Got more of her life story than I wanted to hear, but that happens sometimes. Once you open the floodgates, the pond's gonna drain. She'd come out to the West Coast from Poughkeepsie, New York, about twenty-five years ago. Had a full-ride basketball scholarship from Seattle Pacific U, but blew out her knee early in her sophomore year. School wasn't really her thing anyway, so she dropped out and kicked around a bit. Did the Europe thing. Did the Mexico thing. Coupla bad marriages—at least they didn't have any kids—string of dead-end jobs, yadda yadda, ain't it funny how time slips away?

By the time she was finished, I felt pretty certain I'd gotten whatever there was to get. She didn't have any more idea where Brett Ward could be found than I did, and I didn't have so much as a suspicion.

I walked over to a desk. Six or eight framed photographs were arranged on the surface, mostly family stuff. Rosemary and what figured to be her mother and father sitting at a picnic table together. A younger woman who looked enough like Rosemary to be her sister and what I assume to be her three kids, all smiling like crazy into the camera. Picture of a sailboat on a lake. A black Lab drooling on a tennis ball. Standard family photo stuff. The kind of thing that passes for memories these days.

On the back left of the desk sat a gold-framed Brett Ward. Mr. Preppy in a red sweater vest over a crisp white pullover, braced behind the wheel of a sailboat, Space Needle looming over his left shoulder, hair blowing in the breeze, big, bright virile grin. All very *GQ* bright and shiny.

I picked it up and held it in my hands. "Can I have this?" I asked.

She shrugged. "Take it. I never see that face again it'll be too soon."

I dug out another old business card out of my wallet and handed it to her.

"If you think of anything else," I said.

.  .  .

Despite Rosemary De Carlo's vague recollections, I'd found the place with little trouble. Problem was that Shilshole Marine Yard was no longer in business. A quarter mile of temporary chain-link fence ringed the property from sidewalk to waterline. A red and white plastic sign wired to the front gate said to contact Northwest Maritime if you were interested in buying the property and to otherwise keep the hell out. Somebody had spray-painted a blue Latino gang sign over the phone number, making it impossible to read. Scattered around the property, vessels in varying stages of decomposition slouched on the blacktop like vagrants.

These days, mom-and-pop boatyards are every bit as much an endangered species as Midwestern family farms. Just keeping up with the escalating environmental requirements costs a fortune, and then, to add to the problem, as the potential value of the property increased, so did the size of the tax bite. Unless you happened to be the darling of the deep pockets set, your two hundred feet of waterfront was worth more than the business was ever going to be, no matter how long your family had been there or how good a businessperson you were. All of which made it even more tempting to take the money and run.

And lord knew Seattle had no shortage of newly moneyed morons who'd pay whatever freight was necessary for a glimpse of something wet. Sound, lake, canal, river, bay, sump. It didn't matter. All it had to be was wet. If it was wet, it was scenic, and if it was scenic, they'd build on it. Real estate ads contained phrases like "partial seasonal water view," which meant that if you stood at the peak of the roof in the dead of winter and, at the time, were neither fogged in nor being blinded by sleet, you could just about make out this body of water in the distance.

It was the lure of the salt, I figured. Something in our shared embryonic past calling us back to the warm water of the womb. Didn't matter whether it was distant or dangerous, if it was placid or polluted, the siren song of our collective consciousness kept calling us home to "waterfront property."

In an attempt to stem the relentless tide of gentrification, King County had begun making it nearly impossible to move from a commercial to a residential property designation, which, as far as I could see, was the only reason why this particular piece of property hadn't morphed into thirty or forty luxury condo units at a million-three a pop.

I parked my car in front of the Tides Tavern, crossed Shilshole Avenue, and walked east along the fence line with the sky the color of slate and the icy onshore flow from

Puget Sound jabbing at the back of my neck. I shuddered inside my coat and turned up the collar.

At the far end of the boatyard, almost in the neighbor's parking lot, I found an overturned oil drum nestled among the weeds, rolled it from the bottom side up, climbed on, and boosted myself to the top bar of the fence.

Jumping from heights is one of those moments where you first notice you're getting older, that the balance isn't quite what it used to be, and the knees aren't as nearly as accommodating about absorbing shocks as they once were.

My body acted as if I'd jumped off the Space Needle. I staggered forward on impact and nearly turned an ankle, stumbling spastically through knee-high brush and brambles until I was able to regain some semblance of balance and composure.

I took a minute to count body parts and make sure nobody had seen me staggering around like a drunk. My ear throbbed to the beat of my heart. The impact with the ground had aggravated my shoulder. I cradled myself until it calmed down. I was grateful for something else to think about when out in the street an eighteen-wheeler came growling by. Moving slowly up through the gears until it finally blended into the general hum of the city.

As I saw it, I didn't have the luxury of being surreptitious. If somebody saw me, then they saw me. I'd burn that bridge when I came to it. Nobody had seen Rebecca in something like a week and, even presuming she was out there somewhere mucking around on her own, whatever she was doing, she was doing without her cell phone, driver's license, and credit cards. My gut felt as if it was full of nails.

I cut left around the stern of an old wooden fishing vessel. The *Cheryl Anne*. Blue and white up top, black beneath the waterline. Didn't take a marine engineer to see that the old girl wouldn't be going anywhere. The entire transom had fallen off, exposing her nautical ass in a most unseemly manner.

The yard arrangement was classic. Little boat shed for little vessels with little money. Big boat shed for bigger vessels with serious folding cash. Everybody else was propped up on jack stands outside in the yard, "on the hard" as they liked to say.

Out in the ship canal, an enormous red and white Crowley tug was motoring its way out toward Puget Sound. I watched as whoever was at the helm of the *Response* raised his hand. I thought he was waving hello, as boaties are inclined to do, and was about give the obligatory return wave when the sudden blast of his air horn shook me to my core. I shuddered again and hunched my shoulders against the chill.

What looked to be an eighty-ton travel lift straddled the haulout slip like a giant blue mantis, its polyethylene lifting straps hanging lank above the inky water. If I recalled correctly, a lift that size was good for at least eighty-footers. Maybe as big as a hundred, depending on the make and model.

I followed the "office" arrows around the south side of the building. Twenty feet of old twelve-pane windows and a peeling green door looked out over the yard. The glass was filthy, inside and out, the glazier's putty so dissolute it had fallen out in many places. A single arm of blackberry vine, bristling with thorns and thick as my wrist, wandered unimpeded over the front wall.

I checked the area immediately around the door. No stickers or decals. Apparently, not Zagat rated. No "this business is protected by" such and such security company either. I checked the door and didn't see any obvious alarm wiring, but then again, you're not supposed to. No alarm bells under the eaves. Besides which, this didn't look to me like the kind of property where anybody was going to be willing to foot a monthly security bill. Looked like the metal thieves had already lifted anything ferrous that could be toted off and sold. What was still lying around the yard was either too big to mess with or without value. Tentatively, I turned the knob. The door swung open.

The moment my eyes adjusted to the gloom, I could tell I was too late. Somebody had gotten there before me. Everything that opened was open. A number of things that didn't open had been smashed on the floor, as if destroyed in frustration rather than as part of the search. Whoever had preceded me apparently wasn't having any more luck finding Brett Ward than I was, and was none too happy about it either.

I stepped inside, found a light switch to the right of the door, and flipped it on. Several banks of old-fashioned fluorescent lights began to hiss and blink.

The room was maybe ten by twenty. Fake wood paneling, circa 1950s rumpus room. Metal desk down at the end. Coupla cleavage calendars pinned to the wall behind the desk, three metal file cabinets to the right, and a couple of motel chairs for guests. Couple of other racks and tables scattered about the walls, one piled with paperwork, another with paint cans, and yet another with all the carcinogenic condiments and plastic stirring implements necessary for making truly wretched coffee.

It was, however, the black metal door directly opposite where I stood that hijacked my attention, or rather the collection of waffle-soled boot prints scattered about the surface. Bunches of them, high and low, left, right, and middle. Several of them upside down, where he'd stood with his back to the door and tried to horse kick it in. No doubt about it, somebody had worked up a hell of a sweat trying to get through that door, all to no avail too, which probably explained all the unnecessary breakage.

Now, if you knew Brett Ward, you knew that he was a smooth kind of guy. Not the sort to be lugging around a big set of keys that made lumps in his pockets and screwed up his pleats. No, no. That wasn't Brett at all. What knowing Brett Ward told me was that if Brett Ward had the key to that door, he wouldn't be carrying it in his pockets. No sir. It would be right here someplace, where he could lay hands on it with a minimum of effort. I'd bet on it.

First, I had to lift the desk back onto its feet. That was the hard part. Absolutely amazing what those old metal desks weigh, especially if one of your arms isn't working. On the other hand, the key was exactly where I'd imagined, front and center in the top drawer of the desk, so I guess the aggravation evened out.

I snapped the bolt back and pulled open the door. A narrow trapezoid of light raced across the floor. I felt around both sides of the door but couldn't find a light switch of any kind, so I took a couple of tentative steps into the room and waited for my eyes to adjust. As my pupils expanded, I could make out what looked like a hotel room or, more likely, the master stateroom from a salvaged yacht. Nicely appointed and anonymous. Little fridge. Couple of mirrors. Big platform bed, end tables, lamps, the whole ball of wax. The bed was even made. The pillows fluffed.

Maybe it was just me, but around the time the novelty wore off, the room started to look sad and a bit depressing. Like what was wrong with a grown man who went to this much trouble just to boff the company receptionist. It boggled the mind.

I edged toward the brass table lamps that flanked the bed. Tried one and then walked around and tried the other, neither of which worked, so I followed the wires up the right side of the bed and around the corner, where I found a pair of wall outlets and plugged in.

A warm glow enveloped the room. Maybe a little brighter than I would have chosen for a romantic interlude, but passable nonetheless. I guessed Brett liked to see who or what he was doing. Probably told her she was so beautiful he didn't want to miss a thing. A couple of quick involuntary images of Brett Ward hunched up behind Rosemary De Carlo made my head swim. I hadn't slept much lately and felt a bit woozy, so I leaned against the wall and took a minute to regroup.

I don't know why it caught my eye, but it did. Over in the back corner of the room. A pair of nondescript blue wires jutted from under the carpet, made a quick right turn, and disappeared through the adjoining wall. For what? The room's electricity was obviously on the same circuit as the lights. The digital clock had blinked midnight ever since I plugged in.

Then it came to me, like the proverbial bolt out of the blue. I chided myself for being stupid, blamed it on sleep deprivation, and walked over to the corner of the room. Took me under a minute to figure out. Once I pulled the dresser out from the wall, I found there was no damn wall, just a framed-out rectangle where, if I got down on my hands and knees, I could crawl back into some sort of hidden corridor.

I sighed. I wasn't crazy about cramped spaces, and crawling back into Brett Ward's private porno palace was going to put me a lot closer to him than I wanted to be. I'd have killed for a pair of coveralls and a surgical mask as I got down on one knee and wiggled my shoulders through the opening.

Turned out there was a little Flip HD movie camera secreted behind each of the mirrors. He had a plank set up to hold the Dell laptop that he used to burn his DVDs. I turned the PC on, opened the media player, hit Play, and there he was, Brett Ward, buck naked, with his mouth locked on the crotch of a fleshy brunette, whose impassioned urging seemed to spur him to ever greater ministrations. I had the odd thought that viewed dispassionately and from just the right height, human beings engaged in sex must be a rather confounding sight. I pictured antennae aliens looking down and wondering: "Just what the hell are they doing?"

I chided myself for being silly and ejected the disc, turned off the Dell, unplugged it, and slid it under my arm. A quick search turned up seven DVDs, each of them labeled with a different woman's name or initials. I figured the one marked Rose Mary D to be Rosemary De Carlo. Not much gets by old Leo.

I also figured that none of these women deserved to wake up some morning to find themselves on YouTube doing the horizontal bop with Brett Ward, so I pocketed all the discs, removed the cameras from their mountings and crawled back out into the love nest. I was feeling so queasy I didn't even look around; I just kept walking until I was outside in the yard.

The cold, wet air blowing in from Puget Sound was a blessing.

I'd never felt more like I needed a shower.

■   ■   ■

What should have been a five-minute drive took more like twenty. Rush hour was looming and everybody in town was trying to get a jump on the traffic, which, as might be expected, produced precisely the opposite effect. Seemed like I was always ten cars back at traffic lights and just missed making every one of them.

I followed Google's pulsing blue pin and made a quick stop at Northwest Maritime's office at Fisherman's Terminal. Caught the agent just as he was locking the place up for the night. Guy in a plaid shirt with wild and wooly eyebrows told me if I wanted a piece of Brett Ward I was going to have to take a number and get in line. Said Northwest held the paper on something like eighty boats that were behind in their payments, half of them in Canadian waters. Said he'd been using Millennium to carry out the repos until Brett Ward showed up at the Northwest office one morning with the proverbial offer they couldn't refuse.

Brett said he could save Northwest the twenty-five per-cent "agency fee" that Jorgensen was charging them. Since Brett was the person actually carrying out the repos and already had a working relationship with the pain-in-the-ass

Canadian authorities, and twenty-five percent was, after all, twenty-five percent, Northwest Maritime decided to go along for the ride. Brett said that all he needed was some boatyard space where he could do the necessary repairs, so Northwest gave him the use of Shilshole Marine, on which they also held the paper and which was sitting vacant at the time. Seemed like a match made in heaven.

And for the first six or seven months, it was. As most of the repos were voluntary, it was mostly a matter of dotting the i's and crossing the t's, and then motoring the boats down to Seattle. They were averaging two a week. Seemed like everybody was happy with the arrangement until about the time that damn fool on Vancouver Island started waving a gun around and things suddenly went to shit.

Quite naturally, his talk of gun-waving piqued my interest.

He said I'd have to check with Canadian authorities if I wanted the whole story, but what he'd heard was that one of the owners went psycho when Brett showed up to repo his sixty-foot Hargrave. Claimed he didn't know anything about any fucking repo and wasn't about to give his boat up. Pulled a gun and stuck it in Brett's face.

I suppressed a malicious grin and let him continue.

Quite wisely, Brett backed off and called the Provincial Police and, to make a long story short, they had this big ugly confrontation where the guy ended up taking a shot at a Canadian policeman. Took an extra week to get the boat back to Shilshole and, from that point on, things were never quite the same.

After that, seemed like it took longer and longer to work through the Canadian end of the process, longer to make the repairs, longer for Northwest Maritime to get their money, until, finally, a couple of weeks back, Brett stopped answering his phone altogether and the repos started piling up, at which point Northwest pulled his ticket and put the boatyard back up for sale, which wasn't going to happen unless they could get the zoning changed to residential, which wasn't going to happen anytime this century.

Nobody had heard from Brett Ward since, and, by the by, if I happened to run into that son of a bitch, tell him he was fired.

I shook his hand, thanked him for the help, and started toward my car.

"Hey," he called to my back.

I turned. He walked over to me. His forehead was furrowed. His eyebrows looked like mating caterpillars. "One strange thing."

"What's that?"

"Boat show last week," he started. "I'm manning the company booth when an old friend drops by to say hello. Ronnie Brewer. Runs a marina over on Lake Washington. Tells me he's got a real deal for me."

"Don't they all?"

"Showed me a photo of a Mainship Pilot 30. Said he can let me have it for sixty-five. Just about half the book value." He bobbed his prehensile brows up and down. "Rare boat," he said. "I recognized it right away. It's one of our repos."

"So?"

"So I pumped him a bit. Seems a guy named Brett Ward wholesaled him the rig for fifty-nine nine."

"So?"

"That's the same price he charged us," he said.

"So Brett broke even on the boat?"

"Near as I can tell," he said.

"How could that pencil out?"

"You tell me," he said.

.   .   .

I drove around the lake, moving at the speed of lava, lost in one of those semiconscious states where you manage to operate a motor vehicle without being aware of having done so. That occasional out-of-body experience, where a phantom crawls up in your lap and drives while you're busy doing whatever. Next thing you know you've arrived at your destination, without the slightest recollection of how you got there.

That was me as I slid the Tahoe to the curb a block north of the Eastlake Zoo. I turned off the engine and sat there for a moment, blinking myself back to reality.

I took several deep breaths, checked to make sure I was all present and accounted for, and stepped out into the street. It was dark enough for the streetlights to be doing some good. The air was ten degrees warmer than it had been down by the water. As I ambled along the sidewalk, I slid my hands into my jacket pockets and came upon my cell phone, which got me to trying to remember the last time I'd used it. Sometime during last night's festivities I'd inadvertently turned off the ringer. I had five messages. Four of them from Iris Duval and another from a local number I didn't recognize. As the chances of me calling Iris were slightly less than the likelihood of my winning the lottery, and I had no desire to speak with strangers just about then,

I thumbed the ringer back to off and dropped it back in my pocket.

I didn't know exactly where the boys flopped anymore. At one time, they lived together in an abandoned condo, but that thing had long since slid down under the freeway and disappeared into the mud. For a while, they had a house up on Franklin, but that deal went sour a couple of years down the road and they were back on the street. Lately I think it's been catch-as-catch-can. Anyplace dry and reasonably safe where there's room to bend an elbow and a soft place to crash.

I did, however, know where to find them at this time of day. Whatever their failings—and they were legion—the boys were creatures of habit. If they were broke, they'd scrounge up all the cheap booze they could lay their hands on and go to ground. If they had money, which I knew they did because it was still early in the month and I'd augmented their drinking fund a couple of days before, then they'd be at the Eastlake Zoo yukking it up. As Ralph liked to say, "A fool and his money are soon partying."

By this time of day, they'd already had a couple of eye-openers just to firm the chin and get them up and lurching, followed, at a suitable interval of course, by a medicinal midmorning phlegm cutter or two, intended purely to keep the pipes clear, as they segued into the inevitable few beers with lunch, thus providing a solid-food foundation for several midafternoon bracers as they prepared themselves for yet another evening of enchantment.

The gala was already in full swing when I arrived. As usual, they'd commandeered the floor space back around the corner from the bar. The place where the stage used to be, back before the neighbors got snotty and called the city about the noise, resulting in an official "no more music" injunction. These days, the Zoo didn't hire a band except on special occasions, when somebody's birthday party or wedding reception money made it possible to factor in the $750 fine and still break even.

The two things I'd always liked about the Zoo were the clientele and the jukebox. The Zoo serviced the entire gamut of neighborhood residents. Everything from my degenerate friends in the back of the room, to houseboat yuppies out slumming, to corporate secretaries, to local businesspeople, and aging junky bikers. Everybody was welcome and, for the most part, everyone got along splendidly.

The jukebox was every bit as eclectic as the clientele. Everything from Sarah Vaughn to the Butthole Surfers. Green Day was belting out "American Idiot" as I pulled open the front door and stepped inside.

I stopped at the bar and waited for Louie to deliver a couple of boilermakers to the café racers sitting in the front booth. He smiled at the sight of me, made his way through the gate at the end of the bar, and wandered in my direction.

"Leo," he said, extending his hand.

We shook hands and exchanged pleasantries.

"Your copy machine working?" I asked.

He said it was. I handed him the picture of Brett Ward I'd gotten from Rosemary De Carlo's apartment and dropped a ten-dollar bill on the bar.

"Hows about making me six copies?" I inquired.

Louie palmed the cash and reckoned how it would be no problem at all.

*Don't want to be an American idiot. One nation controlled by the media.*

Two minutes later I rounded the corner with a smile on my face, the photocopies dangling from my hand, and Green Day still blasting in my ear.

*Welcome to a new kind of tension. All across the alien nation.*

I was greeted like Caesar returning from Gaul. I'd have preferred to think my popularity was a product of my stunning good looks and innate charisma, but since my arrival at the Eastlake Zoo always coincided with a free round of drinks, I made it a point not to get too far ahead of myself on that one.

"It's Leo," somebody shouted and the melee was on. A crowd of hand-shakers and back-patters gathered round and collectively pumped and pounded me like a cube steak. As sore as my ear was, the outpouring of affection nearly brought me to my knees, as I glad-handed my way across the room toward the mismatched collection of Naugahyde booths lining the back wall, one of which held George and Ralph and a guy in a red plaid jacket.

George looked up as I approached the table, dug an elbow into Ralph's ribs and nodded in my direction. Took Ralph a minute to process, but eventually he looked over in my direction and grinned that gap-toothed grin of his.

"Fellas," I said.

The third guy was short and stout and greasy. Some kind of Southeast Asian or maybe a Filipino. His sullen eyes said he'd started drinking early today and wasn't going to last much longer. I leaned down, smiled, and looked him in the eye.

"You suppose I could have a private word with these two?" I asked.

"Huh?"

"I need to have a word with these two gentlemen."

He wiped his mouth with the sleeve of his jacket and picked up his beer. "I ain't movin' nowhere," he said.

I gestured toward the bar where Louie was pouring everybody what they wanted on my dime. "Lemme buy you a drink," I offered, patting him on the shoulder. "Tell Louie I said to make it a double."

He shrugged my hand from his shoulder. "Get the fuck outta here," he said.

I'm not making excuses for myself, but I'd had a tough coupla days. The person I most cared about was missing under very scary circumstances and I'd made precious little progress finding her. I was tired; I was beat up. I'd ripped my pants getting back over the fence at the boatyard and, I'm sorry to say, I wasn't in the mood for this guy running his street-person power trips on me. This was one of those guys who waits for the light to turn yellow and then sashays through the crosswalk at one-nineteenth of a mile an hour, because making the fat asses in the fancy cars wait was as much power as he ever got to wield.

Feeling pretty certain he and I weren't going to be Facebook friends, I grabbed him by the lapels, hoisted him out of the booth, and sent him sliding across the floor like a red plaid bowling ball. Somewhere mid-slide, his beer glass skittered off under the snooker table, but didn't break.

As they say in Brooklyn, "Ya coulda hoid a pin drop."

Louie's pouring arm poised in midair. The knot of hip-checking revelers at the bar looked like they were playing freeze tag. They gawked in silence as the guy righted himself, and, without a threat, a remonstration or a backward glance, staggered the length of the bar and disappeared out the front door. The stoic manner of his departure suggested to me that this gentleman had considerable prior experience being thrown out of places and had learned to roll with the flow.

"Woooweee," somebody whooped and then it was over. As I slid into the booth across from George and Ralph, the normal buzz of the place began to rise from the floorboards.

George was bleary-eyed but still in possession of his faculties. "What's wrong?" he asked.

"Why does something have to be wrong?"

He smirked. "Haven't seen you that testy in a long time, kid." He pointed at my ear. "Looks like that smarts."

"Shaving mishap," I claimed.

"What's wrong?" he asked again.

"I got some work for you guys," I said.

"Detective work? 'Cause that friggin' landscaping shit…"

"Detective work," I assured him.

He smiled and poured himself a fresh beer.

Sounded like a cat was purring, but it was just Ralph, leaning against the wall, taking a short siesta between rounds. I slapped the photocopies of Brett Ward's picture on the table and gave George the complete rundown. When I'd finished talking, I took out my notebook and wrote down the addresses of the condo in Madison Park where Brett and Rebecca lived, as well as the address of the Shilshole Marine Yard.

"I need to know if he shows up at either place," I said. "Buy each team a prepaid cell phone. I need to know right away."

I threw a handful of cash on the table. "Take cabs. Do what you have to."

George looked horrified. He and Rebecca were quite fond of one another. "Ya just gotta find her, Leo," he said.

Ralph snorted and bumped himself off the wall. He looked around. "Find who?" he asked.

I pushed myself to my feet and walked over to the bar to settle up with Louie.

. . .

I called the SPD East Precinct looking for Marty Gilbert. The desk sergeant told me Marty was in a meeting until about eight and wanted to know if he could take a message for him. I told him I'd call back later and broke the connection.

No doubt about it, I needed to get the police involved. Every minute made a difference in missing person cases. The longer it went on, the less chance of seeing the person again. Things were every bit that simple and every bit that desperate.

I was hoping that the Rosemary De Carlo impersonation story would be eerie enough to spur the SPD into action. God knew it was giving me the willies. Besides which, I figured I had a small edge with the cops as Rebecca was one of theirs, and they really don't like people messing with theirs.

It was full dark as I strode up the sidewalk toward the Tahoe, making the blinking red light on my voice mail hard to ignore. I stopped in front of the Fourteen Carat Café and checked my messages again. Three more calls from Iris Duval and another from that local number I didn't recognize. Same thing in voice mail. On the off chance that there'd been some sort of recent development,

I forced myself to listen to Iris's most recent message and was treated to a minute-and a-half harangue regarding my lack of character and, if possible, my even more dubious genetic heritage.

Always nice talking to Iris, it was.

That left the other number. It was ironic that now I found myself in the same position as people who hired private eyes. For the sake of my own sanity, I had to make sure I left no avenue unexplored and no stone unturned, so I tapped the mystery number and waited to see who answered, fully expecting one of those riveting one-way conversations with an automatic telemarketing machine.

But no. Somebody human picked up on the second ring.

"Rachel Thoms."

I cleared my throat. "This is Leo Waterman," I said. "My phone seems to think you called."

She even rustled over the phone. "I think we need to talk."

"I'm out and about," I said. "Just tell me when and where and I'll show up."

"You know a place called Tini Bigs?"

"Martini bar down at the bottom of Denny?"

"Yes."

"When?"

"Fifteen minutes."

. . .

I made it in twelve, but she was already there when I arrived, sitting at a little round two-person table along the west wall with what looked to be an iced tea sitting half empty in front of her. Four thirty-something business suits at the far end of the bar were knocking back martinis and eyeing her like a Rottweiler contemplating a pot roast.

"You look quite a bit worse for the wear," she said as I sidled over to the table.

"And here I thought you were in the nurturing business," I joked as I took off my jacket and hung it on the back of the chair.

"I'm in the reality business," she said without a trace of humor.

"Wouldn't look good on a business card," I said as I seated myself across from her. I drew a straight line in the air with my finger. "Rachel Thoms, realist. By appointment only." I shook my head in mock solemnity.

She almost laughed. She was that much prettier up close. God help me if she ever full-on smiled at me. My head might explode.

The waiter made an appearance. I slipped him a ten and asked for the biggest glass of ice water the premises could muster. Her body language told me she thought the tip was excessive.

"It's how I assuage my inherited money guilt," I explained.

She did that shrink thing again, watching my body language and searching my face. I felt like a giant reader board, and she wasn't much liking the message.

"I tried to google you today," she said.

"And?"

"And all I got was your father," she said. "Pages and pages and pages about him."

"He cut a wide swath," I offered.

"And not an altogether legal swath at that."

I shrugged. "He operated the way movers and shakers operated back then. In those days it was a patronage system. You did for him. He did for you. One hand washed the other. As long as he sat on the city council, you always had somebody to call when you needed the potholes in your street fixed, and he always had your vote on Election Day." I showed my palms to the ceiling. "Quid pro quo."

"He apparently did a rather good job of feathering his own nest."

"Hence the inherited money guilt," I said with a grin.

She wasn't buying it. "Really?" was all she said.

"I mean…what's the point of revisionist history?" I asked. "Things are what they are. Why does the past have to conform to the present? That was then; this is now. The rules were different then." I wanted to shrug again, but stifled it. Instead, sensing that I might be getting a little too worked up on the subject, I closed my trap and looked away. An uncomfortable silence settled around the table.

Thirty silent seconds later, the waiter slid a man-sized water tumbler in front of me. Rachel waited until he'd moved two tables down and was completely out of earshot and then leaned across the table. Very proud of myself for maintaining eye contact despite the considerable cleavage surge this occasioned in my periphery.

"I've done some soul-searching since we spoke yesterday," she said.

"And?"

"And I think perhaps these are special circumstances," she said.

"You have no idea," I assured her.

My response troubled her. She frowned and asked, "How so?"

I told her about Rosemary De Carlo. She was suitably appalled.

"Rebecca knew he was having an affair," she said.

"Bunches of them," I corrected. I told her about Brett's little love nest and the collection of DVDs and recording equipment I'd found behind the wall.

"I should have told her," she said.

"Told her what?"

"He came to two of our sessions. He was…" She hesitated, as if she was choosing her words carefully.

"He was what?" I prodded.

"I thought he was a classic psychopath," she said.

"Really?"

"Not like Hannibal Lecter or anything like that. That sort of serial killer psychopath is very rare. The kind of psychopath we deal with day today is…" She stopped again. "He was just so glib," she said after a moment. "And he had all his props in place. The car. The hair. The clothes." She looked me in the eye. "He had no center to him," she said. "It was all a show. The whole time we were together, he was just going through the motions. I could feel it."

She could tell I agreed with her and went on, "A famous psychologist said that psychopaths know the words, but they can't hear the music. They know what to say from listening to other people. They know when to be happy and when to be sad, but they don't actually feel any of it themselves. They're too busy using other people to get what they want to feel anything. They have no conscience. No empathy."

"I've never been able to see what the attraction was," I admitted. "I mean, he looked great and everything, but that guy was a petri dish in the ocean of life."

"That's exactly right," she said.

"How did Rebecca know Brett was dogging her?"

"He left his phone lying around. One day while he was taking a shower, the thing kept beeping, so Rebecca picked it up. A woman was in the process of leaving a message. Cooing at Brett, wanting him to get together with her later. So she checked the phone's memory and found dozens of calls from the same number." She leaned closer. "As I understand it, a friend in the police department got her the woman's name and address."

"Which was?"

She shrugged. "She didn't say."

"And that's why she took a leave of absence?" I asked.

"Among other things."

"What things?"

She thought about it. "She was under a great deal of stress."

A dry laugh escaped my throat. "You ever met her mother?"

"Excuse me?"

I waved her off. "Could I ask a favor?"

She looked me in the eye. She'd heard that one before. "Depends," she said.

"How about you tell me everything you know about what was going on with Rebecca, without me having to pull it out of you one question at a time."

She did the RCA dog thing again, tilted her head and looked at me with new eyes. "I guess I'm still a bit conflicted about my professional priorities."

"That pesky 'sacred trust' thing?"

"I realize it may seem a bit abstract to you Mr. Waterman, but…"

"It's not abstract at all," I interrupted. "It's just that I'm tired and frustrated and scared to death. Everything that's happened so far suggests this thing is going to come to a bad end. I've got a voice screaming inside me that says that if I don't find her pretty soon, I'm not going to find her at all, and it's tearing me up, so please excuse me if I seem a little impatient. I don't mean to be rude or anything."

She sat back in her chair and looked me over like a lunch menu. "You're exactly like she said you were," she said after an interval.

I chugged half the ice water and wiped my mouth. "And how would that be?" I asked.

"Big and smart and maybe a little bit loopy." She started to say something else but caught herself and swallowed it.

"What?" I pressed.

She moved her head in a way that said, "Okay, you asked for it."

"A tad adolescent perhaps."

"It's my immaturity that keeps me young," I said.

Her bemused expression said I'd just proved her point. "Is that what you always do?" she asked.

"What's that?"

"Misdirect a serious question with a joke."

"It's always worked so far," I said.

A laugh escaped her—an unladylike bark. "You sure of that?" she asked, shutting down both laugh and smile, but it was too late.

I was attempting to come up with another joke when it hit me: Christ, what was wrong with me? Rebecca was out there, and here I was panting after her therapist. "So anyway…you resolve your ethical conflicts enough to help me, or not?" I asked.

She must have, because after taking a moment to organize her thoughts, she opened up. I could tell that she was editing herself as she went along, giving me what I needed as far as facts went and leaving out the details of Rebecca's inner life, which, she'd quite rightly decided, I didn't need to know.

The phone calls weren't the beginning of it. They were just the capper. The birthday Strip-O-Gram was the beginning. What Ricky Waters hadn't known when he gave Brett the heads-up about the dancer coming to the office was that the young lady was the daughter of one of Rebecca's friends, and that the first thing the young lady did when she got back from Millennium was to call Rebecca and tell her that Brett didn't work there anymore, and offer to give the money back. Said she'd made out pretty well on tips and felt bad about not being able to do what she'd been hired to do. That was the beginning of the unraveling.

"Did she confront him about it?" I asked.

"Absolutely." She'd told Rachel how Brett spun this long involved story about how he'd been trying to surprise her with his new enterprise. How he figured he'd get the business up and running before he told her about it.

I was incredulous. "And she went for that?"

She put on her professional face. "People believe some ridiculous things when they're trying to save a marriage. Things that they'd normally dismiss out of hand, they choose to believe, for the sake of being able to tell themselves they tried to make the relationship work." She shrugged.

"What then?"

"Then the phone calls."

"And that tore it."

She nodded. "That's when she decided to take the leave of absence." She took a sip of her iced tea. "She said she needed to find out exactly what was going on in her life. The uncertainty was very hard for her to deal with."

"She likes to be in charge of things," I said.

"Which is why she decided to look into this on her own. She wanted to see for herself exactly what was going on with her husband and…" She stopped and thought about what she was going to say next.

"And what?" I pressed.

"We talked about it the last time we met," she said.

"When was that?"

Rachel had seen her only once after Rebecca went on leave. Eight days ago, in her office, which, as far as I knew, made her the last person to see Rebecca Duval alive.

"Did…did she…" I hesitated. I didn't want to ask the question because I was afraid I might not like the answer. "Did she say anything to you that might indicate that she was…you know, scared or apprehensive?"

"Do you mean scared as in physically threatened?"

"Yes."

"If Rebecca had felt physically threatened, she'd have immediately gone to you." She gave me a long, steady look.

Instinctively, I knew she was right, and felt marginally better for knowing it.

We sat in silence, each of us lost in our own thoughts. The waiter made another pass and when neither of us wanted anything, he left the check.

"What are you going to do now?" she asked finally.

"I'm going to try to get the police involved."

"If there's anything I can do…" she began.

I thanked her for sharing. "I know that wasn't easy for you. If I ever get my head shrunk, I hope the shrink takes that 'sacred trust' stuff as seriously as you do."

She nodded, pinched her lips against a smile. "You ever need a referral…"

"You got a team you could suggest?"

That bark again, and I had to get the hell out of there. Talk about ethical conflicts.

■  ■  ■

The sky was starting to spit rain as I hiked up First Avenue toward my car. I tried Marty again, but he was still otherwise occupied, so I decided to make another run by Rebecca and Brett's condo over in Madison Park. What the hell, you never knew.

I beat the rain to the car, buckled up, and drove Denny straight up the face of Capitol Hill, wandering through neighborhoods and around traffic circles until I got to Broadway, where I hooked a right and rolled north for half a mile to Madison. Madison Park wasn't on the way to any-where. If you found yourself in Madison Park, you either were lost or that's where you were going.

The ride down to the water was longer than I remembered and Madison Valley more gentrified than the last time I'd been in this neck of the woods. Wall-to-wall salons and shops and restaurants on the same sidewalks where fly-by-night body shops and barbecue joints used to be.

Not many years ago, the streets on this side of the city were one of the few places I'd ever seen where the very rich and the very poor lived cheek to jowl. At the tops of the hills the well-to-do looked out at Lake Washington and counted themselves lucky. Quarter mile away, down in the valleys, it was strictly "the 'hood," where, as in so many urban areas, the poor were slowly being displaced by an ever-growing middle class in need of new and less-expensive places to live. Columbia City, Georgetown, Sodo, the Central District, it was all the same. Everywhere you looked, what had once been poor and run down and industrial was in the process of becoming hip and trendy and residential.

I chided myself for being so retro. Recently I noticed how I was beginning to resent many of the changes that were taking place around me. As the new was ushered in and the world I'd grown up in slowly faded from view, I'd come to feel as if it somehow wasn't fair, and that the world had an obligation to match my youthful memories. Guess it's part of growing older.

Brett and Rebecca shared a two-bedroom waterfront condo in the old money part of Madison Park. The complex was called Madison Square. No garden. Just Madison Square, an eleven-story edifice hard by the waters of Lake Washington, almost directly opposite Bill Gates's little glass shack over on the eastern shore.

Immediately to the north, a mile and a half of overhead lights traced the graceful arc of the Evergreen Point Floating Bridge as it slithered over the lake, carrying on its back a never-ending line of traffic traversing the lake in both directions.

I turned left on McGilvra and drove it to the end, then let gravity take me to the bottom of the hill. That's when I got lucky for the second time.

I was a block and a half uphill from the condo when what to my wandering eyes should appear but the white Cadillac Escalade, parked exactly where the signs said you absolutely, posatutely, shouldn't park.

Apparently I'd arrived just as the drama was about to unfold. Looked like the building's security guard had pulled open the passenger door and was reading Mr. Moto the riot act, waving his arms, pointing at the signs, and telling him to move the damn car. What the guard didn't see was Koontz emerging from the parking garage behind him.

I put the Tahoe in reverse and backed into the nearest driveway. I doused the lights, crossed a patch of lawn, and peeked around the edge of the fence. Koontz had arrived on the scene. The security guard turned in his direction, said something, and then refocused his attention on the driver.

Without breaking stride, Koontz shouldered the security guard aside, and began to climb into the passenger seat. The guard, outraged at having been brushed aside like a gnat, reached out and put a restraining hand on Koontz's shoulder, a move that proved to be a serious mistake.

In the blink of an eye, Koontz spun in a tight half circle. I don't know what you call the move, but Koontz used the spinning momentum of his body to hit the guard with the back of his fist. I winced at the sound of the impact. The guard went down in a heap, his arms bobbing, stiff and spastic.

Koontz never even looked down at the guy, just stepped up into the Escalade, and closed the door. The cavalier nature of the violence hung in the air like a noxious gas. Before I had time to process my options, the Cadillac was roaring up the hill at me.

I shrank into the wet shrubbery as they rolled by, only half of Mr. Moto's head visible above the window frame, the dashboard lights reflecting blue on the oversized lenses of his glasses. I was seriously conflicted. Part of me wanted to go down and see how the guard was doing, maybe call an ambulance, but another part was telling me to follow them, that I wasn't going to get another chance like this, and I couldn't just let them drive off into the night. Not with Rebecca still unaccounted for.

I hurried over and jumped into my car. I was a block or so behind them, running with my lights off, when they turned onto Madison and headed toward downtown.

■ ■ ■

No matter how many times you've seen Jim Rockford do it on TV, following somebody in a car is not a one-man job. Law enforcement agencies use a minimum of three and sometimes as many as six cars in order to keep from being spotted, and even then, if the subject is even remotely wary, he probably gets wise to them sooner rather than later.

By the time they rolled to a stop, I'd nearly lost them three times and had come damn close to getting myself killed running a red light down by Safeco Field. The only thing that kept me from being spotted was that these guys were predators, and predators generally aren't in the habit of watching their backs.

With the chorus of angry horns still blaring in my ears and my hands more than a little shaky, I pulled over onto the graveled shoulder a quarter mile behind them, and watched as they turned into a warehouse complex on South Fidalgo Street.

I stayed put and watched their headlights bobbing up and down on the side of the building as the Cadillac negotiated the sea of potholes that passed for a road. When the lights disappeared around the back of the building, I hopped out to jog up the street. The old wooden warehouse building sat wedged between Parnell's Custom Cabinets and Victory Plumbing Supplies. The barnlike structure may have dated from the 1940s or 1950s, but the sign on the front was brand new: Saint David's Transport.

As I jogged along, I tried to recall who Saint David was and what he'd done to merit being a saint, or, often as not, what had been done to him. I thought maybe he was the patron saint of Wales, one of those guys back in the fourth or fifth century who was part of the monastic movement, but I wasn't sure. I knew David was an old-time biblical name, but somehow it sounded awfully modern for a saint. What was next? Saint Tiffany, the patron saint of Bergdorf Goodman?

An approaching train whistle jolted me back to reality, reminding me that the Burlington Northern tracks ran directly behind the building and, beyond that, the pestilential Duwamish Waterway snaked its way through the industrial heart of Seattle. It crossed my mind that this wasn't the sort of place that a couple of Canadian thugs would know about unless whoever they were working for was somehow connected to one of the businesses in the immediate area. The train whistle sounded again, closer now, the low growl of the massive diesels seemed to vibrate the air.

I picked up my pace. The St. David building was the better part of a football field long, an uninterrupted wall of metal siding with nowhere for me to take evasive action should the need arise. Were they to come back up the road, I'd be standing there like a deer in the headlights.

I heaved an inward sigh of relief as I skidded up to the corner of the building and peeked around. A black Hummer with B.C. plates was nosed up to the Cadillac. An advertising logo and some kind of slogan were painted on the Hummer's door but I couldn't make them out in the gloom.

Interestingly, Koontz and Moto were nowhere to be seen. I inched closer to the corner and swept my eyes across the rear of the building. Nothing unusual other than a couple of luxury cars sitting nose-to-nose on the gravel with their engines running.

Halfway between my position and the Escalade an old dump truck was backed against one of the loading docks. The four flat tires and briars and brambles growing up and over the rusted hood suggested it hadn't moved this century and was well on its way to full-fledged planter status. The junker truck was cover, and cover was what I needed at that point. I was trying to decide how and when to make my move, when a flash out in the distance caught my eye.

I focused on the spot for a full ten seconds before my eyes managed to pick them out—Koontz and Moto walking back this way. Back from what? The river? That's all that was over there. What in hell were they doing over there?

They were about forty yards out and from the sound of things weren't going to make it back before the train got here. As if to prove me right, another blast of the whistle heralded the train's arrival. I could feel it now, feel the weight of its cargo shaking my feet as the freight cars clicked and clanked over the uneven rails. Sounded like somebody shaking a box of tools. The whistle sounded again as the trio of train engines crept into view, blocking any view of Koontz and his little Asian friend walking back this way.

Each and every freight car had been tagged multiple times and in several hues. Gang signs, elaborately flourished signatures, and anatomically infeasible suggestions, all of it rolling by in living color. "Kilroy was here" on a grand scale. The hip-hop generation rolling through a neighborhood near you.

A pair of small red lights approaching from the left said the caboose was about to arrive, and that I was about to get hung out to dry, so I sucked it up and made a dash for the truck, hoping to find some cover. The rumble of the train covered the sound of my footsteps as I raced to the side of the derelict dump truck and rolled beneath.

My shoulder hated everything about it. I had to stifle a groan as I scrunched myself toward the rear of the truck and wedged myself between the tires. I took several deep breaths and waited for my shoulder to calm down.

The train clatter was fading as I peeked out from behind the tires. The driver's side door of the Hummer was hanging open. The logo was an artsy-fartsy monogram. The letters STE all swirled together. ST Emtman Ltd. in block letters beneath. Below that in smaller letters: Serving B.C. since 1965.

Koontz and Moto were standing there by the open door, listening to whoever was inside the Hummer. Sounded like the mystery driver might be yelling. Koontz said something and apparently the Hummer said something back and then suddenly the meeting was over.

The Hummer's door slammed. The halogen headlights lit up the yard like Safeco Field as the driver threw it in reverse, wheeled around the front of the Cadillac and roared off around the corner.

The Escalade, on the other hand, took its time leaving. A full minute passed before I heard the sound of tires crunching gravel. I stayed where I was. The minute they rounded the corner, I crawled out from under the truck, dusted myself off as best I could, and started jogging back up the access road.

The Hummer was gone. I arrived at the corner in time to see the Escalade bump out onto First Avenue, turn left, and head back toward downtown.

Without actually wishing it so, I began to run. Who knew? Maybe they'd catch a couple of traffic lights and I could get back on their tail. As leads went, they weren't much, but they were all I had, so I put my head down and gave it my all.

The exertion set my ear to burning and made the ache in my shoulder nearly unbearable, but I kept running anyway, sidling along like a Dungeness crab, keeping my eyes glued on the knee-deep potholes, trying not to break a hip before I reached the Tahoe.

Imagine my surprise when I looked up to find a pair of uniformed SPD officers pointing guns at me over the top of my car.

"Put your hands on your head," the nearest cop shouted.

"Hands on your head," the female officer screamed.

I did as I was told, then tried the line again. "Is there an echo in here?" I asked.

They didn't think it was funny either.

■　■　■

Marty Gilbert was the second cop through the door. The first introduced himself as Detective Sergeant Broils and sat down across the table from me. Standard issue detective material. Thick salt-and-pepper hair, thicker mustache, wearing his badge around his neck on a silver chain. Detective Broils made a ceremony out of taking out his notebook and pen and rolling up his sleeves before lifting his baby blues and asking, "You know why you're here?"

"Seems to be National Arrest Leo Week," I said.

He sat back in his chair and folded his arms across his thick chest. "I heard you think you're funny."

"Seems to be the minority opinion."

"Maybe you ought to travel with a laugh track," he suggested.

I was working up a snappy reply when Marty let himself into the interview room. He stood with his back resting on the rear wall and his hands behind his back. Everything about him said that he was only there as an observer and that I shouldn't count on any help from him.

I rattled the pair of handcuffs that connected my right hand to the table. "I'd offer to shake hands, but..." I said to Marty.

He turned his face aside.

Having arranged his pen and notebook and glasses at perfect right angles to one another, Broils put on his serious face. I watched as he slid two fingers down into his shirt pocket and came out with a business card. He threw it on the table, where it landed face up. It was one of mine.

"You want to tell me about this?" he asked.

"Turn the card over," I said.

He hesitated, looked over his shoulder at Marty, and then flipped the card. The back of the card was clean, so it couldn't be the one I gave to Rachel Thoms. That one had another number scrawled across the back.

"I gave that one to a woman named Rosemary De Carlo," I said.

"When was that?" Broils asked.

"Earlier today. Around three thirty or so."

Broils was jotting notes. He looked up. "So you admit to being there?"

"Sure," I said.

"Ms. De Carlo was a friend of yours?"

"Nope."

"So how'd you know her?"

I looked up at Marty, who was making it a point not to meet my gaze. "Marty," I said. "You're going to want to pay attention here."

Marty did his Mount Rushmore impression as I laid it out for Broils. About Koontz and Moto warning me off. About Rosemary De Carlo impersonating Rebecca at the Alderbrook. About how Brett Ward put her up to it. About the late Teddy Healy and getting arrested at the crack of dawn, and then finding Rosemary, and the Shilshole Marine

Yard. About what I learned from Northwest Maritime, and about running into Koontz and his buddy down at the Madison Park condo, and following them to South Seattle. The only things I left out were Rachel Thoms and Brett Ward's secret porno palace, neither of which I thought they needed to know about.

By the time I'd finished talking, Marty had bumped himself off the wall and walked over to the side of the table. "You're being straight here, Leo?" he asked me. "'Cause this is no time to be fucking around."

"Absolutely."

Broils still wasn't satisfied. "What condition was Ms. De Carlo in when you left?" he wanted to know.

"Beat up," I said. "That Healy character slapped her around quite a bit. She had a mouse under one eye and a full-scale shiner in the other. Why? What happened to her?"

"Somebody about beat her to death," Marty said. "She's up at Harborview. They don't think she's gonna make it."

"Wasn't me. All I did was borrow a picture of Brett Ward from her."

"Neighbors said they heard noises around five o'clock. Where were you?"

I thought about it. "I was talking to a guy over at Fisherman's Terminal. After that I was at the Eastlake Zoo from whence I went to Tiny Bigs down on Denny. Then I went to Madison Park and, as they say, the rest was history."

Marty stepped out into the hall. Broils kept at it. Wanted to know what law enforcement agency had picked me up earlier in the day.

"Washington State Patrol," I said. "Guy named Bradley."

"And you claim this…" He checked his notes. "…this Koontz character assaulted the building security guard?"

"Knocked him stiff. Left him on the lawn."

Broils jotted away and then got to his feet, fixed me with what he imagined to be a withering stare, gathered up his belongings, and left the room.

Forty-five minutes passed before the door opened again and a uniformed officer came in, took the cuffs off me, and escorted me down the hall to Marty's office. Marty was on the phone, so I took a seat. Half a minute of yesses, nos, and thank yous, and he hung up.

"Sorry about that, but it wasn't my case," he said. "I told him beating up women wasn't your style, but he had to find out for himself. That's how it works around here. Three witnesses and that business card put you at the scene. It had to be done according to protocol."

I told him I understood. He anticipated my next question.

"We had an assault report from their condo office."

"How's the guard?" I asked.

"Broken jaw and a fractured eye orbit," Marty said.

"That was one punch, man," I said. "This Koontz character is an animal."

"I don't like one goddamn thing about this," Marty said.

"Join the club."

"I've got a call into Missing Persons. I'll get them cranking as soon as I can. I put out a find order on both their cars. I'll have patrol check for their cars over at the condo."

"What about this ST Emtman Limited? And the Saint David company? Can you find out something about what's up with them?"

"I've got a friend in the Vancouver PD. I'll make a few calls."

I started to speak, but he waved me off.

"Go home, Leo. We'll handle it from here." He leaned out over the desk. "I don't want to hurt your feelings or anything, buddy, but you look like shit."

# Chapter 4

By the time I pulled into my garage after midnight, I was slumped over the wheel, steering mostly with my chin. I crawled out and fished around under the seat and found Brett Ward's DVDs and cameras, and stuffed them into my coat pocket.

I live in the downstairs half of the house, and even that portion is about three times as much space as I need. The maid service goes upstairs once in a while to push the dust around and flush the toilets, but I seldom make the ascent myself.

I let myself in the back door, emptied my pockets onto the kitchen table, and stumbled into the bedroom, where I plopped down on the edge of the bed.

I sat staring at the carpet for the longest time, trying to put everything I'd learned into some sort of meaning-ful order, but it was like reading late at night, where three minutes in you realize you've read the same paragraph six times and still don't have any idea what it's about. I stood up, dropped my clothes on the floor, and crawled between the sheets.

The second I closed my eyes, I fell back into that haunted house, can't-quite-get-to-Rebecca dream that I'd had what seemed like a week ago but was only last night. The difference was that Koontz and Mr. Moto had replaced the maniac hillbillies as the heavies; otherwise the plot was eerily familiar.

I awoke sitting up, sweating like a racehorse. Took me a half a minute to realize I'd been dreaming. The bedside clock read two-fifty-nine, and since there was no way I was going back to sleep anytime soon, I pulled my robe from the hook on the back of the door, and wandered into the kitchen.

After I made coffee, I scrounged around and found a container of milk in the door of the fridge. When I peeked inside, the former milk appeared to be waving back at me, so I rummaged through one of the lower cabinets and came up with a jar of Coffee-mate so old it had originally belonged to my father, and he'd been dead for a couple of decades. Stuff had a half-life of six thousand years.

Most of the way through the coffee, I was trying to work up a reasonable scenario wherein Rebecca could still be out there somewhere, but hard as I tried, I couldn't put anything feasible together. I told myself not to panic, that I'd figure it out, that I'd find her if I just had a couple more pieces of the puzzle. That's what I told myself.

I was about to start over when my eyes came to rest on the Flip cameras and the collection of DVDs fanned across the table like a sliced tomato. I wondered once again, what kind of man feels a need to secretly film his lovers. Wondered if somewhere in Brett's little mind he found leching at the digital images somehow more exciting than the sex acts themselves, as if a life lived in the third person held greater appeal to him than simple reality.

I refreshed my coffee, rounded up the cameras and DVDs, and headed for the study. It used to be my old man's office, the inner sanctum from which many a shady deal was hatched, and from which I had been barred right up until the day he died, which probably explains why, even before moving in, I'd had the room razed and renovated. New glass desk in the corner, coupla couches, coupla chairs, and a TV the size of Nova Scotia. If I'd left the office as it was, I'd have seen him sitting there, glowering at me from behind his desk for all eternity. Way I saw it, it was either make it my own, or nail the door shut and forget about it.

As I fired up the TV and refreshed my memory of how to operate the DVD player, I realized that something inside me didn't much want to see what was on these discs, that I was embarrassed to be peeping into the private parts of people's lives...to coin a particularly unfortunate phrase.

I figured I could skip the Rosemary De Carlo show, so I slid the disc labeled Serena A out of the middle of the pack and popped it into the DVD player. Time and date in the upper corners. March fifth a year and a half earlier. Eleven-oh-nine in the morning.

Serena A was a good-looking blonde woman, getting a bit flanky in middle age, but I felt pretty sure it didn't matter to Brett. From what I could see, Brett Ward was an equal opportunity adulterer. Big, small, old, young, six to sixty, blind, crippled, or crazy, it was all grist for ol' Brett's mill.

Despite profound trepidations, I settled into my football chair. Right from the start, I could tell that the sounds were going to bother me more than the images. Maybe it was because Brett liked to talk dirty and made it a point to get his partners doing likewise, or, more likely, because there was something inherently more revealing about what came out of a person's mouth than there was about what went in.

Nonetheless, I resisted the strong impulse to hit the mute button.

What I noticed right away was that there was a definite pattern to his sexual conquests. He more or less performed the same acts, in the same order, regardless of who was naked in the room with him, as if he was directing a fantasy movie in his head and all he did was recast the female lead whenever he took a new lover.

Brett liked to do the undressing for the both of them. His eyes shone like a kid on Christmas morning, unbuttoning this, unsnapping that, peeling it away, fondling the foundlings, apparently without regard to size, shape, or degree of lividity. I reckoned how it was always a pleasure to see a man enjoying his work.

Once he got 'em naked and suitably pinched, Brett became living proof that Oscar Wilde had been right when he'd opined that everything in the world was about sex, except sex, which was about power. What seemed to titillate Brett Ward was pushing each woman a couple of notches beyond her comfort zone. With the shy, it was just verbal. Getting them to beg for it with such prosaic entreaties as, "Give it to me. Give it to me"—or, my personal favorite, uttered five months back by one Amy T, "Oh God, use me like an animal." I don't know why, but plowing came immediately to my mind.

With the more sexually adventurous, things took a significantly darker tone, as Brett seemed to be fixated upon getting the women to perform some sexual act they found abhorrent, the more painful and the more humiliating the better, as if their shame and discomfort somehow validated him. I found it difficult to watch but nonetheless managed to persevere.

I suppose it was predictable that I would know one of the women on the DVDs. I was three discs into the carnal cavalcade when up popped Hillary Franks, one of Rebecca's oldest and dearest friends, splaying herself like a honeydew melon, exposing parts of herself theretofore observed only by certified medical professionals.

Not to belabor the Oscar Wilde thing, but I'm pretty sure he also said something to the effect that a friend is the one who stabs you in the front, which, as sad as it sounds, may be all we can reasonably expect from one another these days.

The times and dates on the DVDs suggested Brett took a new lover about every three months or so. His most recent conquest was still in the camera's memory, so I had to move over to the desk and watch it on my computer. Eleven days ago. Four thirty in the afternoon. Barbara P. A well-tended brunette in her early fifties. She'd shaved her pubic hair into the shape of a heart. She lay spread-eagled, tied to the bed with a red ball gag stuffed between her jaws and a pair of old-fashioned clothespins pinching her nipples. Looked like it smarted.

Part of me wanted to laugh out loud at the sight of this pampered matron bound and gagged for pleasure. Another, better part of me recited the old "different strokes for different folks" mantra, and turned off the camera.

I jumped at the sound of the newspaper hitting the front door, blinked a couple of times, looked around, and noticed gray daylight creeping through the office windows. I yawned, rolled my shoulders, and pushed myself to my feet.

I reached to shut down the iMac but changed my mind and instead opened YouTube and typed the name Jordan Koontz into the search box.

Like I figured, he wasn't hard to find. His greatest hit, six years ago. Four million, three hundred sixty-three thousand, five hundred and nine hits later. I clicked Play and the screen blinked to life. Between rounds at a mixed martial arts fight. McMahon Stadium, Calgary, Alberta, Canada. Jordan "The Terminator" Koontz versus Billy "The Wolfman" Czyz. The camera followed a lithesome young woman in a red bikini as she paraded around the perimeter of the octagon, holding a red number three above her head to signify the round.

Only after she blew a kiss to the cameraman and returned to her ringside seat did the fighters come into view. Koontz was sitting on a stool in the blue corner, looking like he hadn't blinked in the past hour and a half. He was sweaty, and his blond spikes were plastered to his head, but otherwise he was relatively unmarked.

His opponent, on the other hand, looked like he'd been hit by a truck and dragged for several blocks. A cut man was applying cold steel to a hideously swollen area above the fighter's right eye, while his trainer exhorted the fighter in some Central European language, and a third guy poured bottled water over his man's head.

My first thought was that I couldn't believe the referee was going to let this guy come out for another round. He looked to have been threshed and baled. But, after conferring at some length with the ringside doctor, the referee waved the fighters from their corners, and the fight resumed.

Thirty-seven seconds into the third round, the fighters launched themselves at one another at precisely the same instant. Their heads came together with a sickening crack.

Czyz's forehead smashed into the front of Koontz's face, sending both men reeling.

I don't watch enough mixed martial arts to qualify as an expert, but I knew for certain that head butts aren't allowed. To me, this particular butt had appeared to be an accident, the kind of thing that often happens when highly conditioned men come together in the ring for the purpose of beating the bejesus out of one another. Jordan Koontz, however, didn't see it that way. He pawed at his flattened face in disbelief and when his hand came away bloody, he went completely berserk.

The referee was busy warning Czyz that any further head butts would result in the stoppage of the fight, so he never saw Koontz coming.

Koontz threw the ref aside like he was made of Styrofoam, sent him staggering across the octagon, where he lost his balance and fell to his knees. Before the official could recover, Koontz drove a side-kick into his startled opponent's middle, doubling him over, bouncing him off the ropes and down onto the mat.

After that, it got hard to watch. Whoever had posted this version of the fight had slowed things down at the moment of impact. Czyz was on all fours when Jordan Koontz's foot made impact with the back of his neck.

The result was horrific. You could see the hail of sweat and spittle dislodged from Czyz's head at the moment of impact. Watched as his mouthpiece flew out into the stands. Took everything I had not to put my hands over my eyes, as frame by frame, whatever collections of muscles and nerves and bones and sinew that held our heads upright became completely detached from their moorings.

And then…then Czyz died, right before my eyes. Right there on the screen, super-slow motion, high definition dead, as whatever spark, cosmic or otherwise, that animates a human being left his body. I knew it; everybody in the arena knew it. Dead.

Koontz, however, didn't seem to notice. He continued his wild-eyed effort to stomp his opponent's head flat, until the referee, having regained his footing, tried to throw himself onto Koontz's back. Unfortunately, Koontz saw him coming.

Koontz caught the ref in mid-stride, threw an arm between his legs, and lifted the poor guy completely over his head. Every lung in the area froze for a second as Koontz drove the referee headfirst into the mat.

What followed was a melee of epic proportions, as dozens of people threw themselves into the fray, trying to rescue the fighter or the referee or one another; it was hard to tell. Mostly it was just a flailing, churning ball of humanity.

I watched in stunned silence as medical personnel finally fought their way into the center of the octagon and began administering aid.

Koontz had to be subdued and then sedated before he could be strapped to a gurney and wheeled from the venue, with the threats and curses of the crowd raining down on him. At that point, somebody got smart and shut down the camera feed.

I sat back in the chair and took several deep breaths. My phone began to vibrate against the hard surface of the desk and, grateful for something—anything—that would help me push those pictures from my mind, I picked it up.

■　■　■

Marty had managed to promote a cup of coffee from the Mickey D's across the street, which meant he'd been on the scene for quite some time. He had his ears hunkered down inside his collar as he walked my way. He looked cold.

"You wanna have a look before they haul it off?" he asked.

I said I did.

"I spoke with PE," he said, referring to the Parking Enforcement Division of the SPD. "There were four tickets on the windshield and another two in the glove box," he said. "They say it's been here five days. The three officers who do the sweeps down here say they gave her a free ride for a couple of nights." He shrugged, as if to dismiss their largesse. "They figured they'd already written her up four times, you know, maybe enough was enough."

"Remarkable restraint," I commented.

"To protect and serve."

"I don't get how two of the tickets got in the glove box," I said as we walked.

"Not from around here," Marty said. "They were issued early last week over in Wallingford, two days apart."

Rebecca's green BMW X3 was angled into a spot directly beneath the southbound lanes of the viaduct. Two guys from Liberty Towing were hooking it up to the inclined bed of their truck as we approached.

They waited patiently as I opened all the doors and poked around inside the car for quite some time. I don't know what I was expecting to find, maybe just a sense of Rebecca clinging to the carpets or the headliner or something. It was weird, but I just had to do it.

Marty read my mind. "Forensics is gonna give it a full go," he assured me.

"Where in Wallingford?" I asked.

"On Eastern," he said. "Between Forty-second and Forty-third."

I closed my eyes and pictured the neighborhood. Nice area. A mixture of older Victorians and postwar craftsman cottages. One of those narrow-street neighborhoods that was built before the automobile ruled the world. No driveways. If you met somebody coming the other way on Eastern Avenue, one of you had to duck in among the parked cars to let the other guy pass. Strictly single-family residential. No commercial activity of any kind. Nothing to hint at why her car had been illegally parked in that part of town.

"Harbor Patrol swept that area of the Duwamish Waterway behind Saint David's Transport. Came up empty."

"What about those freaks in the Cadillac?"

"What about 'em?"

"Aren't you going to pick 'em up?"

He shrugged. "No probable cause," he said.

"What about the assault on the security guard? That ought to be enough to get 'em in and at least sweat 'em a bit."

"As of a couple of hours ago, the security guard doesn't remember a damn thing. All he recalls is waking up on the lawn with a broken face. The docs say it's a fairly common reaction to a severe concussion."

"I saw it happen."

"You want to spend your day giving depositions?" he asked. "They'll bail out and be back on the streets in under an hour. You know it, and I know it, and they know it." He wiped the idea away with his free hand. "No point to it."

The whine of the tow truck ricocheted among the concrete pillars as they pulled the Beemer onto the bed of the truck and began to chain it down

"I also called a colleague on the Vancouver PD. About ST Emtman and Saint David's Transport."

"And?"

"They're expecting us for lunch," Marty said.

I winced. The trip to Vancouver, BC, was a 180 miles door-to-door, and that didn't account for the border crossing, which could take another hour and a half to four hours depending on the volume of traffic, the current level of terror alert, and how well the countries were getting along at that moment. Pangs of dread were churning my insides to pudding and the idea of spending a whole day traveling back and forth to Canada just didn't sound like time well spent.

"That's gonna kill the whole day," I groused.

He shrugged. "They didn't want to talk about it over the phone."

I didn't say so, but something inside me didn't want to get that far from Seattle. I felt like I was giving up the hunt or deserting my post or something.

Marty sensed my discomfort. He jerked a thumb back over his shoulder. "Everything points in that direction, Leo," he insisted. "If there was anything else to do here in Seattle, I'd be doing it."

I wanted to argue, but Marty was right. Whatever had turned Brett Ward's life upside down had originated up in B.C. Everything from the license plates to the shootout with the Provincial Police that heralded the beginning of the end of Brett's boat repo business. All of it started in Canada.

"Let's go," I said. "I'll drive."

. . .

Looked like a Canadian cop convention. Multiple plainclothes officers represented the Provincial Police, the Vancouver PD and the RCMP. Another six uniformed constables lined the walls. Inspector Anthony Hargress of the VPD handled the introductions. Marty and I shook hands all around, sat down at the foot of the table, and got our notebooks out.

Hargress looked like he didn't get out much. Fifty-something, losing sight of his belt buckle and his hairline at the same time. Poster boy for the Pacific Northwest pallor, that cadaveric hue one gets from living where the sun is, at best, an infrequent visitor.

"ST Emtman and Saint David's Transport are part of Billy Bailey's far-flung empire," Hargress began. An angry murmur crawled around the room. Hargress looked at Marty and me. "Which, in case you were wondering, explains the unusual level of interest in this room today."

As a matter of fact, I had wondered about that very thing the moment we'd walked through the door. Either it was a slow crime day in B.C. or Marty's interagency request for information on Saint David's Transport and ST Emtman had touched an unanticipated nerve within the Canadian law enforcement community.

The name rang a bell, but I couldn't quite put my finger on it. "Billy Bailey?" I said.

"Billy Bud," growled the Mountie on my right.

"Ah," I said. "Not the Melville character, I take it?"

Apparently my comic renown had once again failed to precede me.

Hargress cleared his throat. "For the benefit of our guests..." he began in a tone that reminded me of an annoyed schoolmaster forced to repeat himself.

Billy Bailey, or more formally, William Somerset Bailey III, would go down in history as Canada's most famous and certainly most successful drug trafficker. Billy Bud, as he came to be known, parlayed a small-time pot-growing operation into an international pot-smuggling cartel that supplied major portions of the weed consumed on the West Coast of the United States. Thousands of tons of B.C. bud flowed over the US border and, much to their collective chagrin, nobody on either side of the border seemed to be able to do much about it.

Billy was beyond slick. He understood how to keep his business at a distance. Over the years Canadian and American authorities had arrested an army of mules and seized tons and tons of pot, even taken down some of the movers and shakers within the organization, but had never gotten close enough to Billy to make a collar.

Worse yet, the scope and audacity of Billy's operation had turned him into a national folk hero. Hargress reckoned it was the tunnel that pushed Billy's image over the top. The minute he brought it up, I recalled the headline: Border Breached. Seems Billy and his minions had excavated a tunnel beneath the international border. A tunnel big enough to drive pickup trucks through. Had a nasty winter storm back in 1998 not exposed the south end of the tunnel to the U.S. Border Patrol, it would undoubtedly still be in operation today. Not one, but two *National Geographic* specials had documented Billy's colorful and meteoric rise to prominence.

As if to rub salt into the wound, Billy Bailey then morphed into the face of a national movement advocating the legalization of marijuana, appearing in an assortment of omnipresent television ads, eventually making himself the most recognized face in British Colombia. Another, angrier, rumble of discontent filled the room.

And then, after nearly twenty years of interagency detective work, just at the point where the authorities thought they might make a case against Billy for conspiracy, he did the unthinkable. He went straight. Bought a couple of small businesses and turned them into gold mines. Seemed his knack for commerce proved every bit as successful in the legal sector as it had in the drug business, so he bought a couple more, and then a couple more until he was making more money in his legal endeavors than he was from trafficking drugs, at which point he parceled out the drug-smuggling operation to his underlings, and became a legitimate businessman of national repute.

"Cheeky bastard's running for Provincial Parliament," somebody added.

"Cheeky bastard's going to win," another voice answered.

Hargress laced his fingers behind his back and looked directly at Marty and me.

"The man has been making a monkey of us for twenty-five years, so I'm certain you gentlemen can imagine why any potential opportunity to do battle with Billy Bailey has our undivided attention."

Marty cleared this throat and picked up the conversational thread. He explained that Rebecca Duval was a vital and much-respected force in the Seattle law enforcement community, explained why the SPD had not gotten involved until now and then deferred to me.

I'd jotted down a few notes, so I was reasonably well prepared. Thirty seconds into my little recitation, however—the first time the words "Jordan Koontz" left my lips—the room came unglued.

"That's gotta be Junior," Hargress said.

Crosstalk buzzed like an angry hornet.

"Excuse me?"

"Jordan Koontz and Lui Ng are Junior's little playmates," he said.

"Guess we're a bit behind the curve here," Marty admitted sheepishly.

Hargress nodded toward the Vancouver PD contingent sitting on my left. "Roddy," he said. "A little background perhaps."

Roddy levered himself to his feet. Roddy was 180 pounds of sinew stretched over a six-foot frame. It wouldn't have surprised me to find out that he ran marathons in his spare time. He swept his close-set eyes over the assembled masses and explained that Junior Bailey was Billy Bud's only child. Seems Junior had grown up as heir apparent to the drug-smuggling operation and had more or less geared his career expectations to a life of crime. As luck would have it, however, just about the time Junior reached the age of majority, his father had the unmitigated gall to go straight, dashing the poor boy's criminal hopes on the rocks of respectability.

Not to be denied what he considered to be his birthright, Junior Bailey used his multimillion-dollar trust fund to finance his own life of crime, mostly pimping and loan-sharking operations.

Unlike his famous father, however, Junior showed precious little criminal acumen. Only his father's influence and a crack legal team hired expressly for that purpose had thus far managed to keep him out of jail.

"Junior the Genius," someone muttered.

Hargress pinned us with his gaze. "I assure you gentlemen the designation is purely ironic. Junior Bailey is as dumb as the proverbial bag of rocks."

"Thinks he's a gangster," Roddy added disgustedly. "Keeps Billy Bud busy trying to keep him under wraps and out of the lockup."

"I looked Koontz up on the Internet," I said. "What about this Ng guy?"

"Lui Ng," Hargress explained. He spelled it. "Former leader of the Golden Dragons street gang. Half Laotian, half Chinese. Mr. Ng likes to shoot people."

"He's Koontz's lover," Roddy threw in.

"No kidding?"

"And not the way you imagine, either," he said with a bob of his eyebrows. "Ng's the top. Koontz is the bottom."

My mind offhandedly rejected any image of those two coupling in any manner whatsoever, once again confirming survival as the first instinct of human nature.

"Ng's a person of interest in at least five murders," Hargress added. "Junior uses them as his personal bodyguards, his entourage, as it were."

"So...not to belabor the obvious, but what you're telling me is that whatever is going on in Seattle is connected to Junior Bailey, rather than his father. Is that right?"

"Almost surely," Hargress said. "Billy doesn't break the law anymore. He's too worried about his image and his political future."

I mentioned the black Hummer.

"ST Emtman's company trademark," Hargress said.

"Billy's got fifty of them," someone said disgustedly.

"Fifty-three," one of his colleagues amended.

I segued to what I knew about the boat repo where the owner had pulled a gun on Brett Ward and the Canadian cops, hoping that somebody sitting there at the conference table could throw a little light on the subject, as, somehow or another, that was the moment when things had begun to unravel for Brett Ward and I needed to know the hows and whys of it.

I wasn't disappointed. Seemed that no matter which side of the border you were on, taking shots at police officers was considered extremely poor form.

"On the island," somebody said.

"Dashwood," one of the cops amended. "Out at Cross-Current Marina."

"Local guy named Trevor Collins. Took a nick out of one of our constables," the provincial cop added.

Hargress nodded. "We thought the most interesting aspect of the matter was how quickly Mr. Collins was free on bond. Hard to imagine why someone would put up one hundred thousand dollars to get a lowlife like Mr. Collins back on the street." Seemed like there was a punch line waiting somewhere in the weeds, so I kept my mouth closed and waited for it to arrive.

"We can't be sure...," Roddy began cautiously. "...privacy laws being what they are regarding bonding agencies, but we managed to trace the bond to a law firm. Teglow and Murphy from down in Surrey."

Another murmur of interest swept over the conference table. Seemed the name was familiar to them. Hargress once again pinned Marty and me with his gaze.

"Teglow and Murphy regularly represent Junior Bailey's legal interests."

"How's this Collins guy connected to Junior?" Marty asked.

"They went to high school together. Quite chummy we're told."

"You know," said the other Provincial Police officer, "I'm thinking that Billy Bud might be interested in hearing what Mr. Waterman has to say."

"He does dote on that boy," Roddy noted with an ironic twist of the lips.

For our benefit, he explained. "Junior thinks he's defying his father by being in business for himself. In reality, Billy runs his show for him. Behind the scenes, of course, but they're his old suppliers and cronies. He just lets Junior think he's in business for himself."

I could see where they were going with this. They were thinking they might be able to get to Billy Bailey through his son, and they were hoping I might serve as a handy catalyst to do so. They were quite rightly assuming that leverage on Junior was the next best thing to leverage on Billy Bud himself, especially if they had the likes of Marty and me to run interference for them. Anything went wrong and they could just say, "Oh, you know how crude those Americans are."

Roddy leaned over the table and looked me in the eye. "Would you like to talk to him?" he asked.

"Is that possible?" I asked.

"Billy loves to talk. Mostly about himself. I'm sure he'd be glad to bandy a few words with you."

I thought about it. The sense of urgency that was churning my insides wanted to go back to Seattle. To...to...that was the problem, to what I didn't know; I didn't have a plan anymore. Maybe find the stripper and see if there was anything there. Maybe start all over again. Other than that, I was pretty much at a dead end.

"We've gone to Rome," I said with some reluctance. "Guess we might as well see the pope."

· · ·

Roddy turned out to be his last name. Detective Sergeant Tony Roddy said it would probably take an hour or so to put together the meeting with Billy Bailey. He explained that Billy always insisted on having his attorney present and to just hang in there, they'd make the arrangements as quickly as possible.

Faced with a delay, we asked if he would kindly point us toward a restaurant where we could catch a bite. He recommended the greasy spoon across the street from Provincial Police headquarters. What I had presumed to be a comment on its menu, in fact, turned out to be its given name, the Greasy Spoon. Needless to say, the bill of fare more than lived up to the signage.

It was nearly two o'clock in the afternoon before word came and we finally got under way. By that time, the bacon and eggs were doing backflips in my tract, and I would have gladly walked back to Seattle on my hands, just to feel like I was doing something useful. Mercifully, the drive to Billy Bud's place was short.

Fifteen minutes after we crossed the Burrard Street Bridge, we were rolling through what the locals called Kitsilano, a little village-like area on the far side of English Bay. Billy Bud's manor house stood gray and imposing on a dramatic outcropping of rock, offering a sweeping view of both the Vancouver skyline to the east and the ominous Strait of Georgia to the west.

I don't know why. Maybe I watched too many gangster films, but I was expecting a *Godfather* scene, where you pull up to a locked gate guarded by sixteen fat guys in fedoras, and, after being inspected like a week-old eggplant, you're reluctantly allowed inside the family compound. Not so with Billy Bailey. The gate was open and the massive circular driveway empty as we rolled to a halt. What I imagined had once been the stable and the carriage house was now a ten-car garage.

"Used to belong to William Cornelius Van Horne," Roddy said as we stood looking out over the dark, roiling water toward Vancouver Island. He sensed we didn't recognize the name and helped us out. "Former chairman of the Canadian Pacific Railway," he explained. "Same fellow who built the Banff Springs Hotel." He swung his hand in an arc. "This used to be Corny's little urban *pied-à-terre*."

Looked to be about twenty thousand square earth feet in the Scottish baronial tradition. A great chunk of concrete, faced with stone, standing sentry over the water. Were it not for the trio of security cameras chronicling our every move, it would have been easy to feel as if we'd somehow been transported back to the early twentieth century.

The front door swung open on massive wrought-iron hinges. A brunette in her midthirties stood holding the door in one hand. "Good afternoon, gentlemen," she said. "Mr. Bailey is expecting you." She spoke with an air of detachment, as if, as far as she was concerned, our visit held scant appeal. Great cheekbones and the kind of blue eyes that made men forget about what happened the last time they'd looked into eyes like that more than compensated for whatever she lacked in warmth.

She wore one of those soft, fuzzy sweater suits so popular in the 1950s and 1960s. The sort of clothes that suggested rather than shouted. The robin's egg–blue wool skirt was a couple of inches longer than current fashion but looked real good on her. A single strand of pearls completed the look and accented the firmness of her throat. Albeit retro, all in all a very put-together and alluring package.

We followed the swaying blue skirt down a seemingly endless expanse of flagstone, past what they probably called "the great room," with its panoramic view, soaring ceiling, and stone fireplace large enough to roast an ox with the hair on. All very tweedy and heath and moor and calls to "let loose the dogs." I felt like I was in a Basil Rathbone movie.

If Billy Bud had once been the prince of the counterculture, he'd gotten over it in a big way. No hookahs or patchouli incense. Nary a paisley shirt or Birkenstock sandal in sight. No, this was strictly lord of the manor stuff, all oak-paneled walls and glassy-eyed animal heads staring down at us as we doggedly trekked through the house.

After what seemed like a mile and a half, our tour guide stepped aside and shepherded us inside an expansive room. I glanced over my shoulder as we crossed the room. Rather than going back to whatever she'd been doing prior to our arrival, she remained standing in the archway. I got the impression she didn't think our visit was going to last very long and was saving herself a couple of thousand steps.

The room was a gorgeous Victorian library, floor-to-ceiling beautifully bound books, with a rolling brass ladder to provide access to the more lofty tomes. One of those rooms where the books were all gold-embossed matched sets and you couldn't imagine that anyone had ever pulled one out to read.

Billy sat behind a half-acre mahogany desk with his fingers laced in front of him like an attendant schoolboy. He was a good-looking man. A little older than me. Fifty-something with a thick head of hair parted neatly in the middle and swept back over his ears. Big brown eyes and a little bow of a mouth that made him look thoughtful and perhaps even a bit sensitive. He pushed himself to his feet as we entered the room.

"Ah...Inspector Roddy. So nice to see you again."

"Sergeant," Roddy corrected. "Detective Sergeant."

Billy Bailey waved a dismissive hand. "By all means consider yourself promoted," he said magnanimously. "A man of your talents and obvious charisma..."

Billy rambled on at some length. I had to swallow a smile. Having had vast personal experience annoying the authorities, I could see right away why Billy Bud was so unpopular with Canadian law enforcement. Not only had Billy made them look inept for a quarter of a century, but he'd had a good time doing it as well. The kind of guy who kicked your ass and then made sure you didn't forget about it. Just the sort of attitude guaranteed to piss off serious-minded authoritarian types. Trust me, I've been there.

Interrupting Billy's monologue, Roddy introduced us as "detectives from Seattle."

Billy smiled a welcome and then gestured expansively toward the man standing on his right. "You remember Mr. Spearbeck," he said.

Spearbeck was another matter altogether. Looked like they'd flown him in from Las Vegas. The kind of guy who looked good in a sharkskin suit and narrow tie, both of which he probably wore to bed. He stepped out from behind the desk, as if running interference for his client. He rested a bony hip on the front corner of the desk, leaned back and inquired whether or not this was an "official visit."

"No," Roddy said immediately. "These gentlemen have a bit of a problem…a missing person's problem. They were hoping you might be of assistance."

"Always glad to be of assistance," Bobby said affably.

"Who's missing?" Spearbeck wanted to know.

I told him. The ramifications of a missing member of the Seattle law enforcement community were lost on neither Billy nor his attorney. Not only wasn't it the kind of case that would eventually go away, but it was the sort of case that made for particularly bad public relations in a civic-minded society such as Canada.

"And how is it you imagine Mr. Bailey might be of assistance?"

I jumped in. "Because the events surrounding Ms. Duval's disappearance involve a couple of characters named Jordan Koontz and Lui Ng."

Amazing how those names seemed to stop conversations. Billy Bailey wiped the corners of his mouth with his thumb and forefinger. He noticed that I'd noticed, looked away and folded his arms protectively across his chest.

Billy's politician's smile never wavered, but the corners of his eyes tightened slightly. I'd seen that look before, seen it in my father's eyes more times than I could count. The look of parental disappointment. The sad expression that said I hadn't quite turned out to be what he'd been hoping for, and thus, for my old man anyway, the even sadder certainty that his predator genes were about to skip a generation.

It was almost as if he'd have preferred I'd had some sort of disability. Had I been a dimwit, well, that just would have been the luck of the draw; he could have lived with that. That I was reasonably articulate and in full control of my faculties, and still didn't have any interest in carrying on the family fleecing business, was beyond his most fevered imaginings.

A thick and awkward moment passed before Spearbeck broke the silence. He chose his words carefully, as lawyers are paid to do. "We have no connection to either of those gentlemen."

"Mr. Bailey's son, Junior, certainly has," Roddy said.

"Young Mr. Bailey handles his own affairs," Spearbeck said.

They went back and forth for several minutes, debating what sort of involvement and therefore what responsibility could reasonably be laid at Bill Bailey's door.

"Do you recall a provincial policeman being shot in Dashwood?" Roddy segued.

"When was that?" Billy asked.

"Several months back."

"We might," Spearbeck interjected quickly. "What of it?"

"A gentleman named Trevor Collins wounded a constable in a dispute over a boat repossession."

"And this has what to do with us?"

"We take attacks upon our officers quite seriously," Roddy said.

"I'm sure you do," the lawyer said.

"And rightly so," Billy added. "A healthy respect for law enforcement is the cornerstone of civilized society. Any society…"

Sounded like Billy was prepared to go on at some length, but Roddy cut him off. "Considering the nature of his offense, Mr. Collins was remanded on a one-hundred-thousand-dollar bond."

"And?"

"In less than twenty-four hours, the destitute Mr. Collins was back on the street."

The lawyer opened his mouth to speak, but again Roddy kept talking.

"We have it on good authority that it was young Mr. Bailey who put up his bond."

Billy opened his mouth to say something but a quick glance from his attorney encouraged him to swallow it.

"That used to be your old stomping ground, didn't it?" Roddy pressed.

"Excuse me?" Billy said.

"Over there on the island. Over by Dashwood. That's where you lived before…" Roddy swept a hand in a grand ironic gesture. "…before all of this."

Neither of them said a word. At this point they weren't even willing to talk about where Billy Bailey used to live, which told me that the conversation had reached the point of diminishing returns. These guys weren't going to tell us anything useful. Billy had invited us over for the sheer fun of it. He wanted to parry and banter, to revel in his triumph over the forces of darkness. And then we spoiled the party. Touched a nerve right out of the gate. Ruined everything by bringing up his ne'er-do-well son, the royal idiot as it were, whose ham-handed criminal career was a very real threat to his father's political ambitions.

This was one of the rare instances where being a private investigator had it all over being an actual cop. Despite the obvious manpower and technological advantages enjoyed by modern police departments, policemen adhere to a fairly exacting protocol. They need probable cause. They need warrants. They have to be polite and not step on anybody's toes unless they can prove they are lawbreaker toes, and even then they have to be careful about how they go about their business, lest their quarry get off on some crappy little technicality.

Not so the PI. When things don't seem to be going anywhere, a private eye can start turning over rocks to see what's on the other side. He can annoy people on purpose, show up at the same places over and over, and ask the same questions until somebody snaps and something breaks loose from the log jam.

I was deciding who to insult about what when I was up-staged by the echoing sound of a raised voice, followed by the distant boom of the two-ton front door.

I snapped a look back over my shoulder just in time to see Miss Panty Girdle abandon her post at the library door and hustle off toward the racket.

Another shout, much closer this time, seemed to set everyone in motion. Spearbeck bumped himself off the corner of the desk and straightened his tie. Billy Bailey folded his hands in front of him like he was praying.

A moment passed, and then I heard two voices entwined in conflict. I could hear the sound of their feet scraping the flagstones as they approached. "Like I give a fuck," the male voice said.

He came barging through the door like a black squall, throwing an angry hand in the air, speaking directly to Billy Bailey. "You ought to teach that twat some manners," he said.

Junior Bailey couldn't have been more than a couple of Oreos short of three hundred pounds. A corpulent corpuscle in a hideous purple suit, he looked like a Cuban headwaiter who had been held hostage in a doughnut shop. Except for the rosebud lips, he bore little or no resemblance to his father.

"Bitch forgets she's the hired help," he said.

I snuck another backward peek. Her cheeks were burning, but her ice-sculpture veneer remained intact.

"I told him you were engaged, sir," she said.

Billy unlaced his fingers and showed a "not to worry" palm. "It's fine, Evelyn," he said. "Would you excuse us please?"

There was something about the way he begged her pardon that told me they were sleeping together. Just a tad more concern for her feelings than the standard employer-employee relationship called for. The kind of compromise a man makes only when his dick is involved.

She managed a thin, insincere smile and headed for the hall. She flicked a surreptitious glance my way as she eased by. I flicked back. She pretended not to notice and instead raised her nose an inch and a half and picked up her pace. I had no doubt that Billy would suffer for this little indignity at some later date. No doubt at all.

Junior lumbered back and forth in front of the desk, looking us over like a general inspecting the troops. "These the cops?" he asked his father.

Junior had one of those Jersey City tough guy walks, like his balls were so big he had to walk around them. You could tell he spent a lot of time practicing in front of a mirror, strutting and hitching up his pants.

He pointed at Roddy. "Yeah," he said. "I remember that one there."

"These gentlemen have some questions regarding Jordan Koontz and Lui Ng," his father said evenly. Despite the moderate timbre of his voice and the bland facial expression, Billy Bailey looked like a man sitting on a wasp's nest.

"What about 'em?" Junior asked.

"You know a guy named Brett Ward?" I tried.

"Never heard of him," he said immediately.

It wasn't that he was a lousy liar; it was that he was too arrogant to try, as if he thought it was more important for us to know how little he thought of us than it was to bother with any tawdry attempts at deception.

"That's funny," I said. "Your friends Koontz and Ng spent the last week or so down in Seattle looking for him."

"So what?"

"So...since neither of those guys takes a shit without your say-so, I figured it must have something to do with you."

The fat bulged into rolls on one side of Junior's neck as he cocked his head at me. Appeared he wasn't used to being pushed. "Told you," he said. "I don't know any Warren guy."

"Ward," Marty corrected. "Brett Ward."

"Him neither."

"How about Trevor Collins?" I asked.

"Who's he?"

"A loser from over on the island. A loser who assaulted one of our provincial constables," Roddy said.

"Never heard of him neither," Junior said.

He looked over at his father, seeking approval, trying for what must have been the thousandth time to make a positive impression on an old man who saw him as nothing but a personal disappointment and a political liability.

For his part, Billy gazed out the window. Out over the heaving gray water, where a pair of heeled-over sailboats raced the storm to landfall. The glassy look in his eye said he was somewhere else, somewhere in the past probably, wondering where he'd gone wrong, another wistful expression with which I was sadly familiar.

I shifted my gaze to Junior in time to watch a wave of color travel up his throat and redden his ears. He was staring at his old man. It was like the rest of us weren't there and these two were yoked together, plowing fallow ground for all eternity.

Since I already hated him, and he was already pissed off at his father, Junior Bailey pretty much volunteered to be the subject of my irritability project.

"You think it could be the name?" I asked.

Junior seemed surprised by the question. "You talkin' to me?" he asked.

"Travis Bickle," I said.

His face was blank as a cabbage, so I helped him out.

"You know, Robert De Niro in *Taxi Driver*," I said.

"What the fuck are you talking about?"

"I was just wondering if being named Junior had maybe gotten you off on the wrong foot in life. It's kind of a diminutive, isn't it? Like you're somehow smaller or lesser than others of your kind, assuming, of course, there are any others of your kind. I was wondering if that fresh-out-of-the-chute insult wasn't a bit more that your tortured little psyche was able to bear."

"My tortured what?"

"Psyche." I spelled it for him.

Junior frowned. "What the fuck are you talking about?"

"You already used that line."

Marty used his elbow to dent one of my kidneys.

Spearbeck could see where this was going and didn't like it a bit. He moseyed over next to his client and said to Marty and me, "Well, I guess then that's it, isn't it?"

When nobody said anything, he tried again. "Sorry we were unable to help you with your problem," he said without sincerity. He gestured toward the door. "So, if you don't mind..." He let it dangle.

Junior wasn't ready to let go, however. He walked right up into my face.

"You ain't no cop," he announced.

I leaned even closer, nearly bringing our noses into contact. He smelled of old sweat and new onions. "This isn't going away," I promised him. "A good friend of mine is missing and some way or other you've got something to do with it. I'm not going away until I find out what happened to her."

"You got quite an imagination there, Ace." He peered back over his shoulder at his father. A brief father-and-son staring match ensued before Junior turned back my way. "You know what I'm thinking?" he asked.

"Salad, I hope."

The room seemed to hold its breath. Took him a minute, but eventually he got the joke. He nodded in the direction of the door. "Go on...get the fuck out of here," he said.

Like I said, cops have to respect boundaries. When a citizen says he doesn't want to talk anymore and that you should get your ass out of his house, they either have to make an arrest or beat a hasty retreat. Roddy and Marty started for the door.

I, on the other hand, had an aching in my gut and, as I saw it, damn little to lose, so I stood my ground and asked him again. "Why are those two goons of yours looking for Brett Ward?"

"Never heard of the guy," Junior repeated.

I took a half step back, giving myself enough leverage to wipe that smirk off his face with a good solid right, something with my hip and shoulder behind it, something he'd recall as he sat in the dentist's chair getting his front teeth replaced, but Marty read my mind, and just as I started to cock myself, I felt his fingers circling my wrist.

"Leo," he said.

I was so angry I could feel my body shaking. So could Marty.

"Let's go," he said, using my arm as a lever to turn me away from Junior Bailey's leering face. I took a deep breath and let Marty and Roddy escort me from the room.

■  ■  ■

Marty was a good listener. Must have been three or four minutes before he thanked whoever was on the other end and broke the connection.

We were sitting in the parking lot outside Provincial Police headquarters. We'd tendered our thanks and were getting ready to fight traffic back to the border when Marty decided to check his messages. He pocketed the phone and looked over at me.

"They've been through every piece of real estate Billy Bud owns, rents, or leases in King County. No sign of Rebecca anywhere. We've got requests into both Pierce and Kitsap Counties asking them to do the same. Pierce says it'll be a few days. Kitsap is having trouble finding a judge who's willing to go for probable cause." He made a disgusted face. "Lotta rugged individualists out there," he said.

Before I could respond, a clap of thunder shook the car. Marty and I looked at one another, both of us thinking this was a weird time of year for a thunderstorm. I leaned my face against the side window and looked up at the sky. A sheet of low clouds rolled overhead like a steel escalator. Down on terra firma the ornamental trees decorating the parking lot cowered, as if girding themselves for the oncoming onslaught.

"Junior lied to us about knowing this Collins guy," Marty said. "Kinda makes a body wonder why something like that is worth lying about."

As usual, Marty had a point. Why bother to lie about something so seemingly trivial? So you knew him. So you bailed him out of jail. So what?

The first raindrops were huge. I sat in the driver's seat and watched in glum wonder as they thumped onto the hood of the car. I was about to comment on their ungodly proportions when suddenly, another, much closer, clap of thunder rumbled and roared and, before you could blink, a deluge of biblical proportions poured down on us.

A minute later, the wind arrived, swirling from all directions at once, sweeping up bits of litter and tree debris from the parking lot and spiraling it aloft. The newly sprouted daffodils bobbed and weaved their bright yellow heads like punch-drunk fighters.

The Tahoe rocked on its heavy-duty springs as the deluge reached a hammering crescendo, making it impossible to converse, reducing a couple of grown men to sitting there, gawking out the side windows as the squall swept up and over the city, sitting there watching the high-rises disappear into the front wall of the storm, seemingly evaporated by nature's fury, only to reemerge a few moments later, as the squall raced toward East Vancouver and the mountains beyond.

"You know what I'm thinking?" I asked when the racket died down.

"Almost never," Marty said.

"I'm thinking we ought to go over to Dashwood and poke around a bit. See if we can pick up anything about this Trevor Collins from the locals." I dropped a disgusted hand in my lap. "We already pissed away the whole day. Maybe we can come up with something useful over in Dashwood."

Marty thought it over. "We're here," he said finally. "This is as close as we're gonna get to Vancouver Island." He shrugged. "Why not?"

"Whatever happened to Brett Ward started when he repo'ed that damn boat." I said it as much to myself as to Marty, trying to convince myself that we were making progress, that we weren't just thrashing around and going nowhere.

"How long to Dashwood?" Marty asked.

"Depends on the Nanaimo ferry. If we catch the first ferry, three, maybe four hours. If there's a line, we add an hour for every ferry we don't catch."

Marty sighed. "I'll call Peg," he said. "She hates if I have dispatch call her for me. She always thinks they're calling to tell her I'm dead."

. . .

Four hours flat and we were a couple of miles south of Dashwood, tooling along in a icy rain, on what they called the Island Highway, forest primeval on the left, dark, churning water on the right. According to Google, the Cross-Current Marina was supposed to be somewhere up ahead on the right.

We'd spent the sixty-minute ferry ride drinking coffee in the snack bar and reading the Vancouver PD file on Trevor Collins, who turned out to be pretty much as advertised, a lifetime scumbag, low-level drug dealer, and part-time burglar, with no previous history of violence whatsoever, a fact that immediately caught Marty's eye.

"Shooting at a policeman is way out of character for this guy," Marty commented.

"Repo men and process servers make people absolutely nuts," I said. I knew too. Couple of times in the beginning of my PI career, I'd had to serve process in order to make a living. Hundred bucks a pop and what you learned right away was that there was something about having a subpoena slapped in your hand that brought out the very worst in people. Made 'em do things they normally wouldn't even consider. Crazy things, way beyond what the situation called for. Next thing you know you've got a podiatrist chasing you with an ax.

Marty wasn't buying it. When you've been a cop for as long as he has, you assume everybody's lying to you all the time, and thus operate from the assumption that nothing is quite as it seems. It's why cops have a tendency to hang out exclusively with other cops. That way, at least everybody's on the same page.

"Not that nuts," he said. "This guy's been in the joint a couple of times. He knows how the system works." I watched from the corner of my eye. I could tell he was editing himself, trying not to say something that he thought would make me feel worse than I already did.

"What?" I pressed.

He looked over at me. "Unless there was something that scared him more than a long stretch in the joint."

Ricky Waters came immediately to mind. I could still see the self-loathing behind his eyes and feel his pain.

A quarter moon poked a hole in the cloud cover and oozed its pale blue light down on the dark expanse of water. Otherwise, it was just a rural highway, anywhere in North America, on a cold spring night.

Marty pointed toward the water. Down by the rocky shoreline, several banks of overhead lights glowed in the gloom, illuminating an area about the size of a Little League baseball field.

"Gotta be the marina," he said.

"Shall we?"

"Why not?"

I turned right and bumped down the gravel drive.

New day, new marina, same hard-luck story. Like most of its brethren, Cross-Current Marina had fallen on hard times. The yard was mostly deserted and the weeds along the fence line were chin-high. The half dozen derelict vessels scattered here and there looked a lot like fossil remains in the harsh overhead lights.

The rain had turned to mist and was hissing on the hood as I turned off the Tahoe and climbed out. On the other side of the car, Marty stretched and groaned.

The roll-up door on the big Quonset hut stood partially open. I could see a pair of legs moving around inside. A moment later a cascade of welding sparks began to flow onto the floor like falling stars.

I was about to head in that direction when the office door swung open with a bang and a guy in white coveralls stepped out onto the macadam. Six feet, maybe thirty-five years old, with crude jailhouse tattoos decorating the backs of both hands. He had a lumpy asymmetrical face that looked like it had been assembled from spare parts. The red and white patch on his chest read, "Rudy."

He walked our way. "Help ya?" he asked.

We introduced ourselves. Marty showed him his badge.

"Seattle, huh?" was all the guy said.

"Your friendly neighbor to the south," I threw in, trying to lighten things up.

"Kinda far out of your jurisdiction," the guy noted.

"We're looking into the shooting of that provincial constable," Marty said.

The craggy face closed like a leg trap. "Got nothin' to say about that," he immediately said. "You want to know about that, you go talk to the cops."

And that was that. Without another syllable, the guy turned, marched back to the office and disappeared inside with a bang, leaving Marty and me standing in the wet parking lot, glowering at one another in frustration.

Marty sighed and started for the car. When I didn't follow along, he stopped walking and turned back my way. His face said he was losing his patience with me. I motioned at the Quonset hut with my head. He thought about it, shrugged, and started walking in that direction.

I bent at the waist, grabbed the handle, and rolled the door up over my head. The stern of an old purse seiner was facing us as we walked inside. The *Kelly G* occupied the front right quarter of the space. The rest of the building yawned dark and vacant.

The tall arched ceiling was filled with a cloud of welding smoke and the air was twitchy with molten steel. The leather-clad apparition in the welding hood turned our way. Two feet of scraggly white beard hung below the bottom of the hood. Unless I was mistaken, a thin line of smoke was rising from the bottom of the beard.

"I think your beard's on fire," I said.

"Happens all the time," he said, as he pulled the welder's hood from his head and set it on the bench. The hood had left a red furrow running across his forehead. His pale blue eyes had the red watery patina of a man who'd spent his life staring at the tip of a welding rod. He used his leather-clad hands to sweep an embedded ember from his beard.

He pointed with the welder. "Office is over there," he said.

I said I knew. He picked up on my meaning.

"Barrel of laughs, ain't he?"

"Mr. Personality," Marty said.

"We wanted to ask him a few questions about the shooting incident they had out here awhile back."

"About time," the old guy said.

"How's that?" Marty asked.

The guy draped the black rubber welding cable over the end of the bench and took off his leather gloves. I could see we'd touched a nerve. This guy had a speech stored up, and I felt pretty certain we were about to hear it. He flipped a couple of switches on the arc welder. The lights went out.

"Somebody shoulda asked right from the start," he said.

"Asked what?"

"What the hell he was doing out here, anyway. Everything that son of a bitch knows about boats woulda fit on the back of a fuckin' stamp. Never did a goddamn day's work in his sorry-ass life and all of a sudden he's renting the only shed in town where you can get out of the elements. Wants it all to himself too. Don't want nobody else in the building with him." He spat on the floor, hawked up something from the back of his throat, and then spat again.

We kept asking questions; he kept venting his spleen. Seems that about a year ago, the marina changed hands, which wasn't surprising when you considered how bad business was. The Marino family took the dough and moved to the Azores, wherever the hell that was. Next thing you knew that idiot out there was running the place into the ground. Don't do nothing but sit around the office with his thumbs up his ass, which was probably a good thing since he don't know shit about the marina business. And then, all of a sudden—eight, ten months back—Cross-Current's indoor workspace was no longer available to the general public. Seems it was leased by Trevor Collins, Dashwood's home-grown crime wave. Paid six months in advance. Fifteen hundred a month for the whole damn building. Nobody else allowed inside. Just him and his damn boats.

"So...you knew Collins?" Marty asked.

"Everybody in town knows that little turd. He's our very own village idiot."

"What did he claim he was doing?" I asked.

"Refitting boats for sale." He barked out a bitter laugh. Coughed again, spat again. "Like anybody's buying high-end boats these days. And like he'd know how to refit 'em if they were."

"What do you think he was up to?" Marty asked.

"God only knows," the old guy said. "What I wanna know is where he got the boats to begin with." He waved an angry hand. "Hell, the night he got arrested, he was working on a Hatteras seventy. Local paper said the boat was registered to him. How in hell does a pissant like that come up with a half-a-million-dollar boat? Nobody in his whole goddamn family ever had a pot to piss in or a window to throw it out of, and then, all of a sudden, Collins owns a boat like that. Don't make no goddamn sense."

We mined his ire for all it was worth. Came up with lots of local color but nothing to bring us any closer to finding Rebecca. Mostly just that he was pissed off and, as far as he was concerned, the world was going to hell in a handbasket. I knew the feeling well, so I let him ramble a bit.

"So this wing nut takes a shot at an officer and you know what?"

"What?" I said.

"A week later he's right back here doin' whatever the hell it was that he was doin' before. Like nothin' happened. This time he's got Broward flush deck. Real pretty boat. Three hundred grand if it was a nickel." I started to commiserate but he was rolling now. "And the same prissy bastard he pointed the gun at in the first place..." He paused for effect. "Mr. Fancy Pants is right back here collecting the boats as soon as Collins gets through doing whatever in hell he's doing to 'em. Does that make one goddamn bit of sense? You tell me. Does it?"

I patted myself down. Found the folded up photo of Brett Ward I'd caged from Rosemary De Carlo and held it in front of the old man's face.

"This the guy?" I asked.

He nodded. "That's him. Don't seem like gettin' a gun shoved in his face bothered him very damn much."

"How many boats did he collect from Collins?" Marty asked.

"Least a dozen," the old guy said. "Maybe more."

We kept at it until the well ran dry, at which point Marty asked him if he knew someplace we might be able to get a bite to eat and, after that, maybe someplace we could spend the night.

"Same place," the welder said. "Got a bed and breakfast about two miles down the road from here. Zeigler's Roadside Inn. Probably the only thing open this time of night. This time of year, anyway. Ain't exactly tourist season."

And then, suddenly, his face darkened and he was looking out over my head. I followed the line of his eyes. The guy in the Rudy coveralls stood in the doorway.

"You spent more time working and less time running your mouth, no telling what you might get done," he said.

"I'll talk to anybody I damn well please," the old man said.

An ominous silence swirled the smoke in the air.

"I'd be careful if I was you," Rudy warned.

"You ain't me," the welder countered.

"I'm closing up," Rudy said.

The old guy couldn't believe it. "You said you was working till ten or eleven."

"Changed my mind," he said as he turned and walked away.

"Son of a bitch," the old man said. He spat again and began to pick up his tools.

■　■　■

No room at the inn. All she had was a little cabin out back of the bed and breakfast where her son stayed when he came home from college. Brought his girlfriend sometimes, you know. Privacy concerns. The cabin was part of the original Currents Roadside Cabins. Back before her late husband, Harry, built the big house and tore down the rest of the buildings. Clara could let us have it for eighty dollars Canadian. A wink and a nod. "No tax." Dinner for the guests was long over, but she had meatloaf and mashed potatoes left over from the family meal. By that time, my stomach had partially digested itself and comfort food had seldom been more comforting.

By the time we'd finished filling our faces, the rain had let up. The yard was filled with the sound of percolating water as we drove around the back of the inn, across a wide section of lawn, and parked next to the rustic cabin. The door wasn't locked. I snapped on the lights and looked around.

Knotty pine. I'd forgotten about knotty pine. All those evil little faces and those black eyes staring at me in the night. Used to scare the living bejesus out of me when I was a kid. Always sent me sliding down under the covers. Wasn't like I'd conquered the fear either. I'd just stopped staying in places with knotty-pine paneling.

It had also been a long time since I'd stayed in a motel room with Marty Gilbert. Way back in the 1970s sometime, back when a bunch of us used to go hunting in Ellensburg on the opening day of pheasant season every year. Back when we'd all check into some fleabag motel and live on bullshit and bad whiskey for an entire week. Believe me when I tell you that half-a-dozen hungover suburbanites toting twelve gauge shotguns posed a far greater risk to one another than they ever posed to the birds.

Marty and I traded the obligatory macho jokes about nobody waking up with his shorts on backward. He reminded me that he was armed and dangerous and that I'd better stay on my side of the room, if I knew what was good for me.

I lay there in the dark. A couple of minutes passed before Marty said, "The old guy was right. The story doesn't make any sense. Why in God's name would Brett Ward continue to do business with somebody who pointed a gun at him and then took a shot at a constable?"

"Gotta be money," I offered.

"From what? Selling the boats?"

"I don't think so," I said. I told him what the guy at Northwest Maritime had told me about Brett losing money on one of his boat transactions.

A minute passed. "I don't have to tell you how bad this is, do I?" Marty said.

What he was being kind enough not to say was that we were past the point of no return. The point where any hope of seeing the victim alive again was statistically astronomical. I could feel his eyes on me in the darkness.

"No," was all I said.

He let it go at that, so I lay there on my back, staring at the knots in the ceiling. Awhile later, I heard his breathing change as he drifted off to Neverland and left me in the dark with all those beady eyes taking my measure.

I don't remember going to sleep, but I must have because sometime in the wee hours my eyes popped open. Took a second to remember where I was. Marty was snoring like a chainsaw, and I really, really needed to take a leak, so I rolled out the other side of the bed and cat-footed around the corner into the bathroom.

Trying not to disturb Marty, I closed the bathroom door before I reached for the light switch, which, as it turned out, wasn't on either side of the door, where I'd imagined it would be. In the process of groping around like a mentally retarded mime, I managed to bang my shin against the old cast-iron bathtub.

I was hopping on one leg, alternately groaning and cursing behind my hand, when the universe took mercy on me and allowed the cord from the overhead light to brush against my forehead.

On my way back to bed, I made it a point to hang onto the cord until I had a firm grasp on the doorknob. I simultaneously pulled the cord and eased the door open. Whoever said timing was everything was right on the money. A minute either way and things would have turned out quite differently. Because that was the moment when I heard the sound of an automobile engine and saw car lights swing over a dark line of trees.

I stood there gawking like a fool, watching as the headlights swung in a wide arc, sleep-stupefied, trying to figure out why anybody would be driving a car on the lawn in the middle of the night.

And then the headlights bounced to a halt, bright white halogen beams shining directly at the cabin, lighting the room with blinding silver shafts. I shielded my eyes with my hand and waited for the driver to catch a hint and douse the lights, but instead, he flipped on the high beams.

The hair on the back of my neck immediately stood on end. I opened my mouth to speak at precisely the moment my ears picked up the snick of metal on metal, the unmistakable sound of a cartridge snapping into the breach.

"Marty," I screamed.

The inside of the cabin door splintered as half-a-dozen high velocity rounds tore holes the size of my fist in the wood. Marty dove for the floor about two seconds before his bed was raked to pieces by another sustained volley.

By that time, Marty was flat on his belly, crawling under my bed, his eyes wide as he crabbed across the floor. I reached out, grabbed him by both wrists, and pulled him out the other side. Together we huddled on the floor, slack-jawed, wide-eyed, dazed, and panting.

The air inside the room was filled with bits of pulverized wood and pink fiberglass insulation. Feathers from Marty's bedding wafted down from the ceiling. From the look of it, the front wall of the cabin had barely slowed the rounds before they plowed through the back wall and disappeared into the darkness.

Marty and I exchanged frightened glances in the dark. The firing stopped and all I could hear was my own breathing. Before I could form a thought, another burst of automatic fire ripped into the room, starting down at the far end and moving methodically in our direction, destroying everything in its path. We had to move or die.

With the room exploding behind us, we crawled into the bathroom just before things got quiet for the second time. Quiet enough to hear the shooter slam another clip into the weapon. Instinctively, I grabbed Marty by the shoulders and threw both of us into the bathtub. My head banged against the bottom. My vision swam as high-velocity slugs hit the cast-iron bathtub, ringing it, rocking it on its clawed feet as we huddled as far down inside as we could get, hoping to God the tub could withstand the onslaught. The air was thick with powdered porcelain as the hurricane of bullets scoured the finish from the tub.

I don't know how long it went on for. Seemed like forever, lying there with Marty pressed to my chest, listening to chunks of steel-jacketed lead flattening against the cast iron. I think he reloaded at least once more and raked the room from one side to the other a final time, but I couldn't be sure. It was all a blur.

And then...the eerie silence before the car engine raced and the bright lights swung across the trees leaving us breathless and too scared to raise our heads above the lip of the tub, for fear of having it blown off.

I heard a bell ringing. Maybe two. And then a siren whooping in the distance.

"Cavalry's on the way," I choked out.

Marty didn't answer.

■   ■   ■

Roddy was bent forward, cell phone pressed to his ear, staring at the floor. I was leaning back in the chair, checking out the acoustic ceiling tiles. My hands were still shaky and the sound of gunfire still rang in my ears as I sat in the trauma center of Vancouver General Hospital, waiting to find out whether Marty was going to make it or not. Somehow or other he had taken a slug in the left armpit. Apparently it had rattled around inside him and severed the subclavian artery.

I flew in the helicopter with him and watched as a trio of EMTs scrambled to keep him alive. As fast as they fed fresh blood into his arms, Marty leaked it into his chest cavity. About halfway there, the pace of things got frantic, and I could tell they didn't think he was going to make it, but somehow he hung on until we touched down at the heliport, where an ER team awaited with a fresh supply of blood.

I'd called Peg as soon as they rolled Marty into the trauma center's ER. Tried to talk her out of coming up until we knew something more, but there was no dissuading her. She got their youngest daughter, Stella, to drive. I figured they were somewhere in the vicinity of the border by now.

The squeal of rubber soles on linoleum jerked me to my feet. Roddy whispered a sign-off, pocketed his phone, and levered himself upright.

The doctor was the future son-in-law of every mother's dreams. Tall, dark, and handsome, with a thick head of curly black hair, and a great set of Hollywood teeth.

I held my breath as he squeaked our way.

"Damn near bled out on us," he said.

"But he's all right," I stammered.

"He got very lucky," the doctor said. "The muzzle velocity was so low the slug just bounced off his clavicle."

"It had already come through a wall and hit a cast-iron bathtub by the time it got to Marty," I said.

"Saved his life," the doctor said. "Those AKs usually make a hell of a mess. Pulverize everything in their path. Kill you from the shock alone. We grafted the artery back together. Until that heals, he's going to need to take it real easy."

"Can we...is he?"

He read my mind. "We're keeping him sedated," the doctor said. "They're airlifting him to Seattle in about an hour. Can't think of any reason he needs to be awake for that."

Neither could I.

He walked over to the nurse's station, scribbled something on a piece of notepaper, and handed it to me. "You can call operations for the details of your friend's air transport."

Before I could thank him, the overhead speakers began to squawk hospitalese. He held up a finger and listened intently. "Duty calls," he said with a resigned shrug.

I shook his hand and thanked him for his efforts. He seemed to think it was nothing special and double-timed it down the corridor.

I made the call to operations. Turned out to be complicated. Nobody seemed to know anything about Marty's airlift. I was fighting to retain my composure when the last guy figured out that the Seattle PD was sending its own helicopter for Marty, which was why the flight didn't appear on anybody's manifest. My blood pressure dropped precipitously as I wrote down the details.

I took a moment to calm down and then called Peg. She and Stella were north of Bellingham, headed our way with a Washington State Patrol escort. I could hear the hitch in her breathing as she waited for me to say something. I remembered what Marty said about how she always expected the worst when she got these kinds of calls, so I just blurted out the good news and the details of Marty's arrival in Seattle. She burst into tears and broke the connection without saying good-bye.

When I managed to pull myself back into the here and now, Roddy was standing by my side. "We'll need a statement," he said apologetically.

I told him I understood. He clapped me on the shoulder.

"One hundred and seventy-five," he said.

I said something terribly intelligent like, "Huh?"

"That's the number of AK-47 shell casings they found on the lawn."

.  .  .

Roddy had an officer drive my car back from the island, so by the time I finished giving my statement, the Tahoe was waiting for me in the parking lot.

I don't remember the drive back to Seattle. By the time I got to Harborview Hospital, Marty had already been pronounced to be in serious but stable condition and transferred to Swedish Hospital, about three blocks up the street.

I left the Tahoe in the Harborview parking garage and covered the distance on foot. It was raining buckets. By the time I got to Swedish, I looked like I'd been swimming. The old lady in the information booth took one look at me and started giving me directions to the ER. I assured her that I felt considerably better than I looked and she reluctantly told me where to find Marty. Seven-oh-three. West Tower.

If I'd been expecting another cop convention on the seventh floor, I'd have been disappointed. Two cops in overcoats formed a muttering knot along the right-hand wall. On the opposite side of the hallway a young female patrol officer sat with her hat in her lap. Other than that, the corridor was empty. If you closed your eyes, only the faint hum of electronics and the stale, recycled air reminded you where you were.

The cops unwound themselves and started my way. I recognized the one in the lead. Captain Andrew Hardy, a serious old-school cop and Marty's direct supervisor. Hardy was a nondescript guy just this side of sixty, with a head of salt-and-pepper hair slicked straight back. He had a reputation as being a stickler for detail and a hard guy to get along with. He didn't bother to introduce his toady.

He shook my hand. "What the hell happened up there?" he asked.

I told him. Took me a full ten minutes to get it all in. Like Marty, Hardy was a hell of a listener. "So whose boat did you guys rock?" he asked when I'd finished.

"Gotta be Junior Bailey," I said.

He took a minute to digest what I'd told him. "OK," he said finally. "We're forming a joint task force with the

Vancouver PD." He looked me dead in the eye. "You're out of it now," he said. "We appreciate your efforts thus far, but as of right now, you're no longer part of this investigation."

I kept my mouth shut. This wasn't a guy to screw with. He could put me on seventy-two-hour remand as a material witness with a nod of his well-groomed head and the last thing on earth I needed was to spend the next three days in jail.

"Did you hear me?" he pressed.

"I heard."

"'Cause you've got a reputation as a guy who has trouble taking no for an answer."

"Dogged. That's me," I said.

He leaned in close. "Don't fuck with me, Mr. Waterman. If you still had a PI ticket I'd be obliged to tell you to just stay out of the way. But you don't. You're just a civilian these days, so I'm telling you to get all the way lost here." He cut the air with the side of his hand. "The mother needs an update, tell her to call my office."

"I'm going to keep looking for Rebecca Duval for as long as it takes," I said.

The air in the corridor was thick.

"They were right about you," he said.

"Who's they?" I asked.

He reached a hand back over his shoulder. The toady slapped a manila envelope into his palm. He held it out to me. "Here's what you and Detective Sergeant Gilbert had working on the Duval missing person's case."

I took it from him.

He nodded toward Marty's room. "Peg and the daughter are in there now. Then it's going to be me and a police stenographer." He nodded at the female officer across the hall. "So it's gonna be quite a while."

For once in my life, I took the hint and headed for the elevators.

■ ■ ■

Ten minutes later, I was sitting behind the wheel using a damp roll of paper towels to dry myself and running the car heater on high. Having inventoried my options, I decided to see if I couldn't catch up to the boys, on the off chance that one of their surveillance teams had seen something, anything. What *was* certain was that when "the boys" were your best option, things were about as bad as bad could get.

My frustration meter was redlined. I felt useless, like I was madly treading water and going absolutely nowhere. I had no idea what sort of trouble Brett Ward had managed to get himself into, other than it involved boats and quite probably that scumbag Junior Bailey. Worse yet, I was no closer to finding either Brett or Rebecca than I was when I'd started looking.

I got rock-star parking right outside of the Eastlake Zoo. I stood in the doorway for a minute, letting my eyes adjust to the cave-like gloom and then wandered inside. The place was deserted. One of the younger bartenders whose name I couldn't recall was stocking beer glasses under the bar.

"Rolling Rock," I said.

By the time I reached the end of the bar, he had a cold beer waiting for me. "Half an hour or so," he said to my back as I moved on past. "They been sleepin' in lately."

I took the beer and the SPD envelope up to the mezzanine. I sat, sipping at the beer, looking out the window as

East Lynn Street fell steeply downhill toward Lake Union. Twenty-five years back, in looser times, I used to sit here with my friends and smoke pot and drink beer until the place closed. Nobody gave a damn. That was before the new puritans took over the city. Before political correctness became the rage and melted all of us into a single amorphous dung heap.

I sighed and opened the envelope. Marty had left nothing to chance. Patrol was checking the Madison Park condo hourly. Additionally, they'd gotten an "exigent circumstances" warrant and looked around inside. I read the report. No sign of any kind of violence. Nothing out of place other than the occupants.

Information Technology was monitoring all cell phone and credit card activity. The SPD techie had gone back three months, looking for a pattern of communications or expenditures that might show a pattern of behavior that would point us in one direction or another. The algorithm came up empty.

They'd interviewed everybody down at the morgue, including the janitor. Talked to Rebecca's friends. Even talked to people at the gym where she worked out three times a week. Likewise, *nada*.

At the bottom of the pile was an old-fashioned computer printout. Those green and white striped sheets that were all connected to one another like a paper accordion. Took me a couple of minutes of flipping back and forth to figure out what it was and where it started.

I'd given Marty the names of Brett's lovers, at least the parts I had. Rosemary D, Serena A, Amy T, Kathy K, Lyssa R, and Barbara P. I had no idea of what use they might be, but for my own sanity, I had to make sure nothing was left to chance.

Whoever was working IT for the SPD had gone the extra yard. After exhausting all the normal informational channels, they'd annexed the King County Elections Board rolls and scanned voter registration records for Caucasian women between thirty and fifty years of age, then cross-referenced with the DMV for driver's license photos. There were nine Rosemary D's, sixteen Serena A's, sixty-three Amy T's, fifty-three Kathy K's, eleven Lyssa R's, and a whopping seventy-nine Barbara P's, each accompanied by an address, a current phone number, and DMV photo so muddy and generic the image could have been John Wayne or one of the Golden Girls.

I was still squinting at the first page of Serena A's when the street door burst open and someone shouted for the barkeep. Caesar's lesions had arrived en masse, stumbling in from the great outdoors like lemmings in search of an arctic precipice.

I watched as they assembled at the end of the bar and began to steel themselves for yet another round of debauchery. It was the usual crew with the usual banter about who owed who a drink and what social atrocity so-and-so had committed the night before. George and Ralph and Billy Bob Fung. Large Marge and Heavy Duty Judy with their arms slung around Red Lopez as he bellied up to the bar. Coupla guys I didn't know. And Norman. Nearly Normal Norman stood head and shoulders above everybody else in the room; his great mop of red hair seemed to dust the ceiling as he sluiced around the corner of the bar.

I hadn't seen Norman in some time. Word was he was doing a county stretch for resisting arrest, which was more or less what he always went down for. The original complaint would always be something harmless, like sitting on the sidewalk or pissing in a public place, but when you're six-eight and about two-seventy, when you're determined not to go quietly and it takes a Taser and a half-dozen stout lads with badges to cuff you and stuff you into a patrol car, the original charge tends to get lost in the scuffle and they segue your ass directly into a charge of resisting arrest, which is an ironclad ninety-day misdemeanor.

Once debts, both real and imaginary, had been settled and everybody had a drink firmly in hand, the assembled multitude dispersed itself about the room. Several of them headed for the pinball machines along the south wall. Couple of others started dropping quarters into the pool tables and sighting down warped pool cues. George and Ralph each carried a pitcher of beer toward their usual booth.

I stood up. The movement caught George's eye. He nudged Ralph and started for the stairs. I sat and watched as two guys who habitually lurched from place to place climbed a set of rickety stairs without spilling so much as a drop.

I knew better than to try to make conversation before they'd quaffed a beer or two. I watched in silence as a quartet of secretaries groped their way through the gloom. Looked like they'd never been here before and were having serious reservations about their choice of a hostelry. They took a table at the rear of the bar and waited for somebody to take their orders. It was going to be a long wait.

Norman walked by and waved up at me. "Thanks, Leo," he said.

I nodded and waved back.

George wiped his mouth with his sleeve and set the glass on the table. "You find her, Leo?" he asked.

I shook my head.

"We got nothin' neither," he said. "Had a couple of people lookin' around the boatyard with some real estate guy." He finished his second glass of beer and poured another. "Red and Judy got pinched down by the condo." He shrugged. "Both of 'em had failure to appear warrants out on 'em," he explained.

They'd get pinched for something petty and stupid and then fail to make their scheduled court appearance, which was an offense about ten times as serious as whatever they'd been arrested for in the first place. The proverbial vicious circle of song and story.

Norman walked by a second time, still waving, still thanking me.

"You got any idea what he's thanking me for?" I asked George.

He hesitated for long enough for me to know the answer. He shrugged. "Long as I was down there bailing out Red and Judy, I figured, you know, what the hell, might as well get old Normy outta there too, while I was at it."

"With my money?"

George winked at me. "Is there any other kind?"

"Who's all these lookers?" Ralph wanted to know.

Ralph was pawing through the computer printout. I got the impression that his hazy vision somehow meshed with the blurred photographs.

"Just something I was working on," I told him.

He began to read out loud. "Amelia Tasker, 17334 Cherry Street, Seattle," then shuffled through the pages and read another…and then another. George sighed and made an "if it makes him happy" face.

"Kathy Krause, 2611 Winona Road, Kirkland."

Norman made another pass down below.

"Don't mention it," I told him this time. He waved again.

"Kathy Kahn, 8769 North Sixtieth Avenue, Seattle," Ralph intoned. Shuffle, shuffle, shuffle. "Lyssa Redfelt, 456 Queen Anne Avenue North, Seattle."

"You want we should stay on duty?" George asked.

I told him no. "The cops are all over it now." I filled him in on everything that had happened since the last time I'd seen him. About Koontz and Ng and Junior Bailey and Marty getting shot in Canada. By the time I'd finished, so was the pitcher of beer.

"This ain't good," he said as he chugged the dregs.

"No," I said. "It's not."

"Barbara Peterson, 3614 Rainier Avenue South, Seattle," Ralph recited.

I snuck a peek at the secretaries, trying to see whether they'd figured out that they were going to have to order at the bar, but Red had spotted them first. He was standing next to their table, talking and waving his left hand in the air. I winced. With Red, you always had to wonder what he was doing with the other hand. Didn't take long to find out, because that's when I heard the magic phrase.

"Ain't it a beauty?" Red inquired.

"Barbara Parkland, 4509 Eastern Avenue, Seattle."

Apparently the young ladies were not nearly as enamored with Red's tumescence as was Red. They began whooping and wailing, calling for the manager, and sprinting for the door. I smiled for what felt like the first time in a week. Maybe mirth was the answer, because that's when my brain finally clicked into gear.

I grabbed Ralph by the shoulder. "Lemme see that," I said.

He frowned and handed over the printout. I ran my finger down the Barbara P's until I found Parkland. Forty-five-oh-nine Eastern Avenue. Well la-de-da. Exactly the same neighborhood where Rebecca had gotten those two unexplained parking tickets. I checked the DMV picture. The likeness was better than most. Maybe. Just maybe, I'd seen that face before. Except it had more of a pained expression the last time I'd seen it.

I threw a handful of money on the table. "Buy everybody a drink for me," I told George as I headed for the front door.

.  .  .

The house was set back a little farther from the street than its neighbors. I suspected that whatever grand edifice had originally stood on the property had been torn down and something with a sleeker, greener profile had been built on the lot. They'd used the leftover acreage to put in a driveway and a two-car garage, a modern amenity enjoyed by very few in this "park out front in the street" kind of neighborhood.

Brett Ward's blue Porsche Carrera sat in the right-hand stall. A dusty film said it had been sitting there for a while. I tiptoed back to the street to work up a plan of action. The rain had stopped altogether. The trees were still and silent. A couple of cars eased by on their way up to the main drag at Forty-fifth.

A direct assault was out of the question. Kicking in the front door and dragging him out by his heels might or might not put Brett Ward in the hands of the SPD, but it would sure as hell land me in a jail cell.

Problem was I didn't have time to be screwing around. I needed to find him and find him now, so I hoofed it back to the Tahoe, found what I was looking for in the glove box, and then retraced my steps back to 4509, and rang the bell.

I heard the sound of heels on a hardwood floor. She answered the door on the second ring. Barbara P, Brett's latest lover, the one of the unwitting screen test. Our Lady of the Clothespins. The top half of the door was glass. She pulled back the lace curtain, took one look at me, and closed them again. I strained my ears and listened hard but didn't hear the sounds of retreating feet. She was still standing on the other side of the door.

I knocked this time, hard and insistent. The edge of the curtain quivered. I heard her breath catch in her throat. A moment passed before I heard a chain rattle and the door eased open a crack. A brown, Botoxed eye peeped through the crack.

"What's this about?" she asked.

"It's a DVD of you making love with Brett Ward."

She made a rude noise with her lips and closed the door.

I raised my voice. "In that love nest of his down at the boatyard," I added.

The door opened again. No chain this time. Her face was drawn tight as a drum. "Are you saying he…?"

"He had half-a-dozen women," I said. "Digitally photographed all of you in intimate moments." I shrugged. "I guess that's how he gets his kicks."

"That's absurd," she sputtered without a hint of conviction.

"Can I ask a question?"

She started to close the door.

"Those clothespins pinching your nipples...didn't that hurt?" I asked.

She slapped me hard across the face. I stood there and took it. She drew her hand back again, but managed to restrain herself, which was a good thing, because another would have exceeded my "women get one for free" limit.

I reached out and offered her the DVD. "Probably be a good idea if you didn't let that fall into the wrong hands," I said.

She hesitated and then carefully slipped the disc from between my fingers.

"To my knowledge, that's the only copy," I told her.

"What do you want?" she asked. "You want money?"

"I want Brett Ward," I said.

She waggled the disc. "How do I know this is what you say it is?"

"See for yourself. Go pop it in the DVD player. I'll wait right here."

I stood there and watched as she came to grips with it. It's always hard when somebody turns out to be something other than what you imagined, especially in matters of the heart. Her hand shook as she slid the DVD into her back pocket.

She tried for a snarl, but her voice was unsteady with pain. "That son of a bitch," she said.

I took that to be an invitation and stepped inside the foyer. She spun and took off, clickety-clacking toward the back of the house, with me glued to her backside as we wound our way to what must have been the family room, where Brett Ward was stretched out on a black leather sofa, watching *What Not To Wear* on a big flat-screen TV. Clinton and Stacy were trashing somebody's wardrobe.

She was on him like ugly on an ape, landing in the middle of his chest with both knees, pummeling him with both hands, screeching and screaming unintelligibly as she rained blows on his head and shoulders.

I stood in the doorway and watched the action until he managed to corral her hands, duck out of her grasp, and scramble to his feet.

"What, sweetie? What?" he kept saying.

That's when he saw me moving his way. His face went white. He let go of her hands and showed me his palms, almost as if he was showing me he wasn't armed.

"I…," he stammered. "Leo…"

She balled up her fist and belted him in the face. She was going to do it again, so I took her by the shoulders and manhandled her over to the door.

I took her head in both hands and looked her in the eyes. Her breath came in gasps. Her eyes were twitchy and hard as gravel.

"You don't want to be here for this," I said.

She made a leap toward Brett, but I looped an arm around her waist and lifted her from the floor. I swung her in a gentle arc and deposited her in the hallway.

She gulped air. "Hurt him," she said. "Hurt him real bad."

I closed the door. Brett had backed into the far corner of the room. His eyes rolled in his head like a spooked horse. He was pointing a 9 mm automatic at the center of my chest.

"Where is she?" I said.

"Keep away from me, Leo. Swear to God, I'll kill you," he stammered.

I don't know what got into me. Maybe all the frustration I'd been bottling up for the past few days finally spilled over, because I did something very stupid. I rushed him.

I had to take one step to the left in order to avoid running into the coffee table, a move that ultimately saved my life. I saw the muzzle flash and the smoke leaving the barrel. In the confines of a closed room, the nine sounded like a cannon.

I felt the round tear through my coat as I vaulted forward. At that point, I didn't much care whether I'd been shot or not. All I wanted to do was get my hands on Brett Ward. He was lining up for a second shot when I batted the gun aside and hit him with everything I had, right in the solar plexus.

He went down like a stone. The gun bounced off the wall and came to rest on the carpet. In my peripheral vision, I could see Barbara peeking through a crack in the door.

I bent over and pocketed the automatic. When I looked at the door again, it was closed. Brett was balled up on the floor making an odd, keening sound.

I patted myself down, looking for wounds, but couldn't find any, then checked myself in the mirror, just to make sure. Apparently, I was intact.

Brett rocked back and forth on the floor, braying like a donkey, trying to force air into his paralyzed lungs. He was stiff from gasping as I grabbed him by the upper arms, picked him up, and threw him onto the couch.

I walked over to the edge of the couch and looked down at him. I took the automatic out of my pocket and checked to see if it was loaded. It was. I snapped the safety off. "While your air's coming back, you listen to me," I said. "'Cause I'm only gonna ask you this one time. If you don't tell me what I want to know I'm going to shoot you in the head with your own gun and claim self-defense."

I bent over and grabbed him by the ears. Pulled his face right up to mine. "And I'm willing to bet that your friend Barbara there will be more than willing confirm my version of the story," I said. "I told her all about your videotaping setup down there at the boatyard. Something about being betrayed like that tends to wear on a person's sense of humor." I let him go and straightened up.

"Where is she?" I asked again.

He thought about lying to me. I could see it in his face. Fortunately for him, he thought better of it. "They took her," he croaked.

I bent over and put the gun to his forehead.

He began to blubber. "No, man, no...don't. Please don't..."

I ground the barrel into the flesh of his forehead. "They who?"

"You gotta understand," he said.

I pressed harder. "No, I don't."

He closed his eyes, scrunched up his face, and started to cry. I straightened up and watched as a spasm of sobbing shook his body and a steady stream of tears rolled down over his cheeks. He blubbered something, but I couldn't make it out.

"Say again."

"They fucked me," he wailed.

"Outta what?" I asked.

He began to shake his head. "No...no."

That's when it occurred to me I was seeing the same look in his eyes that I'd seen in Ricky Waters's. Almost like he had amnesia or something. Like he woke up one morning and no longer recognized himself in the mirror. A man who had his mooring lines cut in the dead of night, and now found himself adrift in dark, unfamiliar waters.

"Both of 'em," he blurted. "One of them held a gun to my head while the other one fucked me." He closed his eyes and wept some more. "Sons of bitches traded off on me like I was some cheap whore." He covered his face with his hands.

I decided to ignore the terrible irony of a man with Brett's pornographic predilections being assaulted in such a manner. I opened my mouth to speak, but couldn't nail a sentence together. It's not often that I find myself totally at a loss for words. I mean, what do you say to something like that? I'm sorry? Somehow that doesn't seem to cover it. Hope you at least got dinner and a movie seemed a bit flip, even considering how I felt about this jerk. Nothing in my previous experience with quips and pithy one-liners had prepared me for this moment, so I shut up and waited for him to regain his composure.

"Start from the beginning," I said, when he'd calmed down a bit.

■ ■ ■

The story I'd gotten from the Millennium boat mechanic was pretty much on point. With yacht sales in the toilet, Jorgensen had put Brett to work repossessing boats from

Canada. Since most of the owners were more than happy to get out from under their payments, it was just a matter of keeping the paperwork straight and piloting the boats down to Seattle.

Everything had gone well up until the night he showed up at the Cross-Current Marina and the boat owner went nuts, waving a gun around, threatening to blow him away. Brett called the cops, and then all hell really broke loose.

Took him two days to get the Hatteras released by the Canadian authorities. Since he was already way behind schedule, he skipped his customary mechanical checkout and seaworthiness tests, and started motoring south. Predictably for a boat that hadn't been in the water for a while, the engine kept cutting out on him, probably fuel filters, he figured. He had to baby it all the way back to Seattle, never got it over ten knots the whole damn trip.

In addition to the engine problems, the boat was without water, so the minute he pulled the Hatteras out of the water in Seattle, he started looking for the pump from the holding tank. That's when he found the first packet of pot... and then the second and the third and so forth. The whole bulkhead was filled with what looked like one-kilo packages of meticulously wrapped marijuana. Real high-quality stuff. Coupla tons of it, at least. No wonder the guy with the gun didn't want to give up the boat.

He hesitated in his recitation.

"And, as a civic-minded citizen, you called the local authorities, of course," I prompted.

"I never got the chance, man. I was still working it out when..." He looked sheepish. "I figured...you know... what the hell...the maniac with the gun was in jail." He shrugged. "Wasn't going to have to worry about him for a while. I mean, how was I supposed to know he was working for somebody else?"

"And then?"

"The somebody else showed up."

"Let me guess," I said. "Jordan Koontz and Lui Ng."

His eyes began to fill. I watched as he choked up, cleared his throat, and went on. "After they had their fun with me, they said they were going to kill me."

"Might have been better if they had," I suggested.

"I hadda think of something, man," he whined.

"Such as?"

I watched as he gathered himself for the story. "I said, hey you know maybe we could work something out together. I've got twenty to thirty boats lined up for repo and it's like a 'get-out-of-jail-free' card. I'm just the repo man. How in hell do I know what's in the damn boat? Where's a guy like me gonna get a couple of tons of pot? Either coast guard comes aboard and finds anything, I'm sure as hell going to walk. All you gotta do is get 'em loaded up with whatever you want and I'll motor it down to Seattle for you."

"What did they say to that?"

"That's when the other guy showed up."

"Describe him."

"He stayed in his car. I never got a look at him."

"Anyway," I said.

"We cut a deal. I took care of the paperwork. They loaded up the boat and I motored it down to Ballard. They showed up the next day, unloaded the boat, and drove the stuff off in a rental truck. Everything went like clockwork. Couple of times a week for the past six months or so."

"What was your end?"

"Twenty grand a run."

"And then?"

"And then all of a sudden, things changed," he said.

"Changed how?"

He thought about it. "Things got real serious all of a sudden. I could tell something was special about this last run. Something they weren't telling me. Wasn't just Collins loading the boat anymore. Couple of Latino guys made me stay outside while they buttoned her up."

"And you weren't curious about this sudden change in routine?"

"Like I said, I could tell something was different."

"So?"

"So I motored out into the middle of the strait and took a look around."

"Don't make me pull this out of you," I warned.

"Heroin," he said. "Maybe half a ton of it packed into the bulkhead."

"And that didn't bother you? You didn't have any kind of ethical problem with smuggling heroin into the country?"

His voice got whiney. "What was I going to do? I was already in over my head. They'd have killed me in a fucking heartbeat."

"And then what?"

He looked away again.

"You didn't try to rip them off, did you?"

When he didn't say anything, I knew I'd hit the mark.

"How goddamn dumb are you?" I bellowed. "People like that don't let people like you rip them off. What the fuck were you thinking?"

"I told 'em I got busted by Homeland Security. No way you can check something like that. Those guys have intercepted more dope than all the other agencies combined, and that isn't even what they're looking for. Everybody knows that. And those guys release no information at all. No way anybody could check on it."

He still didn't get it. I could tell.

"Don't you understand? People like that just kill your ass now, then worry about whether you deserved it later."

"I was gonna hide the dope and then get lost until things calmed down. We talked about how we were pushing our luck. I figured, you know, what the hell. One big score."

I pointed the gun at the center of his forehead. He raised his hands as if to shield himself. "Don't, don't, don't," he chanted.

"Where's Rebecca?"

When he didn't answer, I pushed the barrel against his brow again. He began to shake and stammer. "They...they said they'd give me a week to get the dope back to them."

"Or what?"

"Or they'd send her back to me in pieces."

"When's the deadline?"

"Tomorrow," he said.

"And you just sat here in your girlfriend's house passing time while those freaks had your wife?" I recoiled in disgust. "What the fuck is the matter with you?"

"What was I going to do, man? I poke my head outta here, they'll kill me for sure."

"Where's the boat?"

He hesitated just long enough to tell me he was thinking about lying. I shifted the automatic to my left hand and used the back of my right to discourage him. The force of the blow knocked him from the couch. He pulled his knees up to his chest and buried his face.

"Don't make me ask you again," I growled.

"Two doors down," he said. "Ballard Marine." He looked up. His nose was bleeding. "I figured...you know...just in case they didn't buy it..." He shrugged.

"Call them," I said. "Tell 'em we'll trade the boat and the dope for Rebecca."

"I don't..." he stammered.

I backhanded him again.

He struggled to his feet, straightened his shoulders, and stiffened his spine. His nose was bleeding in earnest now. A red sheen covered his teeth.

"You might as well kill me right here, Leo, because I'm not getting anywhere near those freaks." He shook his head resolutely. "I'll call the cops before I get near those assholes again."

I hacked out a short, dry laugh. "And tell 'em what, bright boy? That you smuggled hundreds of pounds of heroin into the country, but now you're sorry and want to make nice-nice? There's fifty or sixty years of hard time for you in there, baby, and believe me, Brett, they're gonna love you in prison. You'll be the belle of the ball."

"They'll kill me, man," he whined.

"Before this is over," I assured him. "You may wish they had."

# Chapter 5

Took forty-five minutes of whining into my phone before Brett Ward looked up and offered it to me. With his red-rimmed eyes and his nostrils packed with toilet paper, he looked like a not-so-wild boar.

I reached out and took the phone. The screen read, "Blocked."

"Yeah," I said.

The voice on the other end was using one of those electronic voice transformers, available for under fifty bucks in any one of a hundred mail-order security catalogues. Turn it up high and you sound like Porky Pig. This guy had it set for low and slow, dropping his voice several octaves, to the point he sounded like he had a brain tumor.

He started to tell me what he wanted…something to do with a truck…but I cut him off, "No," I said. "You're getting it back, boat and all. Everything's exactly where you put it. The exchange takes place out at the end of a dock someplace. You get the boat. I get the woman. You just tell me where and when and I'll have it there."

"Listen, asshole," Robbie the Robot droned. "You're not the one making the…"

I cut him off again. "I want to see her. Face-to-face, Skype…I don't care. You figure it out. I don't see her, you don't see your dope again, and we get the cops involved in this thing."

Long, ominous pause and then he said he'd get back to me and hung up, which was just as well. I needed time to think. Things had happened so fast I hadn't had a chance to work anything out. I paced the room.

I hadn't really meant what I'd said about getting the cops on the case. As much as I would have liked to arrive with a SWAT team secreted onboard, there was no way it was going to happen. The minute the authorities were involved, things would be beyond my control. Hell, I'd be lucky if they didn't clap me in jail. Worse yet, there was no way the powers-that-be were trading a thousand pounds of heroin for Rebecca Duval, even if she was one of theirs. That'd be strictly against policy, whereas I had no qualms whatsoever. So it was no cops. I was going to have to do this on my own.

I checked my watch. Just after three o'clock in the afternoon. Brett was huddled on the far end of the couch, licking his wounds, and staring at the wall. I could hear Barbara P banging around in the kitchen. Sounded like she was lobbing pots and pans into the sink from across the room. I suspected she'd watched the video and was more than a little miffed.

The phone rang. Mr. Blocked calling again. Before I could bring it to my ear, the phone blinked a couple of times and there she was, Rebecca, barely able to stand, propped up between two pairs of hairy hands, her head lolling back and forth as she wavered on unsteady legs. Her face was lumpy and her eyes seemed unable to focus.

The screen went black. "Satisfied?" Robbie the Robot inquired.

"Where and when?"

"You know the Hylebos Waterway?"

He pronounced it wrong. Said Hillybus instead of Hilee-bus, which told me he was getting his information from somebody who wasn't familiar with the area.

"Tacoma," I said.

"Eleven tomorrow night."

"She walks down the dock under her own power," I said. "No more than two people with her."

"You so much as blink and she's dead."

"Where in the waterway?"

"Right after the Hylebos Bridge. North side. You'll see a big pile of scrap metal piled up. Hundred, hundred and fifty feet tall. You can't miss it. There's an old wooden dock along the west side of the yard. Right there. Eleven o'clock."

"We'll be there."

The Hylebos Waterway was one of several heavy industrial canals dredged out of the Puyallup River delta. Its man-made shores were lined with all manner of shipbuilders, scrap yards, recyclers, and receiving docks. Anything deemed too unsightly, too smelly, or just plain too ugly for Seattle had been relegated to Tacoma, and anything too unsightly, smelly, or ugly for Tacoma had been relegated to the waterways.

All in all, it was a good choice for the exchange. The heavy industrial part of Tacoma would be completely deserted at that time of night. Even the bars and coffee shops closed up when the business day was over. That time of night, the only things moving were rent-a-cops and Rottweilers.

Brett looked my way.

"Get up," I said. "We've got a lot to do."

. . .

Sometimes the smallest things tell you all you need to know. The name of the boat was *Yachts of Fun.* Need I say more?

Ballard Marine wasn't happy to see us. You want to splash a seventy-foot boat back in the water, they expect a little advance notice. As a means of expressing their displeasure, they let us stand around for an hour and a half before they got around to dropping us in the drink, so it was six-forty by the time we left the fuel dock and headed for the locks.

The Hiram M. Chittenden Locks negotiated the twenty feet of elevation difference between the lakes and Puget Sound and were a mecca for the tourists, who showed up in droves every year to watch the boats go up and down, and check out the salmon runs in the attached fish ladder. Commercial maritime traffic always has the right of way in the locks, and as a trio of Argosy sunset cruise tourist boats were lined up in front of us, it was another hour and a half before we motored past the last green channel marker.

"Which way?" Brett asked.

"South," I told him.

As might be expected, *Yachts of Fun* was a big, blue party barge. Seventy feet of fiberglass and polished wood, powered by a pair of Detroit Model 60 diesels, capable of pushing her over twenty-four knots, as long as you didn't mind burning the better part of a hundred gallons an hour. Brett settled into the pilot's seat and goosed the engines.

To starboard, the sky was the color of a day-old bruise. The jagged outline of the Olympic Mountains rose black and menacing above the wooded hills of Bainbridge Island. The tide was ebbing and the wind had switched around from the south, which, around these parts, was generally a portent of bad weather. We motored along in silence as the big yacht cut through the chop without so much as a quiver. I could feel the low rumble of the engines in my feet but otherwise the boat was like a floating hotel.

Brett was twitchy. Every time I got within arm's length he flinched and put as much distance between us as he could. His eyes held that same hangdog expression I'd seen in Ricky Waters, as if a major portion of his foundation had suddenly been washed away, casting him adrift in unfamiliar waters.

Wasn't until we motored past Alki Point, when he finally worked up the courage to ask me exactly where we were going.

"Tacoma," I said. "I need to see the place where we're going to make the exchange tomorrow night. Think things through."

"Maybe we could..." he began.

"Just shut up and drive the damn boat," I said.

But, of course, he couldn't do that. Not Mr. Irrepressible. Something in his makeup required that he maintain a constant flow of patter. Mr. Salesman overcoming objections, I figured. It was as if nothing was more terrifying to him than the prospect of silence.

"I didn't mean for this to happen..." He started babbling about how sorry he was. How he was just trying to make Rebecca proud of him. How he never intended...

I tuned him out.

By the time we arrived at the Puyallup River delta the onboard clock read 10:12 in the evening. The two halves of the Hylebos Bridge jutted into the sky like post-industrial church steeples. If I recalled correctly, about ten years back the mechanism that opened and closed the bridge had slipped an irreplaceable gear. In order to keep the waterway navigable, they used cranes and cables to yard the bridge into the open and upright position, where it had remained, signaling touchdown for the past decade or so.

To the south, the Art Deco remains of the ferry *Kalakala* slouched half in, half out of the water, its rounded electro-welded superstructure looking for all the world like a two-hundred-and-seventy-foot Airstream trailer.

Over on the next channel, an honest-to-God Mississippi riverboat bobbed contentedly in the chop, its giant red paddlewheel silent and still. Back in the mid-1990s, the Puyallup Tribe had purchased a riverboat named the *Emerald Queen* and turned it into a Cajun-themed casino, with card games, costumed crew, and all. Six or seven years later, the tribe parlayed their floating foot-in-the-door riverboat into a series of dry-land casinos that now dotted the northern Pierce County landscape like neon mange, making the *Queen* more or less superfluous and relegating it to an ignoble fate alongside this fetid industrial waterway.

Mr. Blocked had been right. You couldn't miss the enormous pile of scrap steel thrusting high into the sky, enough rust to make the surrounding air smell like fresh blood, and to get my nostrils twitching with fear.

Brett idled the engines as we crept in front of the scrap yard, moving only marginally faster than the outflowing tide. The dock was old and falling apart, with a rickety-looking ladder running down the east side. A remnant of an earlier age, before cargo boats grew to the size of small towns and the Port of Tacoma mostly shipped logs from place to place.

Looked like there used to be another dock a bit farther west, but it was gone now, leaving only a series of rotted pilings jutting above the waterline like broken teeth.

I told Brett to hold our position while I looked the place over. From their perspective, the place was perfect. Isolated, deserted that time of night. The minute we handed over the boat and the dope, we'd be faced with a hundred-yard death march back to dry land. A hike I felt certain they had no intention of allowing us to complete. Even if we did make it to terra firma, the broken bridge limited our landside escape routes to one.

Interestingly enough, the place worked for me too. The narrow hundred-yard pier was my own personal Thermopylae, giving me ample time to see who was coming our way and prevent them from launching any sort of frontal attack. The secret was to use that hundred yards to my advantage, which, unless I was mistaken, meant not using it at all. The way I saw it, every step we took on that dock brought us one step closer to being dead.

"Where's the tide?" I asked.

Brett pushed a few buttons on the Simrad chart plotter. "Be all the way out in an hour," he said. "Low, low."

"What about at eleven tomorrow night?"

More button pushing. "Gonna be a minus three," he said. "One of the lowest tides of the year."

I turned it around in my head, trying to look at it from their perspective, as if I was the one plotting an ambush. You had to figure that Billy Bud owned the scrap metal business, which meant our adversaries had the keys to the gates. And what about security? With all the metal thievery going on, there must be some sort of security at night. If I were them, I'd call off security for the night on some pretense or another and lock myself in the yard. That way nobody could walk in on what was going down, and then...then what?

My first thought was that I'd station a couple of shooters on the mountain of steel. Maybe another one laying low in the weeds along the western fence line. Put us in a cross fire. Pick us off the minute the boat and the dope were safely in the channel and out of the line of fire.

Problem was that killing us out at the end of the dock presented a very sticky "what the hell to do with the bodies" problem. Carrying three deadweight bodies a hundred yards was no small feat and required more people than you wanted involved in something like this. Wasn't like they could kill us and leave us lying there for the day shift to find either. Not with Billy Bud owning the place. Too many questions about how the perpetrators got in and out of the yard. And sooner or later somebody was going to wonder exactly who removed the security patrol for the night and why. And what if one or more of us went in the water—what then? A boat standing by? Way too James Bond for these guys.

No. Unless I was mistaken, they were going to have to be neat about this. We were going to have to completely disappear, which meant they were probably going to let us walk back to dry land before they put us out of our misery. That way they could cut us down and cart us off in some sort of motorized conveyance, never to be seen again.

I walked to the back of the boat. No davit, no dingy, no nothing.

"Where's the skiff?" I asked.

"In the garage," Brett said.

I watched as he flicked a couple of switches on the control panel.

"Watch your hands," he advised.

The whine of hydraulics filled the air as the back of the boat began to rise, revealing a fourteen-foot Boston Whaler secreted in a little fiberglass compartment.

"Put us on the dock," I said.

Brett engaged the thrusters and began to cozy us up to the end of the dock. I threw a couple of orange fenders over the rail and tied them off at dock level, and looped a line over the nearest piling and tied it to a cleat.

"We're going to tie the skiff under the dock," I said. "By the time it gets light, the tide will be up and it'll be out of sight."

"Yeah...sure," Brett said. "I'll get it out for you."

"No," I corrected, "you'll get it out for *you*."

No way I was giving Brett Ward the opportunity to motor off in the yacht and leave me behind. I watched as he grabbed what looked like a small TV remote from the dashboard and pointed it my way.

"What's that?" I asked.

"Yacht controller," Brett said. "You can run the whole damn boat with this thing—engines, thrusters, system controls—the full Monty."

"How does the boat know which nav station to respond to?"

He pointed to three toggle switches immediately above the radar screen on the yacht's main console. "To the left, she listens to this nav station here. To the right, she listens to the station up on the flybridge. The one in the middle gives priority to the yacht controller."

"What happens if somebody tries to run it from here when the controller switch is on?"

"The boat does what you tell it, unless the controller switch is on and somebody starts telling it to do something else."

"In which case?"

"In which case it does what the controller tells it to do."

"Tie it up good," I said. "Fore and aft, and make sure you leave enough slack in the lines to account for the rise and fall of the tide."

"Aye, aye, Captain," he sneered.

As he slid even with me I put a hand on his chest and looked him dead in the eye. "Don't get cute here, Brett," I warned. "Remember, I've got your wallet, your cell phone, and your car keys. Just put the boat under the dock and get back on board." I leaned in closer. "I found you once; I can find you again."

He started off. I stopped him again. "I'll make finding you and killing you my life's work." The look in his eyes said he believed me.

I stood at the rail and watched as he used the emergency paddle to move the boat into place. Once he was next to the dock, he gave it a hard paddle, ducked his head, and disappeared from view. A tense minute passed. And then another. I was beginning to worry. He'd been under the dock for what seemed like quite awhile when I saw a hand pop out and grab the dock's ladder. Two seconds later he was scurrying upward like a spider monkey. About halfway to the top, one of the ancient rungs suddenly gave way. I held my breath as he caught himself with his arms and pulled himself high enough for his foot to find the next rung.

"Damn ladder's seen better days," he groused as he climbed back on board.

"Let's get out of here," I said.

"Where to?"

"To see a man about a gun," I said.

•  •  •

The timing was perfect. By the time we motored back to Seattle, tied *Yachts of Fun* to the outside guest dock at the Elliot Bay Marina, and caught a cab back to my car, it was nearly two in the morning, a tad late for the rank and file, but just about the time Joey Ortega was starting his work day.

If the local crime scene were a movie, Joey would be in the credits as the executive producer. That's what he did; he produced things. You needed a cold piece, Joe would produce it. You needed your very own armored car? No problem. A flamethrower? Diesel or unleaded? You name it, Joe could produce it. All for a price, of course.

While I hadn't availed myself of his services in a number of years, and certainly wasn't to be counted among his circle of friends, assuming he had one, which I doubted, Joe and I were nonetheless joined at the hip. Joe's father, Frankie Ortega, had been my father's chief persuader and hatchet man for the better part of thirty years.

Right after their final attempt to pry Big Bill Waterman's estate from my trust fund had failed, a bitter SPD police captain confided to me that the department estimated that Frankie Ortega was, in some capacity or another, involved in something like twenty-five murders and disappearances, nearly all of which were, in some way or another, connected to my old man's dirty dealings.

I think maybe Captain Crunch figured this awful revelation would so unnerve me that I'd feel guilty and call a press conference where I'd tearfully give the money back to the city and apologize for my father's myriad transgressions. Much as I hated to disappoint, I'd long since decided that none of that had anything to do with me. I was just a kid when most of it was going on. Joey Ortega and I used to pitch horseshoes and play Wiffle Ball in the backyard on summer days, while inside the house, Frankie and my father sautéed their schemes. Hell, right after I got my first driver's license, we even double-dated several times. The Lombardi sisters, Connie and Donna.

Unlike me, however, Joey had relished the idea of taking up where his father left off, and unlike Junior Bailey, he was good at it. While Frankie had handled the wet work personally, Joey outsourced. All Joey did these days was produce things.

I didn't have his number anymore, but I knew where to find him this time of night. Ever since we'd grown up and haired over, Joey had operated from the upstairs offices of a gentleman's club on Lake City Way, about five miles north of downtown.

Like every other strip club owner in King County, Joey found himself subject to constant harassment from bluenosed local authorities, whose mission in life seemed to be ridding the world of nocturnally inclined young women and those naughty young men who were inclined to incline them.

As a result, the joint's name had changed innumerable times over the years, as drug and prostitution allegations had necessitated closing down for a week and slinging "Under New Management" banners across the front of the building. The club's name morphed from semi-clever monikers such as Camelot, to somewhat racier titles such as Pole Position and Volcanic Eruptions, and, back in the late 1990s, to my personal favorite, Starbutts. These days, it went by the name of Club Exxxtacy. The management, of course, never changed. Only the banners.

Cost us twenty bucks apiece to get in the door. I nudged Brett along in front of me. The joint was nearly deserted. Without dozens of sweating bodies to soak up some of the sound, the booming music rattled the fillings in my teeth as we shuffled inside. A brace of bored bartenders leered at us like hyenas over a carcass.

Brett immediately became fixated on the prodigiously appointed young woman communing with a brass fireman's pole at the near corner of the stage. I butted him with my chest to keep him moving, bumping him toward the back corner of the room and the little fire hydrant of a guy leaning against the brick wall.

A tired-looking waitress was on us like a lamprey eel, bellowing over the music about a three-drink minimum, but I shook her off and kept nudging Brett forward. The door was painted the same color as the wall and didn't have a knob, making it nearly invisible until you were right up on it.

A pair of high-resolution surveillance cameras tracked our progress across the floor. The guy at the door was as wide as he was tall. Looked like George Raft was his tailor. I watched his eyes flicker as the Bluetooth earpiece whispered sweet somethings in his ear, and then heard the soft snick of the electronic lock.

He nodded at me. "Just you," he said, pulling the door open. The door was wood on the outside only. The rest of it was steel, half as thick as a bank vault.

"Keep an eye on him for me," I told the guy. "He has a tendency to get lost."

"I wouldn't worry about it," he assured me.

By the time I mounted the second stair, the door had automatically locked behind me, and the boom of the music had faded to silence. I mounted the dozen or so stairs and turned left. The office door was wide open.

Joey was alone in the office, which was how he'd managed to stay out of the slammer for all these years. Joey talked to nobody. You wanted to talk to Joey, you had to come to him. And whatever you wanted wasn't going any further than the two of you, because you two were the only ones in attendance.

He spent a great deal of time and money making sure nobody bugged his office and he never, absolutely never, did business on the phone.

He looked a lot like his father. Maybe five-foot-seven and a hundred-and-forty pounds. Same wavy black hair and pencil-thin mustache. Same narrow face and black watchful eyes that never missed a thing.

He came out from behind the desk and threw a bear hug on me. "Hey, big boy," he said with a grin. "Been a long time."

"Too long," I said and pulled him tight to my chest.

He stepped a yard away and looked me over like a lunch menu, smiled, and gestured magnanimously toward the yellow leather chair in front of his desk. "Siddown, siddown," he said as he gingerly made his way back to his desk chair.

I watched as he eased himself onto the seat with extreme care. I wasn't going to ask, but he caught me watching and told me anyway. "Hemorrhoids, man," he hissed. "Gotta have something done."

"Sorry to hear about it," I offered.

"Not as sorry as I am," he assured me. He pinned me with his little ebony eyes. "So what's up?"

I told him. Not all of it. I left out the stuff he didn't need to know. He listened intently and without comment.

"Fucking Colombians," he said when I'd finished. "They're the ones pushing all the scag out of B.C. Up there, you come up with half a ton of pure, you got it from the Colombians."

"I need a gun," I said.

He made a "you gotta be kidding me" face and shook his head. "Not your thing, Leo," he said.

He was right, of course. In the twenty or so years I'd been a private eye, I'd never carried so much as a pocket-knife, let alone a gun. The way I figured it, you didn't need a gun unless you intended to shoot someone, and since I didn't, I had no reason to be heeled.

"Something with a hundred-yard range and serious stopping power."

"I repeat, Leo. Guns ain't your bailiwick."

"Maybe some kind of night vision sight too."

"You need a gun like a fish needs a bicycle."

"And it probably best be waterproof." I shrugged. "You never know."

He leaned back in the chair and thought it over. "Gimme a few days. I can put you on some serious contractors. I can…"

"I haven't got a few days," I said. I pulled out my cell phone and checked the time. "Got about twenty hours."

Joey ruminated for another minute and a half. "Better get you something you can squirt like a garden hose then," he said finally.

"Something easy to use," I said.

"This is coming down at night?"

I said it was.

"We'll get you tracers, so you can see where they're going. Makes it easier to zero in on what you're aiming at." He rolled his eyes. "You know, in case, God forbid, you ain't much of a shot."

I didn't say anything.

"You need it tomorrow?" he said.

"Yeah."

He heaved a sigh and held out his hand. "Where's this boat now?"

"Elliot Bay Marina."

"Over by Magnolia?"

"That's the one," I said.

"What's the name of this barge?"

I told him. He made a disgusted face.

"Cute," he said and got to his feet. "One good thing about the Colombians is that they mind their own business. They got a beef it'll be with this Junior guy. You give 'em what they came for, and they'll take it and leave. Anything happens after that gonna come from this Junior guy. They ain't gonna do his dirty work for him."

I liked the sound of that because it meant Junior and his minions would be on a short leash until the exchange was completed. Whatever Junior and the pervo twins had in mind for us would have to wait until the heroin changed hands. It wasn't much, but if I held any edge at all, that was it.

I got to my feet. "Thanks."

He made a pained face. "Be careful, Leo. You're in way over your head here."

"I know," I admitted.

"I'd hate to see anything happen to you."

"Yeah," I said. "Me too."

At the bottom of the stairs, the door swung open on its own. The pulsing music and the flashing lights hit me on the face like a bucket of spit. I was still coming to grips with the sensory overload when the door closed behind me. Brett didn't notice I was back. He was too busy hitting on the waitress.

■   ■   ■

For want of a better plan, I took Brett home with me. I locked us in my bedroom and pocketed the old-fashioned skeleton key. Because my bedroom windows overlooked the garden and were not visible from the street, my insurance company had insisted the windows be equipped with burglar bars. That meant the only way out of the room was either over or through me, and I didn't figure Brett was up to either. Fortunately for both of us, neither did he.

We slept, if that's what six hours of nightmares could be called, in the same bed, fully dressed, each of us lost in our personal house of horrors, until my eyes popped open and the digital clock informed me that it was 10:07 in the morning.

To my left, Brett lay sprawled on his back, one arm thrown over his bruised forehead, snoring lightly. He had a fat upper lip and his cheeks were scraped up pretty good. Random blood spatter decorated the front of his shirt like a Jackson Pollock painting.

I rolled to the right and dropped my feet onto the floor. My shoulder throbbed. I reached up to scratch the side of my head and inadvertently hit my ear. The pain nearly blinded me. I groaned and flopped back onto the mattress, gritting my teeth, waiting for the red cloud to clear.

By the time I was ready to sit up again, Brett was groaning himself to consciousness. While he was in the shower, I threw his clothes in the washing machine. By the time we'd dried his duds, cleaned ourselves up, and choked down breakfast, it was damn near noon. All the while, a little voice in my head was counting off the hours. Ten hours and fifty minutes, it whispered as we backed out of the garage.

I'd seen the exchange site from the water, now I wanted to see it from the landside. No matter how this came down, assuming we were still alive, we were going to need a way of getting out of there when it was over. Working that out was going to be the hard part, because, once the action started, things had a habit of taking on a life of their own, scattering your best laid plans like windblown leaves. I had to be ready for anything.

Half an hour later, we rolled off the freeway at the Fife exit and followed 509 around the loop. Soon as we rounded the corner onto Marine View Drive, you could see the scrap metal trucks queued up, belching diesel in the turn lane, awaiting their turn to pass through the gates and dump their loads.

Miramar Metals, it was called, and, like I'd figured, they had some serious security in place. As nearly as I could tell, the pair of uniformed security guys checked every truck's paperwork before rolling back the heavy metal gate and allowing it into the yard. They weighed the trucks both coming and going. One in, one out. That's how it worked. All neat and under complete control.

Not wishing to attract undue attention, I kept the Tahoe moving past the yard, all the way to the end of the spit where I should have been able to turn left and cross the Hylebos Bridge but couldn't because the bridge was kaput.

I U-turned at the bridge approach and eased back the way we'd just come, moving at lost tourist speed, trying to take it all in, while not looking like I was casing the joint.

Across the street from the security gate, a car upholstery business had filled the dirt shoulder with a dozen or so cars. I pulled into the parking area, stopped directly in front of the shop entrance, and got out. Shop hours were posted on the door. Six to six, six days a week.

An eighteen-wheeler rolled out of the Miramar lot and roared up Marine View Drive in a cloud of dust. From this vantage point, I could see the old pier jutting out into the water and beyond that the *Emerald Queen*, whose bold colors and ornate woodwork looked about as out of place as a barnacle in béarnaise sauce.

I used my phone to snap several photos of the Miramar security gate as we inched by in the street. When one of the guards stopped what he was doing and took notice of me snapping pictures, I fed the Tahoe a little gas and headed back up the street. Around the loop in the opposite direction, rolling down Taylor Way until I was directly across the waterway from Miramar Metals.

The south side of the Hylebos Waterway was utterly deserted. Twenty years ago, the EPA had declared it a Superfund cleanup site, complete with a bevy of skull and crossbones signs announcing that the ground should be considered highly dangerous to your health. I got out of the Tahoe, walked over and read the fine print, which warned of the presence of PCBs, PAHs, arsenic, hexachlorobenzene, hexachlorobutadiene, and a host of other tongue-twisting carcinogens left over from the last couple of centuries.

If this thing was going to come off as I envisioned, this spot was where we needed a car. Problem was, I couldn't leave one here. Port of Tacoma Security would be all over it like ugly on an ape, so the car was going to have to get there just about when we arrived. If, for some reason, the car wasn't in place when we got here, if something went wrong, it was "kiss your ass good-bye" time. With the Three Stooges crew I was about to assemble, some kind of mishap was just about guaranteed. I shuddered at the thought.

I wandered back to the Tahoe and climbed in. Brett was huddled against the door looking out over the Puyallup River delta. From this angle, you could see the brown runoff from the river mixing with the slate-blue waters of Puget Sound. What had last night been only a vague plan to rescue his wife, was working to become a reality and he was getting scared. Couldn't say I blamed him either.

"You want to tell me what we're doing?" he groused.

"No," I said as I dropped the car in gear.

■ ■ ■

The Zoo was hopping. Della Reese was crooning how it was "almost like being in love." Pool balls clicked, pinball machines squawked and rang and whistled above the low-register drone of voices and the clink of glassware.

"I found her," I whispered to George. I leaned in close and gave him the details. "She looked to be all doped up, but at least she's alive. I need your help to get her back."

Down below the mezzanine, Heavy Duty Judy had decided Brett was *très* cute and she was all over him, draping her arm around his shoulders, pinching his butt, and drooling in his ear. He kept looking up at me for help. I pretended not to notice.

"Anything," George said. "Gotta get Becca back."

"I'm going to need you to stay sober."

He gave me the Boy Scout's honor sign. For what it was worth.

"'Cause, if we don't pull this off, we're going to be dead. All of us, and I don't mean dead out of luck. I mean dead as in shot to pieces."

"No shit?"

"No shit."

"There's gonna be shootin'?"

"Probably." I told him about the 175 rounds somebody had pumped through our knotty pine cabin in B.C. About Marty being in the hospital. "These guys are into overkill."

He swallowed hard and ran a hand over his pouchy face. Twenty-plus years of alcoholism had robbed him of his self-confidence. The mention of gunfire scared the shit out of him. I could see it in his eyes.

"You still got a driver's license?" I asked.

As I'd hoped, he was annoyed by the question. Get George pissed off and he tended to forget about everything else. Although he hadn't owned a car for the better part of twenty-five years, he'd always maintained his driver's license as a matter of pride. "Damn right, I do," he barked above the din.

"Good," I said. "Here's what I need you to do."

I laid it out for him. Showed him the photos of the Miramar security gate that I took on my phone. With this crowd, visual aids were pretty much *de rigueur.*

"Where we gonna wait?" he wanted to know.

"There's a car upholstery shop across the street. Bunch of cars they're working on parked in front. It closes at six. Long as you lay low, one more car shouldn't attract undue attention."

"You got all the stuff I need?"

"The lock and the chain are in the car."

He wiped the corners of his mouth. His expression said he wasn't sure he was up to it. Especially sober. "I don't know nothing about that area down there," he said.

"I drew you a map. It's in the car too."

I slid my car keys across the table. "Bring Normy in case there's any trouble."

He nodded.

"Can you handle it?" I asked.

His eyes darted left and right, before he said, "Guess I gotta."

I waited while he came to grips with the situation.

"Quarter to eleven?" he asked finally.

"That'll give you plenty of time to get around to the other side," I said.

I reached in my pocket and pulled out Brett's cell phone and slid it across the tabletop. "Use this to keep in touch," I told him. He swallowed hard again and nodded. "We gotta rescue that girl," he said, as much to himself as to me.

Down below, Judy had wiggled her hand down the back of Brett's trousers. Brett looked like he was tiptoeing through the tulips.

For the second time in a week, I smiled.

·   ·   ·

The full gravity of the situation began to wash over Brett as we cabbed our way back to the Elliot Bay Marina, settled up for the use of the guest slip, which included taking a raft of shit from the marina manager for leaving a seventy-foot boat in a fifty-foot slip, after which we walked out to the end of the dock and climbed on board *Yachts of Fun*.

Actually, it had started earlier. On the way back from Tacoma, he'd gone silent and sullen on me as whatever meager store of courage he possessed began to ebb. That's why I decided to spend the last hours before the exchange on the boat. I figured I best keep him in a restricted environment, lest he decide he was more afraid of Koontz and Ng than he was of me, and did something stupid.

We were making our way through the salon, headed up front to the pilot station, when Brett suddenly screeched to a halt. I heard his breath catch and watched the color drain from his neck. I leaned over his shoulder, trying to make out whatever had stopped him in his tracks.

It wasn't hard to find. There, right in the middle of the big wraparound settee, a plain white envelope lay propped up on a wicked-looking assault rifle. I shouldered my way around Brett and grabbed the envelope. Inside was a single typed sheet of paper that read:

Model AX9

Caliber: 5.56 x 45 mm

Action: Gas operated, rotating bolt

Overall: 838 mm in basic configuration, butt extended

Barrel length: 508 mm in sharpshooter version

Weight: 2.659 kg empty in basic configuration

Rate of fire: 750 rounds per minute

Magazine capacity: 30 rounds (STANAG) or 100-round double drum. Five double drums included.

Short bursts work best. Good luck!

When I looked over my shoulder at Brett, his hands were balled into white-knuckled fists, his face the color of oatmeal. "I don't know...," he stammered. "I don't think I can..."

I grabbed him by the shirtfront and pulled him close to my chest. "This is your doing, asshole. Your greed and stupidity got her into this, and you're going to help get her out."

"I don't...," he stammered.

I shook him hard. His head flopped back and forth like a life-sized bobblehead. "We're going to do this," I said. "We're going to give the Colombians back their dope, grab Rebecca, and get the hell out of there." I pulled him up nose-to-nose. "Either that or we're going to die trying."

•  ■  •

We were idling at the mouth of Quartermaster Harbor at the south end of Vashon Island, directly across Commencement Bay from the Hylebos Waterway, maybe a fifteen-minute motor from the Miramar scrap yard. Brett looked like he'd shed ten pounds in the past twelve hours. His cheekbones threatened to slice the skin as he paced back and forth across the cabin at flank speed. The control panel clock read ten thirty.

The wind had died. It was raining hard, straight up and down, making the surface of Puget Sound look like it had been digitized and was pixelating.

I had Brett's 9 mm jammed in my belt and the AX9 assault rifle banging against my chest as I walked to the stern, brought the Pulsar Digisight up to my eye and surveyed the area. Other than a Foss tugboat steaming north past Dash Point, the surrounding waters were devoid of maritime traffic.

I walked back into the cabin. "Fire it up," I said.

He started to say something, but I sawed it off.

"For the next hour or so, I'd suggest that for once in your life you shut the fuck up and do exactly what I tell you to do."

Believe it or not, he opened his mouth to say something.

"Let's go," I growled.

As Brett engaged the transmissions and fed the boat some diesel, I pulled out my cell phone.

"What's your cell phone number?" I asked him.

He told me. I dialed it. George answered on the first ring. His voice was thick with fear. "Yeah?"

"They show up yet?"

"Nope. Ain't nobody inside at all."

"Call me when they show," I said.

I heard him clear his throat. "Will do," he gargled.

Ten minutes later, as we motored across Commencement Bay, the tension inside the cabin was thick as concrete.

Brett's face was gray and hard. His breath came in short irregular bursts, and he began to sweat.

As for me, adrenaline overload had my cheeks tingling like a funny bone, and I could feel the beating of my heart. I came a foot off the deck when my cell phone rang.

"They just went in," George said. "Two cars. One of them Humper things."

I figured he meant a Hummer. The clock read ten fifty.

"Lock 'em in and get over to the other side," I said.

"Party time," I said to Brett, with more bravado in my voice than I actually felt. He put the hammer down, and the boat rose up on plane and roared across the water.

. . .

Brett used the thrust to ease the boat alongside the dock. I didn't bother to put fenders out. Seemed a good bet that a couple of scratches on the hull weren't going to bother anybody at this point.

The clock said eleven, straight up. The dock was empty.

"Where's that yacht controller thing?" I asked.

He pulled open a drawer beneath the chart plotter, pulled it out, and handed it to me. "Set the switch for the yacht controller," I said.

Brett skittered across the cabin and flicked the center toggle into the upward position. The little red light at the center of the device blinked.

I dropped the controller in my pocket. Checked the dock through the scope. Still nothing.

The depth sounder said we were in six and a half feet of water. The clock read 11:02. The volume of the rain had increased; a hissing a wall of sound pounded down onto the fiberglass roof of the boat. I looked through the scope again. The eerie green light wavered for a second and then came into focus.

"Here they come," I said.

At the far end of the dock, a trio of hazy figures lurched our way. They had Rebecca by the elbows, forcing her along from behind, using her more or less as a shield as they short-stepped over the uneven boards.

I thumbed the AX9's safety to off, wiped my sweaty palm on my pants, and stepped onto the dock. I had the extra double-drum magazines jammed into every pocket. I rattled like a car wreck as I moved out onto the pier.

"Come on," I said to Brett. "Don't get between me and them," I whispered, not that I really imagined he would.

He didn't move. Looked like he was welded to the deck.

"Unless you want to sail off into the dawn with those two, I'd suggest you get your skinny ass out here."

Apparently the idea of a romantic moonlight cruise didn't appeal to Brett. Next thing I knew, he was standing beside me on the pier. The rain was unrelenting, pouring down from the blackness overhead in torrents. Took all of thirty seconds to soak us to the skin.

Rebecca and her captors were a quarter of the way down the dock. A big, thick Hispanic guy in a yellow raincoat and a pimply white guy that kept popping his head out from behind her to see how close they were getting.

"Collins," Brett said.

"Trevor Collins?"

"Guy I used to get the boats from."

"You know the other one?" I asked.

He squinted through the curtain of raindrops. "Never seen him before."

I figured Trevor Collins was along to drive the boat, which made the other guy Colombian muscle. I stepped over to the far rail, putting as much distance between the muscle and me as I could get.

Above the static hiss of the rain, I thought I heard a clap of thunder. Then it happened again and a third time before I realized that what I was hearing were bursts of gunfire out in the street. Dread rolled down my spine like an icy ball bearing.

The trio approaching us was about thirty yards away, still hazy through a steady curtain of rain, moving slowly and deliberately, making sure they kept Rebecca in front of them as they approached our position. Neither Collins nor the Colombian seemed concerned by the weapons fire behind them. Just another day at the office.

I reached in my pocket, grabbed my phone, and started to call George.

Another, longer burst of automatic weapon fire sounded from the street. Thing was, my left ear heard the burst of fire in real time. My right ear heard the same burst from the phone's speaker half a second later. George hadn't broken our last connection. The line was open, preventing me from making another call. I heard George scream and then another burst of gunfire.

"Shit," I said, and jammed the phone back into my pants.

Collins finally looked back over his shoulder, wondering what the hell was going on on Marine View Drive. A metal-on-metal crash, an interval, and more gunfire and another earsplitting crash. The Colombian never twitched. From twenty yards away I could feel his shark eyes on me. Parts of me contracted like a dying star.

Rebecca's knees suddenly buckled. She would have gone down, but the big Colombian grabbed her around the waist, set her on his left hip, and kept walking without breaking stride or removing his right hand from the raincoat pocket.

They were twenty feet away when I called out, "Leave her right there."

They stopped walking, but that was all. No move to set her down.

"Everything's just where you left it," I said. "I just want the woman. Got no desire to spend the next twenty years looking over my shoulder, waiting for you guys to show up and blow my brains out."

The Colombian nodded his understanding. "That's the smart money move," he said in a flat, expressionless voice.

"Just set her down right there," I said again.

He shook his big head resignedly. "Gotta see the product," he said.

He looked at Trevor Collins and nodded toward the boat. Collins put his back against the opposite railing and began to sidestep past us.

"Check him for weapons," I told Brett.

For once in his life he kept his mouth shut and did as he was told, stiff-legging it across the dock, and patting Collins down like he'd seen cops do on TV.

I kept both eyes glued to the Colombian and my trigger finger just outside the guard. I figured there was no way either of us would survive a shootout at this range, and I was hoping like hell he saw it that way too.

"He's clean," Brett said.

"Hurry up," I prodded.

Collins hustled over to *Yachts of Fun* and jumped aboard.

"Just business," the thug said.

I told him I understood.

A tense minute passed. Then I heard Collins's voice. "It's all there."

The big guy set Rebecca gently on the dock and began to move toward the boat. He inched along the rail slowly, never turning his back or taking his eyes from mine, until he ducked into the cabin and disappeared from view.

Within seconds, Collins had reversed the thrusters and the boat started to float into the current. I got as much of me as I could behind the rail and watched through the scope as the big boat began to churn forward.

"Get the skiff," I whispered to Brett.

I didn't have to ask twice. At that point old Brett would have done just about anything to get off that frigging dock. The words were hardly out of my mouth when he was over the side and working his way down the rickety ladder.

I crossed quickly to Rebecca. Her eyes were closed, her breathing shallow. She had one arm curled across her forehead. The inside of the arm had enough needle tracks to start a trolley line.

Out in the waterway, Collins fed diesel to the engines and the boat started to come up on plane. The Colombian stood sentry on the stern. He gave me a curt nod before stepping inside and sliding the door closed.

I brought the AX9 to my shoulder and shot out the overhead light, sending glass and metal debris showering down on the end of the dock. Turned out it was probably a good idea, because a second later the first incoming round arrived, and any thought that these guys were smart enough to wait for us to get back on shore before they whacked us was gone. Apparently, I'd seriously overrated my enemy.

Whatever they were firing must have been about three million caliber. Something in the howitzer family of weapons. The first incoming took out a whole section of dock railing, reducing it to splinters in the nanosecond before the sound of the shot arrived. Took me a second to realize what had happened. Those crazy bastards were shooting at us with a rocket launcher.

I raced to Rebecca, scooped her into my arms, and sprinted toward the missing section of railing. The subsequent incoming round passed about six inches above my right shoulder. Sounded like a flock of Canada geese on the wing. If I'd loaded Rebecca into my arms facing the other way, the round would have taken her head off. I watched the rocket hit the water about halfway across the channel, sending a fountain of spray powering into the night sky. The hundred yards of moldering dock beneath my feet shook from the impact.

I veered toward the missing section of railing, pulled down a final gulp of air, and launched both of us out into the darkness. I was five feet from the edge of the dock, hanging in midair with Rebecca cradled in my arms, when it occurred to me that I had no idea what was waiting for me in the water below; images of old, splintered pilings just below the surface raced through my brain in the split-second before we hit the water. Last thing I heard was the sound of the skiff's outboard motor sputtering to life.

Even to a man already soaked to the skin, the frigid water was a shock to the system. My muscles spasmed. My knees involuntarily drew close to my chest as I sunk to the bottom of the channel, hugging Rebecca to my chest, trying desperately not to swallow any of the carcinogenic water.

And then my feet hit the muddy bottom and I used what little power I could still summon from my legs to push off, sending us upward, until what seemed like a week later, my head breached the surface, and I could gulp another breath and shift Rebecca so that we were parallel and our heads were at the same height.

Brett and the Boston Whaler were about ten feet away.

"Get her," I yelled, kicking my legs, trying to keep both of our heads above the surface. "Come get her!"

He used his hands to propel the dingy from under the dock. That's when Rebecca's autonomic nervous system jolted her into consciousness and she began to swim for her life. Her frenzied thrashing pushed my face below the waterline; I held my breath and lifted her upward for all I was worth.

After what seemed like an hour and a half, I felt her weight begin to lessen and knew Brett had ahold of her, so I let go and kicked my way to the surface, where I grabbed the side of the dingy with one hand and Rebecca's belt with the other. We got her over the side in two tries, but I didn't have enough muscle power left to force myself that high, so I swam around to the stern and launched the top half of me up onto the transom. The outboard belched exhaust fumes into my face as I inched my way on board.

Having rolled Rebecca into the bottom of the boat, Brett reached back and grabbed me by the shoulders. Together we hauled the last three feet of me on board the skiff. Between labored breaths, I could hear the sound of footsteps thundering along the dock. Lots of heavy footsteps coming our way.

"Go, go," I shouted to Brett. "Get us the hell out of here,"

No hesitation this time either. He threw himself behind the wheel, jammed the throttle lever all the way forward, sending the boat roaring out into the channel.

Rebecca babbled incoherently and rolled from side to side fighting off dream demons, as I crawled to the rear of the dingy and brought the rifle to bear on the dock.

"Go, go," I still chanted as I brought my eye up to the night vision scope. Even with night vision, the figures running toward the end of the dock were muddy and indistinct. Before I was able to steady my weapon, muzzle flashes lit up the night, and the water around the speeding boat began to boil.

I aimed and squeezed the trigger. Looked like I was shooting fireflies. Each round glowed phosphorous green as it arced in their direction. Joey Ortega was right. I wasn't much of a marksman, but when you could see where the rounds were going, it was easy to make adjustments.

I raised my aiming point two feet and let go another burst. My second attempt sent our pursuers flat-bellied onto the deck, as the AR began chewing up the locale. I kept my finger on the trigger until the magazine ran dry, ejected the empty clip, and slapped another into the breach.

Brett slalomed the boat back and forth across the channel, trying to make us harder to hit. Before I could loose another burst, a halogen-white muzzle flash the size of a trash can lit up the dock, and the Boston Whaler shuddered violently as the whole bow of the boat disappeared in a scream of tortured metal.

By the time I recovered my wits, the boat was beginning to sink. From where I sat, it looked as if we surely were on our way to the bottom.

"Back here! Everybody back here," Brett shouted.

I grabbed Rebecca and slid past him, half carrying, half dragging her to the extreme rear of the skiff. By the time I got both of us as far aft as we could get, the boat had taken on the better part of a foot of water and our speed was down to nothing. And then, slowly, almost imperceptibly, our combined weight began to lift the nose just enough so that we were no longer plowing water. I ducked a hail of small-caliber rounds buzzing by. As the bow cleared the surface, the accumulated water in the boat sloshed toward the stern, leaving us hip deep as the boat labored across the channel.

We were three-quarters of the way across the waterway. The thirty-horsepower outboard began to smoke from the strain as we slogged toward the far shore. A flash of movement pulled my eyes to the left.

I guess Collins saw that his pals' plans for us had gone awry and had decided to help them out. *Yachts of Fun* had turned around and was on plane, screaming toward us at something like twenty knots. No way we were going to make it to shore before she cut us in half and ground us to fish bait.

"The controller," Brett yelled. "Gimme the controller!"

I fished the yacht controller from my pocket and handed it to him.

"Take the wheel," he screamed.

I levered myself onto the seat next to him and took the helm.

Rebecca was on her hands and knees, trying to struggle to her feet. I reached over and pushed her back to the bottom of the boat as another round screamed overhead. I watched in terror as it plowed into the far bank, sending a geyser of stone and dirt spiraling high into the air.

When I looked up again, Brett was madly pushing buttons on the controller. I snapped my eyes to the left just in time to see *Yachts of Fun* turn sharply to port, sending a wall of spray high into the air as it veered into the middle of the channel.

And then the red light on the yacht controller went out.

"He figured it out," Brett yelled and pitched the controller over the side.

I snapped my eyes forward. We were no more than forty yards from the south bank of the waterway. Our maneuver with the controller might have bought us the time we needed. From the look of it, *Yachts of Fun* had given up the chase.

"Not enough water in here for him," Brett screamed.

As we approached the shore, I kept the throttle pegged.

Twenty yards from shore. Then ten.

"Hang on," I shouted.

Brett threw himself into what remained of the bow in the instant before we plowed headlong into the bank. The impact sent him sprawling out onto the muddy slope and flipped me completely over the steering console. I landed on a pile of life jackets in the middle of the boat. I groaned, grabbed Rebecca under the arms and started pulling her up the bank, hoping like hell I didn't take one in the back of the head as we struggled up the slope. She was trying to walk with me, but her legs were like linguini. Coupla steps, fall down, and slide back. Coupla more steps and slide back. My leg muscles screamed from the effort.

We got to the top and I realized nobody was shooting at us anymore. I checked the opposite shore. Looked like a body lying out at the end of the dock. Otherwise it was deserted. I was contemplating the possibility that I'd actually hit somebody when two sets of headlights went roaring up Marine View Drive. I couldn't make out the first, but the second vehicle was a big black Hummer. My breath froze in my chest. So much for plan A. Somehow or other, they'd broken out of the yard, and were on their way over here to finish what they'd started.

I pushed myself to my feet and looked around.

No George. No car.

Brett struggled to the top of the rise. The front of him was crusted with mud and gravel. His nose was bleeding again. His mouth hung open as he swiveled his head in nearly a circle. Took his fear-addled brain a second to figure it out.

"Where's the car?" he wheezed.

I shook my head and pointed to the *Emerald Queen* riverboat. "Take her over that way," I said. "Get some cover."

I reached into my belt, pulled out the 9 mm, and handed it to him.

"The boat," I said. "Get her to the boat."

Brett liked the idea of getting to cover. That was right up his alley. He pocketed the nine, lifted Rebecca into his arms, and staggered toward the deserted riverboat on the near shore. I could tell by the way his legs quaked and quivered that he wasn't going to be able to get her there on his own.

I pulled my phone from my pocket. The noise coming from the phone's speaker sounded like George was strapped to the wing of a 747 during takeoff. "George," I screamed. "Answer me, goddamn it! George. Do you hear me, George?"

Nothing. Just more of that screeching wall of sound.

I pushed the End button over and over, hoping to break the connection so I could call 911 and get some help because the minute Junior's troops got over to this side, we were going to be dead. But nothing happened. The screeching and squawking continued unabated. I cursed again, pocketed the phone, and looked around.

Out in the waterway, *Yachts of Fun* was a half mile away, rocketing past the Hylebos Bridge, heading out into the darkness of Puget Sound at full throttle.

I was still deciding what to do next when my peripheral vision picked up the shower of sparks, a great yellow rooster tail of molten metal fanning up into the night sky like a thousand Fourth of July sparklers. "What the...," I whispered.

I was still collecting my lower jaw when the Tahoe came fishtailing around the corner, three of the tires completely gone, running on the rims. Even from two hundred feet away, I could hear the rims shredding the asphalt and the big engine screaming as the car bore down on me like a crippled rhinoceros.

I dropped to one knee, thumbed off the safety on the AX9 and put my eye to the scope. I couldn't quite make out who was driving, but from the size of the passenger, I knew it had to be Norman riding shotgun. I eased my finger from the trigger, scrambled to my feet, and waved frantically.

The car slid back and forth across the road, shaking its rear end like one of Joey Ortega's dancers as the one remaining rear tire alternately gained and lost traction.

George locked up the brakes and plowed to a halt about fifty feet in front of me. The relentless rain hissed and spattered as it came into contact with overheated metal.

I raced to the driver's door and jerked it open. George's face was white with fear.

"They seen us, Leo," he yelled. "Caught us chaining the gate."

I pulled him out of the car. Pointed at the retreating figures of Brett and Rebecca, barely visible through the curtain of water. "That way," I shouted. "Go that way!"

Norman stumbled around the front of the car, his left arm bloody and hanging limp by his side. I pointed at Brett and Rebecca again. "Normy," I shouted. "Help him get her to the boat."

He took off running in long, slow-motion strides. Looked like Frankenstein doing the hundred-yard dash.

George was frozen in place. His eyes looked like pinwheels. He held his hands in front of his body, his fingers still clenched around an imaginary steering wheel.

"Go," I yelled.

He looked at me as if I was speaking Turkish, then shook himself from his stupor and went skittering off after the others.

That's when the first of the pursuit cars came roaring around the corner.

I brought the AX9 to my shoulder and pulled the trigger. The automatic spewed a glowing arc of tracers. The car's windshield instantly disappeared; the car drifted lazily to the right. I watched as the Lexus blasted off the edge of the embankment, hovered in midair for a long moment, its wheels spinning, and then belly flopped into the Hylebos Waterway, where it sank nose first into the dark waters.

Having witnessed its predecessor's fate, the Hummer wasn't taking any chances. I heard the screech of tires and watched as three figures threw themselves from the car and ran for cover. One guy ran to the right, the other two to the left. Koontz and Ng were easy to spot, their comic book profiles unmistakable as they hustled over and put portions of the bank between us. I ducked behind the Tahoe, ejected the empty magazine, and slapped in another.

When I peeked around the fender, the blood began to eddy in my veins. Koontz and Ng were lying on their bellies pointing what looked like a rocket launcher my way. My survival mechanism sent me crawling backward, keeping my car between us, trying to put as much distance between the Tahoe and me as I could get.

Good thing too. A second and a half later, I heard the launcher's ignition whoosh and then, in another half a second, the Tahoe was blown to pieces. The shockwave drove me face-first into the ground. Flames shot twenty feet into the air. I covered my head as big chunks of molten metal and glass and plastic rained down from the skies. When the overhead onslaught subsided, I pushed myself up to one knee and looked around. The last mortal remains of my car had been reduced to the size of a VW bug and were engulfed in flames.

At that point, I got smart and began to act counterintuitively, trying to do something, anything they weren't expecting. Instead of running for cover, I crawled back up and got as close to the Tahoe as the roaring flames would permit. Close enough to smell my hair beginning to singe. I shielded my eyes from the heat and peeked around the edge of the burning wreck.

Like I figured, all three were sprinting hard in my direction, thinking there was no way I could have survived the explosion. I had a better line of sight on the guy on the right, so I started with him. I set my sights low and allowed the natural pull of the weapon to bring the barrel up as I emptied the clip. I watched as the firefly slugs stitched him from crotch to chin. He went down in a heap and stayed there.

Seeing their compatriot go down sent Koontz and Ng scurrying back over the bank. I squinted through the rain. Ten seconds passed before I saw the rocket launcher reappear. I took off running, keeping the remains of the car between us. And then—bang—my car exploded again. Two direct hits had morphed my former Tahoe into little more than a pile of flaming metal, ready for the Miramar scrap heap.

In front of me, Norman had Rebecca tucked under one arm and was loping toward the *Emerald Queen* with George zigzagging along in his wake. Brett was nowhere in sight. He'd dropped her on the ground and run for his life. I silently cursed myself for trusting him and especially for giving him back his gun. My ire was short-lived, however. Movement in the corner of my eye said Koontz and Ng were setting up to launch yet another rocket-propelled grenade in my direction, so I made a dash for it. Holding the assault rifle tight against my chest, I gave it all I had in a sprint for cover. I'd barely gotten started when another massive round whizzed by my ear, missed the *Emerald Queen* by a foot and a half, and disappeared into the darkness. I threw my head back and ran for my life. I don't sprint much these days, so by the time I arrived at the *Emerald Queen*, my breath was about gone and my legs felt like they were about to rotate out of the sockets.

Norman had kicked in the casino's double front doors. He and George and Rebecca lay scattered on the casino floor like fallen poker chips. I stayed outside, ducked behind the ornate rail, and flattened myself on the deck.

The combination of terror and oxygen must have had a regenerative effect on my brain, because that was the moment I realized that coming to the boat was, in all probability, going to be the last dumb decision I would ever make.

What had kept us alive thus far had been the fact that we were out in the open. When you fire at somebody with a rocket launcher, you're not trying for a direct hit. That's not what the weapon was designed to do. What you're hoping to do is to blow up something in your quarry's immediate vicinity and take him out as part of the collateral damage of the explosion.

As long as we were in the middle of the Superfund site, there was nothing for the grenades to hit, nothing to blow up. Either they scored a direct hit and vaporized one of us on the spot, or the rockets just flew off and eventually dropped into Puget Sound. What they really needed was something substantial that would create enough shrapnel to shred anything and everything in the immediate impact area, and that's just what running to the boat had given them. I cursed again and waited for the final rocket to punctuate the sentence. But nothing happened.

An eerie silence settled around us like a shroud. A minute had passed when I heard the riverboat's engines roar and felt the rumble beneath as the boat came to life. Had to be Brett, I figured. Scrambling to save his own life. I cursed again, and then duck-walked a hundred feet up the deck and peeked over the rail.

Koontz and Ng must have heard the engines too. They worked their way up the south bank of the Hylebos until they were parallel with the boat. I saw a yellow muzzle flash and waited to for the end to come. And come it did, but not in the caliber I'd imagined. No rocket. Just a long burst of automatic weapon fire tearing up the section of deck where I'd been half a minute ago.

"Stay down," I screamed to the trio inside. "Stay down!"

Why they had switched weapons was beyond me. They had us right where they wanted us and they…Then it came to me: They must be out of rockets. How many of those things could anybody lug around, anyway? A short, dry laugh escaped my throat.

Now, if there was any strategic advantage, it was ours. They were seventy or so yards away, with nothing but open ground between us, and we might actually be able to motor off into the sunset and save our collective ass.

I popped my head up, sighted and let loose a short burst of fire designed to keep their heads down as I crawled forward, untying the lines as I went along. Not surprisingly, another prolonged burst of fire from shore pulverized the area I'd vacated. I pulled another line from its cleat and crawled some more, working my way from cleat to cleat. By the time I reached the back of the boat, the red paddle-wheel had begun to churn the water like a giant eggbeater.

Just above my head, the woodwork and windows were shredded by another prolonged burst of automatic weapon fire. I flattened myself, covered my head with my arms, and hoped to God that everybody inside was doing the limbo.

And then suddenly we were moving. I could feel it. The big boat began to slip out into the waterway just as the next salvo slammed into us. Not down here on deck this time, but higher. Up at the pilothouse where Brett presumably was at the helm.

I popped up, put the scope to my eye, and let loose everything I had at the bright green muzzle flashes. Above the roar of the engines, the drumbeat of lead crashing through the boat and the tinkling of broken glass, I thought I heard a scream, something long and high pitched, and final.

Wasn't until we'd both stopped firing that I heard the sirens. A bunch of them headed toward us, their pulsating light bars painting the undersides of the clouds with splotches of red and blue.

I crawled into the casino on my hands and knees. Rebecca was still out of it, rolling on the floor, flailing her arms, duking it out with her demons. Norman was on his back cradling his wounded arm, and humming a song known only to him. George had crawled under a discarded food service table and assumed the fetal position. From the movement of his lips, I guessed he was praying.

Took me a couple of minutes to find the stairs. Red and white sign on the door: Authorized Personnel Only. By that time, the sirens and lights were all around us. I was halfway up the set of stairs leading to the pilothouse when the *Emerald Queen* came to a crashing, glass-mashing halt, throwing me onto the stairs, busting my mouth open like an overripe pomegranate.

I felt warm blood run down my chin as I grabbed the handrail, righted myself, and clawed up the remaining stairs. The pilothouse was in shambles. Shot to pieces. As I looked around, two things became readily apparent. First off, the *Emerald Queen* had run aground on the far side of the Puyallup River. The big boat shuddered as the paddlewheel tried to shove us up on the shore. I walked over and pulled the transmission levers into the neutral position and turned off the engines. The shuddering ceased.

The other thing wasn't as easily fixed. Brett was spread out across the floor like something requiring assembly. The bottom half of his left arm was missing. Blood was everywhere. Looked like he'd been hit three or four times. The baseball-sized wound an inch below where his left eye used to be would surely have been sufficient.

I pulled a South Puget Sound chart from the nav table and put it over his face.

George crawled out from under the cart and was puking on the rug. Rebecca, who somehow struggled into the sitting position, was holding her head in both hands. She didn't recognize me as I walked by. Norman was still humming that lonesome song.

I heard the flat static crack of bullhorns blaring. I brought a hand to my face and gingerly felt around my mouth. My upper lip was the size of a rutabaga. At least one of my front teeth was missing. I spit dark blood down on my shoes before folding my hands over the top of my head and walking out on deck.

Half-a-dozen red-laser sights bounced over my body. "Hands, hands," a cop screamed. "I want to see those fucking hands."

I figured, what the hell? "Is there an echo in here?" I inquired.

# Chapter 6

"You stole a fucking casino," Hardy bellowed.

"Well, not exactly stole," I amended. "More like requisitioned."

In actuality, the words didn't sound that way at all. The ruined state of my mouth made enunciation nearly impossible. But owing to the fact that Captain Andrew Hardy and I had been bantering back and forth for the better part of an hour, he'd become quite adept at translating the thick utterances that spilled from my mouth like porridge.

When I said, "Ellll, no zacly tole," he knew precisely what I meant.

Day before yesterday, as I'd languished in the medical unit of the King County lockup, the county doctors had discovered my missing front tooth lodged inside my upper lip, from whence they removed it, leaving the area around my mouth with more stitches than a set of slipcovers.

By that time I'd already called my lawyer, Jed James, and, had I been able to speak, I was, on the advice of my attorney, no longer answering questions.

First thing Jed told me was that we were in no hurry to converse with the cops. Quite the contrary. If they wanted to talk to me, they had to get medical clearance first. Independent medical clearance too. Not from the collection of county quacks they kept on retainer. He figured we could put any interrogation off for the better part of a week with medical issues alone.

"I...i...i...i?" I inquired.

"'Cause you're all the buzz, man. There's an army of reporters and a *Dateline* crew outside. Maggie had to hire extra help with my phones. There's a rumor you're going to be the *People* magazine cover for the coming week. This thing needs to simmer down a bit. Right now, it's way too telegenic." He threw a hand toward where a TV should have been but wasn't because this was jail. "You turn on the boob tube these days and there's either a twenty-year-old picture of you with a crew cut and all your teeth, or file footage of that friggin' paddle wheeler toting a bunch of drunken idiots around Puget Sound." Jed patted my shoulder. "You just lay back and get to feeling better." He grinned. "Besides..." His blue eyes twinkled. "Trust me on this, buddy, you don't want your face on television. Right now you've got a radio face."

So five days later, and while my cherubic countenance still didn't have a good side, we decided to do our impression of good citizens, and finally agreed to chat with the boys in blue. Jed leaned against the south wall of the interview room with his stubby arms folded across his chest. We also decided that the best policy would be to give it to them as straight as we could without involving anybody we didn't need to.

The final tally, counting Brett Ward, was five dead, four by gunshot, one by drowning, and two soaking-wet Canadian citizens taken into custody while hitchhiking north on I-5 and listed as "persons of interest" in the ongoing Pierce County homicide investigation.

Lui Ng was found among the dead, but Jordan Koontz was nowhere to be found. Every cop in two countries was turning over rocks looking for him, but thus far he had managed to avoid detection, a feat of no small magnitude when you looked like he did.

George and Normy were still guests of King County, which, in their cases, probably wasn't altogether unpleasant. For those guys, three square meals a day and a warm place to sleep amounted to *Lifestyles of the Rich and Famous.*

News on Rebecca was sketchier. Jed had asked around, but the cops screwed the lid on tight. Scuttlebutt had it that she'd emerged from her drug-induced coma and was resting comfortably, with Iris no doubt hovering buzzardlike by her bedside.

The Coast Guard had located *Yachts of Fun* moored in the Longbranch Municipal Marina. Trevor Collins was found on the engine room floor, with his throat cut and an X carved into his forehead. No heroin. No Colombian.

The interview with Captain Hardy went better than I'd expected. We'd hit the yelling stage a couple of times when Hardy suddenly changed course and wanted to know where I got the AX9. That's when things took on a more contentious air.

I shook my head. "Na...owin...dere," I slurped.

"What do you mean you're not going there?" Hardy demanded. "That gun was stolen from the Silverdale PD storage warehouse. The property locker cop got his head bashed in. Poor bastard's still in intensive care, and I want to know where that fucking gun came from."

I turned my face toward the wall.

"Let's move on," Jed said. "If the DA files weapons charges, we'll deal with the matter at that time."

"D…ooo…ead…by…tatemen?" I asked.

"Yes, I read your goddamn statement. For all the fuck it's worth."

I'd written it all out for them and signed it. Blow by blow, so to speak. The only things I left out were Joey Ortega and the Colombian—for obvious survival-related reasons—and Rachel Thoms for reasons I couldn't quite specify. I guess I figured that if Rebecca wanted them to know about her therapist, she could tell them herself.

"Aah dinna hoot a anabodi who wann't hooting a me."

"Self-defense?" Hardy sneered. "I've got four dead bodies, three of which are a ballistic match to your weapon, and you're claiming self-fucking-defense?"

"Ay weer tyin to kill me."

Hardy made a rude noise with his lips. The muscles along the side of his jaw rippled like snakes. His frustration was palpable.

What I knew, and he knew that I knew, was that both the Pierce County and the Washington State Patrol evidence collection teams had pretty much verified my version of the story. As usual, Jed had been right on the money when he told me I was going to skate on the charges. That they'd screw around, threaten me with a host of lesser charges until the story fell off the front page, and then kick me loose.

"I told you to stay the hell out of it," Hardy said angrily.

"Aaam no so goo a dat," I admitted.

. . .

They must have kept Brett's body in a freezer, because it was a week and a half since he'd been killed, and he still looked fresh as a daisy. I hadn't realized that the "looks good in clothes" thing of his persisted even after death.

I'd parked my rental car on Tenth Avenue East, walked up the alley that separates the ball fields from the Broadway storefronts, and snuck in the back door of the Bonney-Watson funeral parlor, where I tiptoed past the corpse cooler and the stainless-steel embalming tables, down a long, brightly lit corridor, and into the viewing room.

The lights were on in the richly carpeted room, subliminal organ music was seeping from overhead speakers, and the clock on the wall said it was ten minutes to one. I slithered between the sprays of flowers and peeked down into the casket. Last time I'd seen Brett Ward, half of his face was missing. They'd done a good job with the reconstruction. His death visage was a little fuller than he'd appeared in life, but if you didn't count the waxy pallor, and the fact that he wasn't talking, it was pretty much Brett Ward.

The way I told the Great Tacoma Shoot-Out story, Brett's heroic actions had ultimately saved our ass. I mean, what the hell? Huh? No sense in speaking ill of the dead. If not for his sake, then certainly for Rebecca's. When she came out of her drug-induced stupor, she would remember what a weasely little shit-head she'd married. That was bad enough. No sense in rubbing her nose in it.

I could hear a symphony of hushed conversations and a horde of feet milling around outside the double doors and then I suddenly picked up the sound of Rebecca's voice telling somebody, "Thank you for coming today."

I wasn't in the mood for company, and I took her voice to be my cue to exit. I wound my way out the back door, around the corner and out onto Broadway, where the air was ripe with water and streets were alive with Seattle Central Community College students going to their classes. Even their backpacks had backpacks.

It was too early for me, but on this day I needed a drink, so I walked down the hill, past the statue of Jimi Hendrix kneeling on the sidewalk and across Pike Street, under the Egyptian Theater marquee, down to Brody's Place, where I found a nice, dark table in the corner, ordered a double Stoli on the rocks and told the bartender to send another along about every fifteen minutes.

By the time I'd brooded my way through six doubles and all the couldas, shouldas, and wouldas surrounding my present predicament, more than two hours had slipped away. It was three-thirty, and I was seriously wasted. I didn't even think about driving. I called for a cab. At this point, if I got a DUI, they'd probably give me life without parole.

When I got in the cab, I had every intention of going home, of taking a hot shower and maybe even a short siesta. In the front parlor of my brain, the lace curtains were drawn, and I was turning off the lights. Apparently, however, my brain also had a steamy back room, where they were having a meeting and hadn't bothered to invite me.

We were rolling down the steep part of Denny when a voice told the driver, "Get on the freeway. Go north."

I looked around to see who said it, but found myself alone.

The graveside service was winding down by the time I got there. Ashes to ashes and dust to dust and all that rot. Couple of guys from the mortuary were lowering the casket down into the hole with some kind of mechanical contraption.

Iris and Rebecca and a cadre of her closest friends stood stiffly at the head of the grave as the pastor droned on about coming into this world with nothing and going out the same way. I kept expecting somebody to spontaneously start singing "Bringing in the Sheaves." Standing directly behind Rebecca, intermittently rubbing her back for comfort, was Hillary Franks, she of Brett's little love-nest fame. Apparently, the hussy had no shame.

Brett's family had flown in from the East Coast. Mom and Pop, looking old and thin, and three sisters, two who brought their families, eleven of them altogether. Wasn't until I lost my focus and looked out over the youngest sister's head that I spotted the pair of them, standing inside a small copse of ornamental cedars, passing a bottle back and forth.

I made eye contact with Rachel Thoms as I skirted the mourning multitude and made my way over to George and Nearly Normal Norman. George was hunkered down inside his collar. Normy had his left arm in a bright blue sling. They offered me a pull of the world's worst whiskey, but I waved it off. "Been there, done that," I said.

"I didn't think you was coming," George said.

"Neither did I."

The Ward family was shaking the pastor's hand, thanking him for his services and probably slipping him a few bucks. Everybody else was headed for the cars. Everybody except Rebecca, who was headed my way. Back over her shoulder, I saw Iris standing along the edge of the road, next to the limo, a scowl on her flinty face and her mouth clamped tight as a leg trap.

I met Rebecca halfway.

She wore a gray wool overcoat and a black skirt that came down past her knees. Hair piled on top of her head. No jewelry.

She waved, but not to me. "Hi, Georgie," she called.

Then toodle-ooed with her fingers. "Norman."

When I peeked back over my shoulder, the bourbon brothers were grinning from ear to ear.

We came to a stop about a yard apart. I don't know what I was looking for in her eyes, but it wasn't there. Neither was she. At least not all of her. Her ordeal had dimmed her flame a bit. Her slate-gray eyes lacked their usual steely focus.

"I just wanted to say thank you," she said.

"No need."

"I'm guessing there is," she said evenly.

"I was but a pawn upon the playing field."

"That's not what I hear."

I was guessing she'd used her SPD contacts to find out what the cops were saying about it, a story which probably bore scant resemblance to the carefully contrived bullshit Jed and I had been feeding the media for the past week or so.

"Sorry for your loss," I lied.

She nodded, but didn't say anything.

Cars were starting all around us. People were heading home.

"Maybe...," I began. "You know after a while...a suitable interval...maybe we could..."

She said, "We'll see," when what she really meant was, "I don't think so."

Neither did I.

"Becca," Iris's voice grated from afar.

"We've got a reception," Rebecca said.

"Go. We can talk later."

But we both knew we wouldn't. Some things in life you just have to erase. If you're going to go on with your existence, you have to drop them into a deep dark well somewhere in your soul, and trudge onward as if they never happened.

Otherwise, you end up too lacerated to go on, like George and Normy over there finishing up that fifth of rotgut whiskey. You end up with a hole you can't plug and a pain even an ocean of cheap booze won't cure. Seemed like a certain amount of self-delusion was prerequisite to what we collectively defined as happiness.

I watched Iris shepherd Rebecca into the back of the limo, and climb in after her without so much as a backward glance. I turned away. I wasn't looking for one of those, "and their eyes met as the car slowly pulled away" scenes. No way.

Half-a-dozen mourners lingered around the grave. Professionals, I guessed. Part of that odd fraternity who attend funerals as a hobby. Standing cheek by jowl at the foot of the grave, a trio of middle-aged women looked as if they might have come to the service together. A bald-headed black guy, fingering a set of rosary beads; a big dude, with his back to me, wearing a blue Helly Hansen parka shell; and, over by the tree, a thicker specimen in a black hoodie sweatshirt.

Out on the cemetery road, a gold Acura pulled to the curb. The window slid down. Rachel Thoms was behind the wheel, looking at me with those green eyes of hers.

"You need a ride?" she asked.

I gestured with my head toward the deadly duo lounging under the trees. "We're gonna get a little fresh air," I said. "Thanks anyway."

She was smart enough to know that the fresh air part was probably a good idea.

"Give me a call," she said.

"Wouldn't that be conflict of interest?"

She shook her head. "Rebecca's not my patient anymore. I referred her to someone I know." She anticipated my next question. "I do family and relationship counseling."

"Ah," I said.

She rolled up the window.

I stood where I was and watched as the car slid soundlessly out of sight, then strolled over toward George and Norman. The bottle was history. They dropped it on the grass. Just another dead soldier.

"Come on," I said. "We'll walk out to the entrance and call a cab."

■  ■  ■

Twenty minutes of stumbling through the shrubbery brought us to the front gate. The sky was oozing a steady drizzle, as George and Normy lurched over to the cemetery offices and disappeared into the men's room. I pulled out my phone and ambled uphill.

Out on Fifth Avenue the cars hissed along inside shrouds of mist, wipers slashing to and fro, headlights darting over the wet pavement. Not even five o'clock and it was dark as night. Visions of sandy beaches flitted through my brain.

I guess I had a lot on my mind, which probably explained how somebody had managed to shadow us across Holyrood Cemetery without me noticing.

I was about to speed dial Yellow Cab when a rustle of fabric pulled my head around. He was ten yards away. The guy in the black hoodie, from back by the gravesite.

I figured he was probably another reporter who wanted a story. I'd been ducking and dodging the press for over a week, so I assumed this was a scrivener looking for an exclusive.

"Listen, pal," I said. "I don't mean to be impolite, but if you're…"

The black hoodie fell back the second he propelled himself in my direction. Jordan Koontz had shaved his head to stubble and was coming at me like a locomotive.

It's hard to describe the high-pitched keening sound that escaped his chest as he bounded in my direction. Something primitive and pre-language.

On my best day, and this sure as hell wasn't it, I wouldn't last a minute in the octagon with Jordan Koontz. The best you could say was that I had a puncher's chance—that I was big enough and strong enough that if I happened to get lucky and catch him with a haymaker, I might be able to put out his light.

As he rushed forward, instinct sent me diving for his ankles. I missed. He drove a knee into the top of my head. My vision swam. Felt like my neck was broken. I rolled over onto my back in time to see the bottom of his boot descending toward my upturned face. I rolled right. The boot powered down onto the grass with a resounding thud, missing my face by inches. He backed off, bouncing on the balls of his feet, grinning that snake grin of his.

"Get up," he said. "Gonna break you, boy," he hissed. "Gonna break you open."

I scrambled to my feet. My arms felt paralyzed, my knees weak and unsteady. I had no doubt he was going to beat me to death. Right here. Right now.

And then, suddenly, he stopped bouncing, the reptilian smile was replaced by a quizzical expression as he dropped to his knees. I watched in wonder as an exit wound the size of a quarter bloomed like a flower on his forehead. He hiccupped once and fell facedown on the grass. His body twitched once and he didn't move again.

As my brain tried and failed to process what was going on, the big guy in the Helly Hansen parka stepped out from behind a massive rhododendron. A small-caliber automatic dangled from his right hand. He used his left to pull the hood from his head.

The big Colombian from the other night.

I watched as he walked over, bent at the waist, and put another round into the back of Koontz's head. The sound of the report was swallowed by the roar and hiss of the traffic. He dropped the automatic into his coat pocket, fished around and came out with a wicked-looking curved blade with a wooden handle. He dropped to one knee and carved a seeping X into Jordan Koontz's forehead.

Satisfied with his work, he got back to his feet. His black eyes met mine. "People gotta know," he said.

I kept my mouth shut. He sensed my terror.

"It's over," he said.

I nodded.

I watched in silence as he pocketed the knife and walked out through the gate. A dark green Mercedes sedan pulled into the mouth of the driveway. The door opened and he disappeared inside. "It's over," I said under my breath.

■　■　■

"I made up a new word," Ralph was saying.

"What word is that?" I asked.

"Kari-aki."

"What's that mean?"

"Singing with your mouth full of chicken," he said.

They yukked it up. Rocking back and forth and pounding the table with the flats of their hands. It had been a tough few days for George and, although I'd heard the joke a dozen times before, I was happy to see him having a good time.

The cops had turned us loose early that morning. I'd given the Colombian a two-minute head start and then, instead of calling a cab, I dialed 911. Under Jed's watchful eye, I told the cops that Jordan Koontz had knocked me cold, and that when I woke up, there he was, lying on the grass with a couple of bullets in his head and an X carved in his forehead, all of which were a complete mystery to me, as I'd been unconscious at the time and had absolutely no idea who or what had done that to him. That was my story and I was sticking to it. Needless to say, the cops had been dubious.

They kept the three of us for half a day while they searched the area for the murder weapon. Dogs. Metal detectors. The whole nine yards. Two spent cartridge cases from a Beretta .765. That was it. They swabbed our hands for evidence of gunshot residue, and when we came up clean, had very little choice but to turn us loose, despite not believing a word of what I was telling them.

First thing in the morning, before I'd rolled out of bed, Detective Sergeant Roddy called from Vancouver. They'd found Junior Bailey out on Vancouver Island. An unpronounceable Indian reservation. Their medical examiner said he'd been dead for at least a week. Four bullets in the head will do that.

"Colombians cleaning up after themselves," I mumbled.

"You'd think so, wouldn't you?"

Something in his tone got my attention. "Any reason not to?" I asked.

I could almost hear him shrug over the phone line. He cleared his throat. "The murder scene used to be one of the safe houses Billy kept for his drug mules. Way the hell out in the middle of nowhere."

"Yeah?"

"Quite an elaborate security setup. Motion detectors, high-tech security cameras, every camera with a backup. The whole ball of twine, so to speak."

"And?"

"And not only are all the security tapes missing, backups included, but there's also absolutely no sign of forced entry."

"So whoever showed up, Junior must have let them in."

"So it appears," Roddy said.

"Hard to imagine him opening the door for a Colombian hit man."

"As you say, hard to imagine. And whoever it was must have been familiar with the design of the security system," he added. "Way too elaborate for somebody to just get lucky."

"Really?"

"No flourish either. None of the usual signs that they leave."

Like X's carved into foreheads or the horrific "Colombian necktie" of song and story, wherein they slit the victim's throat from ear to ear, reached in and grabbed his whole tongue assembly and pulled it through the hole, leaving the stiff with something akin to an organic ascot.

"Just doesn't look like their work," Roddy said.

I thought it over as I put my feet on the floor. I remembered the faraway look in Billy's eyes as he gazed out over the Strait of Georgia from behind his desk and wondered how bad things had to get before you had your own son killed. Kind of made me wonder about my old man. About how far I would have had to push him before he decided I was just too much of a liability to keep around.

"You don't suppose Billy Bud finally had enough, do you?" I asked.

"We'll never know, will we?"

. . .

The Zoo was quiet, mainly because half of the usual suspects were missing. Norman had taken the bus to Harborview to get his arm dressing changed. Big Jack, Heavy Duty Judy, Large Marge, and Little Felix had gone along for the ride, leaving a skeleton crew to man the bastions of bacchanalia.

Red Lopez played eightball with Billy Bob Fung and a couple of locals. Yelling and screaming every time he made a shot. The jukebox was hammering out "Whip It" by Devo when Rachel Thoms walked in the front door. All of a sudden, I could hear my pulse. She stood for a moment, as everyone does, allowing her eyes to adjust to the darkness, and then strode confidently along the bar, moving toward the commotion in the back of the room.

I had no idea how she knew to look for me here, and, unless I was mistaken, the Zoo wasn't her kind of place at all. She spotted me sitting in the mezzanine and walked in my direction. As she passed the pool table, somebody said something. She hesitated and turned toward whoever had spoken to her.

I read her lips. "Excuse me?" she said.

That's when I heard the magic words.

"Ain't it a beauty?" Red inquired.

The bar went freeze-tag silent. No chuckles or clicks or bangs or bells or whistles. The assembled multitude remained frozen in place, waiting for the moment to play itself out. They'd seen this movie before. This was the end of Act Three. The part where whoever found herself gazing down at Red's appendage ran screaming into the street. A shiver of morbid anticipation ran through the room like a funny-bone current.

Only, inexplicably, that's not what happened. Instead of staging the oft-witnessed elbows-and-assholes retreat, the gorgeous Rachel Thoms looked vaguely amused and steadfastly held her ground. As she leaned forward and peered myopically into Red's palm, the crowd leaned forward with her. After a nearly unbearable interval, during which she gazed at the organ from several angles, she reached into her coat pocket and pulled out her reading specs. Settling the red half-glasses onto the end of her nose, she once again peered down at Red's now puckering package. After yet another uncomfortable moment, she raised an eyebrow, nodded knowingly, and waved a stiff finger at the rapidly retreating rod. "You know…," she said, looking Red in the eye, "…that looks just like a penis…but much, much smaller."

For the briefest of seconds, it was as if the air had been vacuum-pumped from the room, leaving the throng bug-eyed, collectively gasping for oxygen that wasn't there.

Then the place came unglued. People slid out of chairs and rolled among the gum wrappers and peanut shells littering the floor. Billy Bob Fung threw himself onto the pool table, where he rolled from rail to rail like a beached whale, scattering the brightly colored balls hither and yon as he thrashed about, spouting his laughter to the ceiling. Back by the front door, somebody pounded on the bar and brayed like a donkey. A glass shattered on the floor as the wave of laughter and derision rose to the rafters like a tsunami.

Just as things began to settle down, somebody repeated the punch line at top volume. "…but much, much smaller," he bellowed, and the place erupted again.

By that time, Red had packed himself back into his jeans and beaten a muttering, head-shaking retreat to the men's room. When I looked over at the narrow stairway, Rachel Thoms was standing there. "Nice crowd here," she commented.

"Never a dull moment," I assured her.

I offered her a seat. She nodded past my right shoulder, where Ralph leaned against the wall. Together, we watched him nod off with his mouth so wide open you could have dropped a pool ball inside. His brown and broken teeth reminded me of those old pilings sticking up from the Hylebos Waterway.

"How about someplace we don't have to shout?"

I swept my arm across the room and grinned. "But you've achieved full icon status here today," I said. "They'll talk about this for years."

She grinned back. "I'll have to remember to include it in my bio," she said.

I wobbled as I got to my feet. She noticed.

"I shouldn't be driving," I admitted.

"I've got a cab outside," she said, and let her smile loose on me.

I kept my feet, but just barely. "Pretty sure of yourself," I managed as she turned away.

She smiled and started down the stairs. "You coming?" she asked, without looking back.

I said I was.